THE CUNNIGHAM ARRESTS

J. RICHARD WAKEFIELD

SIGNALMAN PUBLISHING

THE CUNNINGHAM ARRESTS
By J. Richard Wakefield

Signalman Publishing
www.signalmanpublishing.com
email: info@signalmanpublishing.com
Tampa, Florida

ISBN: 978-1-940145-85-3

Typeset in Garamond Premiere Pro
Interior design by Joel Ramnaraine

Dedicated to my eleven grandchildren.
May this be a legacy to make them proud.

ACKNOWLEDGMENTS

I wish to thank the following for helping me write this book.

The London Writers Group: Ruth Zavitz, Pat Brown, Clarissa Harwood, John Jeneroux, Ian Gillespie, Mitch Lenko and Carl Zvonkin. Throughout the past eight years, these people have been instrumental in honing my writing skills.

Also, Christopher McGarry, for his editing and proof reading.

Cover art by Shelyse Richard, storybrushstudios@gmail.com.

Finally my family: Jeremy, Charaxes, Jennifer, Brent, and most of all, my loving wife Dorothy for their helpful input and patience.

TABLE OF CONTENTS

THE CUNNIGHAM ARRESTS

J. RICHARD WAKEFIELD

Synopsis

In this sequel to *The Barn*, Chicago Detective Marg Cunningham must investigate how her father obtained hundreds of thousands of dollars, which she found in her mother's home.

Expecting to have a two-week vacation, she is ordered back to the Division. She is transferred to homicide to investigate the recent murder of a witness she interviewed for the case of missing Nick Easton. This puts her up against the Outfit, the mob family of Chicago.

In this fast pace, emotional roller coaster ride, she discovers the reality of being a homicide detective, which severely challenges her worldview.

CHAPTER 1

THE ABDUCTION

Two men walked into Roberto De Luca's front office on the twentieth floor of a downtown Chicago office tower. The receptionist asked, "Do you have an appointment?"

The men stopped short of the door to De Luca's office. "No, but I'll make one right now." He pulled out a Glock handgun with a large silencer on the end. He nonchalantly fired two shots into the receptionist's chest, instantly killing her.

They barged into the large spacious office. The same man pointed the pistol at De Luca, who was behind his desk.

"What the fuck is this?" De Luca screeched.

"Our boss wants to talk to you. Now."

The second man walked behind De Luca, grabbed the back of his suit, forcefully lifted up out the chair and puppeteered him out of the room.

He gasped at the sight of his secretary; her head back against the headrest, mouth wide open. Her lifeless eyes stared blankly at the ceiling. Blood oozed from two perforations in her white blouse.

The second man picked up the spent 40cal casings.

They went down the elevator to the underground parking lot without saying anything to the nonstop babbling, and pleading from De Luca.

They put a black bag over his head, and stuffed him into a vehicle, in which two additional men were waiting. They drove off as if nothing was unusual.

When the bag was pulled off, De Luca found himself in an old factory. Two men were standing behind him. A third was in front.

"Why am I here?"

"Shut the fuck up," the man in front said.

De Luca looked around. Two lanterns on tables on each side of him were the only light. The rest of the room disappeared into darkness.

De Luca continued to plead, but no one listened. The only reply was the hiss of the two naphtha lamps.

In the distance he saw a red glow, then it disappeared. A large man emerged from the gloom. He expelled a great cloud of blue-white smoke, then stuffed the Cuban back into his mouth.

Chewing on the stogy, he said, "Roberto, good to see you again, my friend." He pulled up a chair and sat only a few feet from De Luca. He patted De Luca on the knee. "How've you been?"

"Joe. Um, Joe. Good to see you too," De Luca said nervously. This was not the first time he had met the Outfit's enforcer, but not under these circumstances.

Joe "The Rib" Ribaudo let out a humph. "Well, we'll see if it is good. Have you heard? My son was arrested."

De Luca looked at the other men, then nervously back at Ribaudo.

"No, sorry, I hadn't."

"Well, I think you did, and I think you had something to do with it." He leaned back in the chair.

"How? I haven't seen Russell, I mean, in months."

Ribaudo gave a withering look at De Luca. "You're lying."

"I'm not, you gotta believe me!" De Luca knew what it meant to be caught lying to the Mob boss. Life would become very short, very quickly.

"You got a visit by two cops in your office. Right after that visit my son got arrested. You ratted out my son."

"No. No. That's not true. I mean, yes, er, hum, I did get a visit by the cops, but it had nothing to do with Russell. Honest. They were looking for Nicky, my business partner. He's gone missing."

Ribaudo took a long drag of the cigar, then blew the smoke into De Luca's face. "Liar. I don't like co-incidences."

After a few coughs, De Luca said, "Look, just ask him. Russell will tell you the last time we met."

Ribaudo's bulk enlarged, his body shook as his eyes pinned. "He's dead."

Oh, shit, De Luca thought. This wasn't going to end well for him.

"He got denied bail. One of those fucking gang-bangers killed him in prison as he waited for his hearing."

There was silence in the room for a few moments. De Luca tried to figure how he was going to get out of this.

Finally, Ribaudo spoke. "I need to know what you told the cops. And these three gentlemen here are going to help you remember." He nodded at one of them, got up, and disappeared into the darkness.

Each of the men took one of De Luca's limbs and zip-tied them the wooden chair's arms. Then they zip-tied his legs to the chair. Sweat started to pour down his face. His entire body was trembling.

"No! I didn't tell the cops anything, I swear it!"

From the darkness came, "We'll know for sure in an hour."

The third man in front started to punch De Luca in the face. Not hard at first, but enough to make his lip catch a tooth and start to bleed. Each blow got harder, and more frequent, as De Luca broke down pleading between the crying and screams.

After thirty minutes, his eyes were so swollen they were almost shut. Blood dripped relentlessly on his shirt, mixing with sweat, tears and mucus.

They poured water on his head. It seemed to have revived him a bit.

"So tell us what we want to know."

In a high-pitched, strained whimper, he said, "I didn't tell them anything."

The man doing the punching turned to one of the others. "I'm tired and my hand hurts. Your turn."

The second man came in close to De Luca's face, spitting on him as he said, "I won't be gentle like he was."

De Luca whimpered louder. "I didn't tell them anything."

"Liar." He started into De Luca, this time the punching was into his torso. Ribs cracked. He lost the ability to breathe. They revived him again with more water dumped on his head.

"Please, stop," is all he could get out.

"You still have that hammer in your car?" the third man said to one of the others. He nodded. "Get it."

It wasn't just a hammer. It was a small mallet with a wide face. All the third man said was, "Toes."

"No! Please. No! I didn't tell them anything. I swear!"

"We need to be sure. Toes," he said to the man again.

The hammer yielding man moved in front of De Luca, and knelt. He raised the mallet over his head, then stared into De Luca's eyes. De Luca just whimpered, shaking his head.

Down it came. De Luca screeched out so loud the third man cringed and covered his ears. "Again," he said.

The scream from the second wallop could have shattered glass.

De Luca sat there, half crying, half unconscious from the pain. Urine formed in the chair, then drained onto the floor.

The man was about to deliver a third blow when from the void came, "Enough."

Another red glow formed in the black, then fainted to nothing. Ribaudo emerged from the dark.

"Well, ready to tell us the truth there, Roberto? I really don't like to see you in this state. But I have no choice."

A barely audible voice whimpered, "I didn't tell them anything. Please stop."

Ribaudo shook his head. "You know, you've been a thorn in our side for a long time. You pretend to be our friend. You even try to emulate us with all your trinkets, guns and news clippings under glass. All lies of course. All bullshit. But that's the way it is with you. All lies, isn't it Roberto." He gave De Luca a mild couple of taps on the face.

Then he went nose to nose. "I know you talk to the cops. How else have they not been able to jail your ass? How many times is it?" he said leaning back. "Twenty, I think it is. One does not elude criminal prosecution twenty times without making a deal with the cops."

He got in close again. "And yet, in all those years the cops have come down on us hard. They've put a number of our boys, even our boss, in prison. Hell, they almost got me a couple times. But funny, their witnesses just conveniently disappeared. If you know what I mean."

He leaned back. "Of course you do."

"I didn't tell them anything. You gotta believe me," came a quiet high-pitched squeak.

Ribaudo shook his head. "I have to hand it to you, Roberto, you sure are a good liar. Doesn't matter, if you did, or you didn't. You're never going to be able to again."

He got up, and nodded to the men. Then disappeared into the dark, a cloud of smoke trailing, with De Luca screaming.

CHAPTER 2

TWO WEEKS OFF – NOT!

I got home early afternoon after Mom's funeral. There must have been a hundred people there. Just about everyone was from the Chicago Police Department, including our Deputy Superintendent, James Strong and Superintendent of Police, Dan Dillane.

They paid their respects to both my mother, and by saluting my father beside her. It was a moving, very emotional, event. Bagpipes played. Everyone was in dress uniforms. A few, including the Superintendents, gave eulogies.

I tried to show a brave face. I tried to hold back the tears. But I couldn't hold it in any longer.

Deputy Strong was my father's partner for a number of years, good friends of the family decades ago. He gave some great examples of their time together, some of which brought laughter to the mourners.

That helped with controlling the grief, the realization that I had become an orphan, the recognition I no longer had a mother.

They all wanted to shake my hand and give their condolences.

I was also officially on my ordered two-week vacation. I was still fuming from my meeting with David Doroszuk, our Division captain, to give up my investigation of missing Nick Easton.

The FBI would take over the inquiry. Second time those fuckers stole one of my cases. They weren't going to find out any more than I did. I'd be surprised, after reading my reports, they'd even do anything.

I poured myself a rum and coke, and sat in front of the TV. Tomorrow I had an appointment with the lawyer to transfer my mother's bank accounts and my father's stock certificates into my name.

Then there was all that cash we found at Mom's house. Being alone, staring at the metal box full of greenbacks, having nothing but my thoughts, it started to haunt me that my father was not the upstanding honest cop we thought he was. Every moment I got angrier with him.

I took a sip of my drink. It was an attempt to drench my anger, but it wasn't working.

I had to know, but on vacation, there was no way I was able to track down his notes and files.

However, my biggest concern was Pam. She and Angel had gone to Florida and were looking for a house. She did fly in for the funeral, but headed back an hour ago.

Tomorrow I would also get the cash from the sale of Mom's house, plus her bank accounts – minus the inheritance taxes, fucking government – I should have enough to buy a house for Pam to start her new family.

What else would I do with the money anyway? Might as well invest it in real estate. I couldn't see home values dropping more than they already had.

The news was, again, its usual depressing information. A cop in Salem, Oregon, killed a black teenager. Seemed the kid had pulled a knife on the cop. They scuffled. The kid tried to get the officer's sidearm when it went off, killing the kid. That happened yesterday.

All day today, demonstrations were taking place denouncing the killing, saying it was racially motivated for the cop to even pull the kid's car over.

This could get ugly quickly, I thought.

The next bit of information was also depressing. More footage of ISIL killing people in Syria and Iraq. More bombing runs were shown taking the insurgents out. Plus a segment on insurgents emigrating from Europe, Canada and the US to fight against us in Iraq. Homegrown traitors, one commentator said.

I just hoped this wouldn't happen here. Except they interviewed someone who said the FBI knows ISIL was in the States recruiting for local attacks.

The last bit I watched was on the business report. The price of oil was up again, after dropping to low levels last year. That, the commentator said, was not good news for the economy.

More banks in the EU were charging negative interest rates. What the hell were "negative interest rates?" I thought. I'd have to pay to keep money in my bank account? What the fuck was that?

I fell asleep after the news, in my chair, reading my book.

Took me an hour at the lawyer's to get all the paperwork done, then another hour at each of the three banks in Chicago to transfer those funds into my account. It was rather impressive to see all those digits in my own bank book. But then I remembered about those negative interest rates. Swell. If that ever came to the U.S. there would be a run on all the banks.

One mystery solved, though. I found out where the money for all my mother's accounts came from when I transferred the stocks. They were getting their regular deposits from dividends on the stocks my father had. Those deposits stopped some ten years ago, just before my father retired from the force, according to the records.

Instead they were all diverted to my mother's checking account.

That's what she was living on, or trying to.

With the economy tanking the last few years those dividends were much reduced. Some of them even went ex-dividend. So I was right, even with the reduced amount of my father's pension, she was living on the edge. Month to month.

Finally, I ended the trek around town with a one-way airfare to Florida, leaving first thing in the morning. I figured, once I settled Pam, I'd spend the rest of my vacation checking into my father's military history and how he won those medals.

I had just entered the arrivals at the airport in Miami when my phone played the Dragnet theme. "Hello."

"Marg, where are you?"

"Hey, Derik. I just landed at the airport, just about to meet Pam."

"We need you back here, ASAP."

"I just went on vacation, ordered by David."

"The order was rescinded. We need you back, now."

Swell. Pam and Angel came up to me, taking my bag from my shoulder. I pointed to my phone.

"Derik, what the hell is going on? I just got here."

"Orders. We need you here. De Luca's missing, and his secretary was shot dead point blank."

"That's awful."

"What's awful, Mom?"

"Just a second, Honey. Derik," I said into the phone, "That's homicide."

"Yep, and you just got transferred. Welcome to your first case."

Wow. I got my transfer to homicide. That was damn fast. Something was up with that.

"Marg, I'm looking at the airline schedule, and there's a return flight in thirty if you hurry."

Pam was furious, but they helped me with my bags as I went to the departures counter.

I kissed her on the forehead, "I'll be back as soon as I can. In the meantime, you two look for a house. I've got what we need to buy it outright."

"You're going to live with us, Mom? That's wonderful. Isn't that wonderful, Angel?"

He gave a small yes, but his eyes said he wanted my daughter to himself, with no mother-in-law in the way. Couldn't blame him.

"Maybe, we'll see. They said I got my promotion to homicide. You know I've been waiting for this."

The PA system announced my flight was boarding.

"Gotta go. You two have a good time. I'll be back soon."

Off I went.

First order of business, soon as I got off the plane, I went to the Cook County morgue to see the body of De Luca's secretary.

Derik called me as I got off the plane saying they were doing the secretary autopsy today. They needed the lead detective present.

It was my first time seeing a dead body on the slab. Well, that's not actually true. In our cadet days we went to a number of autopsies to see how it was done. But I was way in the back and couldn't see much.

This time there was no one to hide behind.

Dr. Wilson, an elderly balding African-American man with thick glasses, and in the typical white lab coat, greeted me in the hall.

"You ready for this? Your first time, isn't it?"

I nodded.

"That's OK. Just make sure you barf into the sink. Or you can clean it up from the floor yourself. This way."

We went into the room. It was like walking into a brick wall of offensive smell. It brought back the memory of my first day into one of these chambers.

Several stainless steel tables were in the middle. On each side were freezer doors for the cadavers. A body of a female was on the far table.

"This is her." He looked at his clipboard of documents. "Tara Ronsetti. She was thirty-four. Unmarried." He looked at her. "Events beyond her control, and she was selected against. Too bad, pretty woman."

The body was completely naked. She was laid out, eyes closed, with her head on a wood block. Her right breast was perky, no sag at all. But her left breast was almost completely deflated.

"You can see the two wounds here." He pointed to the one in the middle of the sternum first. "And here," pointing to the one just above the left nipple.

"I'm not sure which was fired first. The one through the sternum fragmented and wrapped itself around the vertebrae. The second one perforated her implant, then, missing the ribs, passed right through the left atrium, and flattened out on the scapula.

"Looks like a .40 calibre by the size of the entrance wounds, but the bullets have no jacket. They're lead. So they mushroomed pretty well. I doubt we'll get any rifling on them. But I'll dig them out for you."

He got a scalpel off the tray.

Swell. My in-flight lunch wanted to return to my mouth. "Ah, Doc, if you don't mind, I just ate on the plane."

He laughed. "I've done that and lost my lunch in here a few times. I tell you, a splattered head from a shotgun will turn anyone's stomach..."

That was it. I left the room before I upchucked something on the floor I'd have to clean up.

"I'll send the bullets to your Division," is all I caught going out the door.

In my car, I had to come to grips with what I was going to have to see when in homicide. Dad never gave us the gruesome details, but I'd seen enough cop shows to know I was going to be exposed to the graphic, horrific deaths of some people.

I arrived, instinctively, to my old building. Someone else was at my desk.

"And you are..." I said as politely as I could.

"Oh, good, Marg, come in here," Chief David said before the young man could answer me.

I entered his office, and closed the door. "You've replaced me already? That was quick. Guess you thought I was serious about not coming back."

"Oh, come on, Marg. We would never do that to you. All your stuff is at the homicide building in Area South. They're expecting you." He got up and held out his hand. "Congratulations on the promotion. You deserve it. Your ol' man would be proud."

I was at a loss for words. I shook his hand, finally saying, "Thank you."

"Now, off you go. You've got a big case waiting for you."

"Do I get Derik as a partner?"

"No, I'm sorry. I've reassigned him to someone else. He's not going to homicide. He told me he doesn't want it. Not yet anyway. I'm sure Hollenger will give you a new partner. Say hi to Ron for me, will you?"

I started to leave the room.

"Don't be a stranger now," he said.

I looked back and smiled.

Ron Hollenger was the Area South Commander of the homicide unit on East 111th Street. Like David, he was a strictly by the book cop. He was a short, somewhat balding, part Asian featured, middle-aged man.

I walked into the homicide unit room and looked around. It was chaos. People were on the phones. People were typing on computers. Others were discussing their cases with each other. The Commander's room was empty.

A woman looked at me from her desk. She got up and came to the door. She was quite petite, with blondish hair done up in a bun. A pretty young girl. I was sure she was a magnet for the guys around here.

"You must be Marg Cunningham. I remember you from the funeral. I'm so sorry for your loss."

"Thank you."

She held out her hand. "I'm your partner, Becky Clarke."

Ok, this didn't make sense. A rookie like me in a new position would be a partner of someone senior, not the other way around. She was younger than me.

"I'd ask how you got into homicide, but maybe I don't want to know."

She looked at me sideways. Then she said, "I came in with the last group of hiring."

"Fresh from college?"

"Yes, let me get you up to speed on your case."

Blind leading the blind or what? To save money the City redistributed the areas of the Police Department, as well as allowing people to come straight from the Police Detective College without any street experience. With the work overload of the beat cops the Brass didn't want to dilute the street cop ranks.

No wonder many homicide cases weren't getting solved. The detectives were just too inexperienced.

We went to our desks, and she explained what they knew about De Luca. I was assigned the case because it was both a missing persons and a homicide. So it was a transition from one unit to the other. Even though his secretary was executed, he could still be alive.

I was senior detective in the case because of my previous encounter with De Luca, or so Becky said.

They had nothing. No leads. No witnesses.

"They're ripping his office apart as we speak. I think we should go there, and then to the morgue."

"I stopped by the morgue on my way here," I said.

"Oh. Ok. Good. Well, let's go. I presume you know the way."

As we began to leave, Hollenger came back from lunch. "Ah, you must be Marg Cunningham. Welcome to homicide. Have you met the rest of the crew yet?"

"Just Becky here."

"That won't do." He walked into the middle of the room and said, "Listen up, this is our new member, Margory Cunningham. Make her feel at home boys and girls."

One by one they introduced themselves to me. There was a dozen members of the team, four of which were out on assignment.

It hit me standing in front of De Luca's desk. When Derik and I visited him he recognized who I was. I remembered he said he helped my father. I wondered what that help meant. Likely never know now.

"Detective Cunningham?" one of the forensic guys said.

"Yes."

"Al Halliday, pleased to meet you. We're about to cut open his safe. You may want to wait in the other room while we torch the hinges off."

The office was full of blue smoke and smelled awful, once they got into the safe.

There was money, about a hundred grand, plus a number of documents, mostly deeds and property papers. But some financial documents too.

They were bagged, labeled and headed off to the financial guys at HQ.

"He has no relatives that we can find," Halliday said. "I wonder where all this will go?" He looked around the room at all the Mob paraphernalia. "That Tommy gun would look great over my bar," he joked.

"I'm sure the History Museum would be interested in it. I'll call them," Becky said.

I asked Halliday, "Any evidence?"

"Not sure. Doesn't look like it. They even policed their brass."

"Could it be a revolver?"

"Maybe. A forty cal? Could be."

"No need for them to look around for a shell casing," I said.

"Makes sense. Maybe the bullets will give us a hit. Pardon the pun."

"I'll check some the other offices. Maybe they heard the gunshots," Becky said, then left the office.

"The coroner said they were lead, and likely mushroomed," I said.

"This was a professional hit, no question. I'd wager the Mob was behind this. Kinda ironic don't you think?"

Next Becky and I went to De Luca's downtown condo. Again, there was no indication of anything. It was as he left it that morning. However, after one of the forensic guys dusted for prints, we found something interesting.

"Look at the desk top," he said.

"There's a void in the prints," I replied.

"Yep, the size of a laptop. They've been here and took it."

"How do you know that? He could have taken it."

"Not likely. If he took it regularly, we would see some prints on the vacant spot. But there's none. That computer had been there for a long time unmoved."

"But nothing else is missing?"

"Doesn't look like it. No sign of forced entry, the door nor the windows. They had a key."

"His key. They kidnapped him, then used his key to get in."

"Makes sense. They wanted his computer."

We wrapped up the scene, then secured the door shut with a CPD evidence seal.

One of the consistent names off the documents was a lawyer. De Luca used the same one all the time. James Rudd. A well- known real estate lawyer, also familiar to police.

Becky and I went to see him first thing in the morning. His office was in a two story building on West Cermak Road west of the city. We had no appointment, of course, we just badged the secretary.

Rudd came out of his office to meet us. He was in a suit that looked like it had been slept in a few nights in a row. He had thin-rimmed bifocals. His thinning hair was streaked with gray.

"You're here about De Luca aren't you? I heard what happened. Damn shame about Tara, you know. I'm a friend of her family. Know her father well. He's also a real estate agent, you know. Come in."

His office was nothing special, unlike De Luca. Many shelves around the room were full of legal books. Numerous books were even on the windowsill. His desk was cluttered with folders, upon folders. The room felt claustrophobic.

"Coffee anyone?"

We declined. I wasn't going to trust the sanitation of this place. Who knew how long ago any cups were even washed?

He sat behind his desk. We sat at two rather uncomfortable chairs.

"When was the last time you saw De Luca?" I asked.

"Couple days ago. I mean, I finalized a sale he did."

"What did he buy?" Becky asked.

"No, he sold. It was a building on Central and 23rd. It's a three-story apartment building with business on the street floor, you know."

"Who did he sell it to?" I asked.

"Oh, I'm sorry, you'll need a warrant for that information. Besides, I mean, if you got his documents from his office, you'll have the legal papers of the sale."

"Do you have any idea why he'd be kidnapped?"

He paused. It looked like he wanted to say something, but held it back.

"C'mon, Mr. Rudd, you're holding things back. Who did this?"

"I mean, I don't know."

That was a lie. He knew we knew. Clearly he was scared shitless. He played with the rings on his fingers. Then he aimlessly shuffled some papers as if pretending to organize.

He wasn't going to give us anything.

I asked one more question. "Who else do you think we should contact?"

He lifted his right hand as if he was going to his keyboard, but hesitated. "No, I'm sorry. I don't."

We stood up. I handed him my card. "Call if something comes to you, Mr. Rudd. Thank you for your time."

"Hope you find De Luca. He's a great guy, you know."

Right, I'd bet he wasn't. Maybe great with giving him business, but with no De Luca I'd wager his income would plummet.

On the drive back to the Division, Becky opened up to me.

"You've been on the job a long time?"

"Twelve years next May."

"How's it been being a woman on the job? Has it hurt your advancement?"

Clearly not since I've done well. She would know that.

"You having a problem in the office?"

"What do you mean?"

"Look, we're going to be partners for a while. I demand honesty from my partners. No holding back. You're having a problem with the guys on the job?"

She reluctantly nodded. "Since day one."

"Want to know my secret?"

"Sure."

"No makeup. You look like a Barbie Doll. No offence, but you look like you're ready to party. You want the hounds to stop sniffing your butt like dogs in heat?"

She laughed. "No makeup is the trick?"

"Worked for me for twelve years. But then again I haven't been looking for a man."

"You're gay?"

I laughed. "No. Just no time. I'm married to my job. For good and for bad."

"No makeup. Interesting, I'll try that tomorrow."

CHAPTER 3

SO THIS IS HOMICIDE

First thing in the morning, 7:00AM actually, I arrived at the Cook County Morgue. I stood at the double door, with my hand about to push it open. I took a deep breath and pushed the door to enter.

Dr. Wilson was there. A number of bodies were on the table. He was dissecting one of the cadavers. All the internal organs were neatly lined up on another table. He was weighing the brain.

"Detective," he said surprised. "One of these yours?"

"No..." I hadn't eaten breakfast, just in case. "I... Look, Doc, I need to get used to this."

"I don't understand."

"I'm in homicide now. I'm going to have to be here for my cases. I don't want to be upchucking on your floor."

He put the brain down and came over to me. "Well, that's definitely how you will get desensitized. So, come in, come in."

He turned, then stopped. He looked back at me. "I have to confess.

That time I told you about the shotgun? Well, I tell that story to all new people. It helps them not feel so bad."

"So that was a lie?"

"In a way. It happened, but it was a long time ago."

We went through the cadaver he was working on. He was very good at explaining things, one organ at a time. I still wanted to barf but I was able to keep it down.

The hard part was the realization that the young boy on the table was someone's son, someone's brother, someone who was supposed to have a future to old age. Instead, he had been stabbed at his school the day before.

That part was going to be more difficult to get desensitized to.

After an hour I had to get going. "Thanks, Doc. I'll come back again."

"Look, detective. I'll be honest. For people like you, this never gets easy. Regardless of how much you think you're used to this, a body will come in here which will remind you otherwise. Welcome to homicide."

Swell.

I was at my desk looking through some of the De Luca documents when this young woman arrived. She was in a plain light blue shirt with worn blue jeans. Her blondish hair was down around her shoulders. It was Becky.

"Wow," I said. "You look perfectly plain! This will be interesting to see if the guys pick up on you now.

"Not so far. They didn't even look up from their computers when I came in. Thanks for the advice."

She sat down at her desk. A couple of the guys looked over with crunched up faces, as if trying to figure out who the person was. But then they just kept doing their work.

"Now we can concentrate on the cases," I said winking to her. The desk phone rang.

"Cunningham... Ok... Where? Got it, thanks." Looking at Becky I said, "We've got a murder." I got up.

"Here we go," Becky said.

We pulled up to the South St. Lawrence Avenue apartment behind a long line of police cars.

Hordes of people were all around. A black woman was crying in the arms of two cops. This wasn't going to be good.

We went into the apartment. A young black man lay dead on the kitchen floor.

A female cop said, "Single gunshot to the chest, Detective."

This was no young man. This was a boy. Blood had congealed under his body. He was wearing blue jeans, and a striped shirt soaked in blood. I turned away, trying not to look.

"Do we have a name yet?," I asked.

The cop looked at her notepad. "Darnell Flournoy. Sixteen."

My heart sunk. So young to die so violently.

"What happened?" Becky asked.

"We're not sure. There was a party going on here last night. The boy's cousin came to pick him up. Some fight broke out, but no one knows who shot him," the cop said.

"Of course they don't," I sighed.

"When did the fight break out?" Becky asked the cop.

"Someone said around 11PM last night.

"And we only got here now?" I said.

"We only found out about it an hour ago."

"So he bled out," I lamented.

"Looks like it."

"They left him on the floor all night to die?" Becky asked.

"That's what they do around here, detective."

"What were they fighting about?" I said.

"What else, a girl. We have her in a cruiser."

"Tell me you have the shooter." I said.

"Nope, he fled."

The coroner showed up, and declared the boy DOA. Two women brought in a stretcher jabbering on about something.

"I laughed at Leonard and Penny about the money. Great idea to use the money for their wedding," the dark haired young woman said.

The other, around the same age, mid twenties, had brown hair streaked with blond strands. "I liked it when Sheldon was in the basement experimenting for being in the mine."

The women opened up a body bag next to the corpse. As they rolled the kid into it...

"Oh, that was funny when he ran out when the basement when the rats showed up, leaving poor Raj behind," the dark haired women said.

As they lifted the body, with little effort, onto the stretcher, the dark haired woman said, "That was so accurate about Howard not doing the dishes. This is so true of men. They think they're helping us but they will do as little possible so they can go back to playing, what ever."

"I laughed at Howy getting the star for making the bed."

"Yeah, it's either that or we have to give them sex for doing their jobs at home."

As they rolled the stretcher out...

"Ah, and notice that's how they made up at the end. Men and their sex."

"That's how we control them, girl. That's why I love that show. The women so control those men. And they don't even know it."

As they disappeared through the door, the blondish woman said, "You got that right."

I had to wonder if I would become that insensitive, that cavalier, that habituated to dead young boys gunned down before they get a chance at life.

We interviewed everyone we could; the cousin, the girlfriend, and the tenant of the apartment. They gave us a good description of the shooter.

"We'll get him," I said to Becky.

So this was homicide: the senseless murder of kids.

I finally got some time to myself at the end of my shift. I went down to the archives to look for my father's notes. The archivist was great. Better than I expected. I had to sign in, but that was it. She didn't seem to care why I wanted to look through these old records. She even helped me find the box amongst decades upon decades of thousands of cops' notes.

It was one brown colored box. All his notepads were there, each one with the year on the front. Each pad was some one hundred pages. Each page appeared to be one event, at the least. That meant at least four notepads per year, for forty years. One hundred and sixty of them in total.

It was going to take a long time to read each one. I allotted one hour per day during the week, and eight hours on the weekends, to read every one in chronological order.

I started with the first book. His first year, 1969, he was a beat cop. I figured fresh from returning from Viet Nam.

He was assigned to a corporal who, in his words, "was well seasoned." The days were just normal issues. Traffic violations. Domestic issues. Neighbor complaints. Nothing outstanding.

I decided this was going to take too long. De Luca said it was in the seventies. So I jumped a few years, and started to read.

There were notes about an investigation into some racketeering complaints by shop owners. There were so many names, so many items in those hundred pages, I realized it was going to get complicated fast.

I went up to the archivist. "Can I take these home?"

"You're not supposed to."

"Who can I see to get them out for a few days?"

"I can ask for you. Come back at the end of the week."

The following day, Becky and I were piecing together the details of the previous day's killing. A number of people were brought in for questioning. The shooter may have been picked up during the night.

We called in the girlfriend of the dead sixteen-year-old. We put a number of people into a line up, including the man picked up.

She picked him out in a heartbeat.

He was read his rights, and off he went to the holding cells for processing.

Gee, that was fast. Easy too. I hoped they would all be like that. But I also realized I shouldn't get my hopes up.

Later in the afternoon a riot started when former garbage men, who the Mayor fired in September, were protesting in front of the Capital building. It got out of control.

We suited up and headed to the area to help.

It was déjà vu for me. Becky was petrified. Though this time I wasn't on the front lines. Becky and I were tasked to get the videotapes of the rioters. Those could be used to identify the perps who were causing the problems.

Shop windows were smashed. Cop cars were torched. Rocks were flying. We hoped most of that was caught not only on surveillance cameras, but people's cell phones. It didn't take long for those to end up on YouTube.

Eventually, as the day wore on, the cold won. By the night everything had died down as people froze as the deep winter enveloped the whole Midwest.

I finally got home after 2am. It was too late to do any reading. I just crashed.

I came into the Division, half asleep, with a double sized coffee in my hands. Becky was there. She looked worse than I did.

"Let's hope we don't have to go through that again," she agonized.

"Don't jinx us by talking like that."

My desk phone rang. "Cunningham." I sat down. "Where?" I wrote an address. "We'll be right there."

"How come we get all these cases?" Becky asked.

"Because this is Chicago, the murder capital of the country it seems."

"No, Flint, Michigan is again this year."

I looked at Becky sideways.

She shrugged, "Something they told us in detective college."

Off we went to West 63rd street. "What do we have?" Becky asked on route.

"A shop owner killed a robber."

We arrived at a food and liquor store. The body of a man lay on the westbound lanes of the street. Traffic was stopped in all directions. We had to go into the oncoming lanes to get around. Only one other cop car was there, but more could be heard coming.

An elderly man was in cuffs at the front of the store guarded by one of the cops. A revolver lay on the sidewalk.

The other cop was questioning the driver of a bus that was parked in front of the store.

"What happened?" I asked the cop guarding the old man, but he interrupted.

"I've been robbed over and over, and you people do nothing. It's the same fucking assholes every time. You arrest them, and they go free. I've been robbed five times this year so far. I'm tired of being the victim."

"OK, calm down," I said. "What's your name?"

"Mike Ashfield. This is my store. I've been here for thirty years. Never before have I ever had this problem. This used to be a good neighborhood. Now all the good people are gone. But where could I go? This is my home."

"Tell me what happened, Mike."

"That piece of shit pulled a gun on me and tried to rob me. That's what happened. It wasn't the first time. He did it last spring, and you people arrested him. Now he's out again? Not anymore."

"Where did you shoot him? On the street?"

"No, in the store. He walked out here and collapsed in front of that bus."

"And the gun on the sidewalk? How did that get there?"

"I followed him out the door. In case I had to make sure he didn't come back."

Becky came over. "Single gunshot to the chest."

"In the front?"

"I don't see an exit wound."

"Does he have a gun on him?" I asked Becky, but Mike interrupted.

"It's in the store on the floor."

I sent the cop in to pick it up. He emerged with a Beretta 92. So his story seemed to pan out.

The cop who interviewed the bus driver came over and said that is what happened. The man staggered out from the store, then collapsed right in front of him.

I went to the cop guarding the old man. "Un-cuff him. Mike, I need you to come to the station and make a statement. Can you do that?"

As he locked his store he said, "And who is going to pay for my lost income?" He got into one of the cop cars.

The coroner showed up, and loaded the body into his vehicle. The fire department hosed down the street ridding it of the evidence someone died.

I got home early. I was spent from not getting enough sleep. But I had to read some of my father's notes.

There it was, 1975, in August. De Luca was stopped for driving a vehicle with a broken stop light. Turned out he stole the vehicle. Dad arrested him, according to his notes.

Once at the Division, Dad interviewed De Luca. There were three names in the notes with a comment "Go see in morning."

I was too tired to read any more. I poured myself a rum and coke and watched some TV.

The news was about an attack on a cop in retaliation to killings in Atlanta of a black man. The backlash against cops was starting. Apparently the female cop was run over by a pickup truck. She was in critical condition in the hospital.

The vehicle had taken off. They didn't have the attacker.

I was incensed at some of the interviews from people of the black community who praised the attack.

After that, they showed more of the attack in France by Muslims on some newspaper who published articles and cartoons which were far from flattering of Islam. It happened the night before. Ten people were dead, including the two Muslim attackers.

Anti-Muslim protests were happening in the UK and Germany. Pro-Muslim protesters were also out in force. Accusations were flying about who was to blame.

I couldn't take it anymore. I went to bed.

The next morning started my weekend. Time to get more into my father's notes.

I wrote down the names of the two people De Luca gave up. I got on my computer and logged into the police database. Checking their names, both were deceased, some ten years after my father met with them.

I checked more, but they were not in prison until five years after 1975. So they didn't get charged from my father's investigation.

I read more of my father's notes.

The two men were found in a drug house. But according to my Dad's notes no drugs were found. He wrote "Bad info, nothing here." But he did note another name given up by one of the perps. There was nothing in his notes they took these guys to the Division for interrogation.

By the end of the weekend, I had some dozen people who were found by cascading from another. It looked like three of them were still alive.

One was still in Chicago according to our database. I had the address. Off I went to South Merrill Avenue.

It was a small house. A car was in the drive. I knocked at the door. A young black boy answered it. "Paul Helton?"

He turned to look into the house. "Grandpa, someone for you."

An old gray haired man slowly came up to me. I introduced myself. I said I was investigating cold cases, and asked if he remembered getting arrested by my father.

He invited me in.

We sat in the cramped living room. "My grandson lives with me," he said in a slow monotone voice. "I'm the only family he has left. His father is in prison for murdering his mother."

"I'm sorry. Do you remember that day?"

He thought. He gave a few answers, but they didn't jive. This wasn't going anywhere. He clearly didn't remember, and was confusing different events of his past. I pretended he was a great help and excused myself.

I got into my car but sat there. He looked about eighty, maybe more. The kid wasn't more than ten. I wondered what would happen to him when his grandfather couldn't look after him anymore. Maybe he couldn't already.

It also dawned on me that many of these earlier arrests and interviews were so old, that most will be like this old guy. I was getting a bit depressed I wasn't going to get answers. I went home.

I was woken up by my phone. I looked at the clock. It was 1:30am.

Groggy I said, "Cunningham."

"Hey, Marg, it's detective Ross Conboy. We met the first day you arrived?"

"Sorry, I don't recall. I'm half asleep."

"I know, and I'm sorry to call you, but you're next in line. I need some help with a homicide."

I took down the address, got dressed, and headed out. So this was homicide... Perps don't care what time of the night it was.

I arrived at the corner of South Princeton Avenue and West 114th Street. It was an out of the way dead end of two streets, circumvented by a railway line. Several cop cars were there. Ross greeted me as I pulled over.

"Glad you could come. We've got a lot of people to interview."

"Where's the body?"

"On route to Advocate Christ Medical Center. But it doesn't look good. He was shot four times close at range. One was in the face, but also in his back and butt. He was right over there when he was found. The neighbor in that home on the corner heard the shooting."

"Got a name yet?"

"Yes, Ronnie Sawyer. I've got his wallet."

"Did anyone see who did it?"

"No, it was a drive by. They sped off up 114th. Some kind of dark car."

"So who am I interviewing?"

He directed me to a house a few blocks up. It was the victim's grandmother's home.

I went inside. Two cops were in the house. Several people were crying in the living room. I ordered the cops to leave.

One woman came over to me. "We want to go see our boy. But they won't let us until we answer questions. Do you know how Ronnie is doing?"

"I don't know." I called the cops over. "Take these people to see their son, or whoever he is. It doesn't look like he's going to make it. Get them over there fast."

Everyone was stuffed as best they could into three cop cars, and off they went.

I walked over to the bloodstained sidewalk where Ross was standing. A train went by obscuring his voice. We waited.

I told Ross I sent them to the hospital.

We did what we could interviewing people in the area. There were six 9mm shell casings found on the road. They were photographed and put into evidence.

I went home.

In the morning Becky and I interviewed the family members. Ronnie died in surgery during the night.

I talked with Ronnie's mother.

"He didn't have enemies. To be shot that many times, it's just... I don't know," she said rubbing tears away. "He's my oldest. I have four children. He was the cornerstone of the family." She sobbed.

"What was your son doing there?"

"His father's mother lives up the street. You were there. He loves... He loved his grandmother. The violence, it needs to stop," she wailed.

"He was thirty?"

"Yes, last spring."

"Does he have a family?"

"Ronnie loved kids. He didn't have any children of his own. He's step-father of three. His fiancé is on her way. Ronnie loved kids. He used to help me with my day care business. The little ones will miss him." She started to sob again.

"So your son was there to visit his grandmother. That was two blocks away. Why was he down where he was shot?"

"I don't know."

I interviewed Ronnie's sister. The two of them had moved out of the area years ago, but came to visit often. She said Ronnie was paying for her tuition at Chicago State University as a nurse. "He always made sure I did my homework at school." She continued, "Ronnie wasn't an angel, 'cause none of us are, but what did he do so wrong that they took his life?"

This seemed such a normal family, which got destroyed by senseless gunfire. But there had to be a reason.

Becky interviewed an uncle. She met me in the hall. "Got anything?" I said.

"Nothing. The guy liked cars. According to his uncle he was a great mechanic. He wanted to start his own dealership with his uncle. That's where he worked."

We got all we could written down, so we sent everyone home.

"You find who did this to my nephew, or I will," the uncle hissed.

"Don't take the law into your own hands," I replied forcefully.

"Then do your job." He left holding Ronnie's mother in his arms.

"What do you think?" Becky said. "So tragic."

"So tragic, it is. Look into their businesses."

Becky and I were assigned to more homicides that month. The previous year's November had forty-five murders. This month wasn't over yet, ten days to go, and we were already at forty-three.

I looked at the compiled list for the month. I couldn't believe the ages. Some as young as sixteen, some as old as eighty. But the vast majority were black men in their twenties. So young.

It certainly hit home every time we had to go to the Cook County Coroner's office. We made the dreaded trek at least once a week.

As always, Dr. Brad Wilson would take us through our cases. Every crypt had a body waiting for autopsy. Every table had a cadaver on it. Most were young kids, all were black. Two were female. Ronnie Sawyer was one of them.

I had to wonder how these people would feel if they knew how indignant their final days before their burial would be: naked, exposed, cut open, organs weighed.

Wilson was returning Sawyer's organs into the chest cavity when we arrived. He gave us the three nine millimeter bullets sealed in an evidence bag.

Becky seemed to be interested in the anatomy aspects. It didn't seem to bother her one bit. I was getting used to it, but that I thought was a bit sad. To be used to dead people robbed of life so soon.

Ballistics later matched the bullets from Sawyer to a Glock used in another murder by the Latin Kings. Clearly we had a motive, Sawyer must have intruded into their turf.

Becky and I drudged on for the rest of the month with murder after murder.

CHAPTER 4

THANKSGIVING WITH A FAMILY

A note was on my desk when I got in Monday morning to call the financial forensic department.

I called the number.

"Ah, yes. I'm Alan Sang, of the Financial Crimes Unit. I've gone through De Luca's books, can you come here so we can talk?"

I was directed to the third floor of the headquarters downtown.

His office was small, against a window at least.

"Ah, you must be Marg. Come in. Can I get you anything? Coffee?"

"Coffee would be great, thanks."

"Have a seat, I'll be right back."

His desk was loaded with documents. Behind it, on the wall, was a diploma. He had a PhD in mathematics from Duke University. That was impressive.

He had a picture of his family on the desk. Him, his son and daughter, and his wife. All oriental. That kinda fit, I thought, in stereotypic fashion. Math, oriental...

He came back in. "Here." He sat down handing me a hot cup of steaming java.

"You have a PhD in math? Why are you not a university professor somewhere?"

After sipping his cup, he laughed. "I was, for a short time. I love mathematical puzzles. A friend of mine in the Boston Police asked me to look at some books from some company who was embezzling funds. He couldn't figure it out and asked if I could.

"I did – figure it out that is. I was hooked. People do very creative things to hide money. I found it intriguing to figure out how they do it.

"A job opportunity came up here twelve years ago, so I applied. And here I am. I love it. I get to play with numbers and figure out complex puzzles. This one was pretty easy, though.

"OK, so this is where we are with De Luca's accounts. He had a couple mill in his personal accounts. Plus the usual stocks and bonds. He owned seventeen properties. Here they are." He handed me the list.

It was mostly small apartment buildings, but he also owned a few storefront properties.

"And this is a list of companies he owned, five."

I looked at that list; one carwash company, one laundry mart, one billiard hall, and one transmission repair shop. But there it was, Chicago Student Housing. Nick Easton's name was there as co-owner.

"Hmm, with all his advertising over the years, I would have thought he owned more than this."

He did at one point. But he'd been buying and selling at a fairly regular rate, from what I can see. Making a profit for the most part. The last two years, he wasn't though. Guess the economy hit even him.

"Now, the interesting thing about the properties he still has, except the Student Housing, is they are all co-owned with known members of the Outfit."

I looked up.

"That's right," he said. "The Mob."

So his little museum was more than just a hobby.

"According to his financial statements we found in the safe, he also lent out money to a number of people, businesses mostly. At nine and ten percent. Guess to people who couldn't get loans at the bank. That's typical of the Outfit. We've seen this before."

I looked at the list. None of the names rang any bells.

"Maybe someone couldn't make a payment, and decided to take De Luca out?" I asked.

"Wouldn't be the first time that's happened."

"Anything else?"

"I didn't see anything about drug money, nor anything about firearms smuggling. Just real estate holdings for the most part. Oh, and he was covering up some of his income from the Feds. Seemed he was declaring just enough income to pay enough taxes to not trip any alarms. But he was definitely making money under the table. Mostly through those loans.

"Now, he was funneling the income from all his properties through three banks. I called them all to get their records. They're in that envelope."

"Well, this gives me a list to start with. Thanks for this."

"Any time."

"Oh, before I forget. Did you do the finances of Insur-Data?"

"No, Wayne did. Here, come with me."

We went a few booths along the wall. "Hey, Wayne, you finished the finances of Insur-Data didn't you?"

"Hi, Alan. No, not yet. Not all of it anyway."

"Can you get Marg here up to speed? She was the lead detective in that case." Turning to me he said, "Nice to meet you. Have a good day."

Wayne and I exchanged greetings. Seems Insur-Data was being investigated for fraud and embezzlement. No indictments had been served yet, but soon as he was done they would. He said a couple months more. "It will make a nice Christmas present for the company," he joked.

"Oh, you'll like this," he continued. "Insur-data was paying Easton's wife a salary, but she didn't log in any hours, nor is her name on any projects. Clearly they were trying to income split to save on taxes."

I smiled at the thought her perfect world was about to come crashing down. I felt for the kids, though. There's always collateral damage to the innocent when there's crime.

I thanked him, and I left with a thick envelope.

I got back to the office and informed Becky we were going on the road.

Our first stop was a transmission shop on West 34th Street. The store-owner wasn't there, but we got his number from the shop manager.

Becky called it as I looked around. She came up to me a few minutes later. "He hasn't seen De Luca in a couple weeks."

"Great, we're done here. What's next?"

"A car wash on West Chicago Avenue."

"Hmm, not likely anyone will be there. But there could be a number to call."

Again, that operator hadn't seen nor heard from De Luca in a month. I was expecting the same at the rest.

The billiard hall was closed, permanently by the look of it.

Becky looked at the list of homes in the Chicago Student Housing. "There's twenty two homes on this list. We're going to visit each one? No one will be home during the day. And with Thanksgiving coming, I doubt most will be around if they're all students."

I agreed.

We spent the next week visiting each home at night. No one had seen De Luca. One even asked if he still had to pay rent.

So there we were, the Friday before Thanksgiving and we hadn't made any progress.

"What are you doing for the weekend?" Becky asked.

"I'm visiting my daughter in Florida. I leave in a couple hours. And you?"

"Family in DC. I leave tomorrow. I'll be gone the whole week. So have a good trip."

I arrived at the Miami Airport two days before Thanksgiving. Pam and Angel met me there. Pam was starting to show her pregnancy.

The weather was great, compared to the deep cold I'd left in Chicago. So this was what it's like with no winter. Moving here was compelling.

We drove towards the Keys to the small metropolis of Florida City. Angel's uncle's villa was just west of town.

A villa it was. It was at least five acres in a village setting of other homes. But none had the property size of the villa. It was walled all around the living area, about a quarter of the property. The rest of the land was a mix of banana trees, orange trees, and even avocado trees. A large garden of vegetables ran along the south side of the wall.

We passed through a solid wood and iron framed gate into the center concourse. The courtyard was a circular drive, with a fountain in the center. Banana trees neatly adorned around the perimeter of the drive.

A large mansion was directly opposite of the gate. It had a three double garage doors on the left side of the house. A second floor took up the entire length of the garage, with a balcony hanging over the drive.

The front of the house was three stories, with six thick pillars holding up the overhang so people exiting their cars were covered. The right of the house was a large greenhouse two stories high.

On either side of the concourse were two identical two-story houses.

Not as huge as the mansion, but themselves much larger than a "normal" home.

"Each of those two homes are where my other uncles and their families live," Angel said.

As we drove under the canopy, a short stalky man with a mustache came out of the door. He took his sunglasses off and opened my door. "You must be Marg. I'm Luis, Angel's tío and head of the familia. Welcome to my humble casa."

My only thought at the time was Pam just married into wealth. I would never have thought it possible. Angel didn't look the part in Chicago. He was working at the local food store, likely at minimum wage.

We entered the main entrance. I was astonished. It was like in the movies.

"I don't want to be rude, Marg. Is it OK to call you Marg? We're going to be familia soon," Luis said holding my right hand in both of his.

"Yes, of course."

"Good. Good. That's good. I'm sorry, but I must leave. Angel here will give you the tour. I'll be back for cena. Then we will talk and get to know each other."

Turning to Angel he said, "You know which room she is to get right?"

"Yes, uncle, the one overlooking the pool."

Luis turned back to me. "The best guest room in the villa." He left in a hurry. Something was up.

The tour took an hour. They had enough bedrooms to sleep twenty people. Every bedroom had its own en-suite bathroom. There were nine guest bedrooms in all. Those rooms dominated the second floor. There was one central living room on that level.

On the main floor was a kitchen the size of my apartment. It overlooked the pool and back yard. Luis' wife, Zamira, was there with a few other women making the evening meals. She looked like Luis without the moustache and with longer, fuller hair. I wondered about the old tale that the longer people are together the more they start to look like each other was true.

She seemed a wonderful woman, offering me all kinds of tastes of what was to come for dinner.

The dining room, off the kitchen, had a table that could seat twenty people. People were setting it up with dinner ware and flowers.

There were five sitting rooms, each with full sized flat screen TVs. Off the back of one of those rooms was an exercise room, fully equipped.

We went into the basement next. There was a two-lane bowling alley, a twelve-seat theater, where each of the four lounge couch rows were elevated, just like a movie theater. The games room was off that, just past the stairs. There were two pool tables, and a card table for poker. A set of couches surrounded a number of flat TV screens with computer game consoles for each.

One thing I noticed was that this was a very religious family. A crucifix hung in every room. Not only were there religious paintings in most of the rooms, but also a number of religious sculptures were scattered around the premises. I was raised Catholic, so it wasn't unfamiliar. But it certainly was a bit overbearing.

We ended our tour back up at the second floor, at my bedroom. The room was bigger than my apartment. It had a small bar/kitchenette, an en-suite washroom, a huge walk-in closet, plus a sitting area with high-back chairs and a sofa. The king sized bed appeared puny in the oversized room. On the opposite wall to the bed, like in every bedroom, hung a large flat screen TV.

The south facing double glass doors exited onto an outside balcony, which had a view of the rectangular pool below. Beyond the pool were immaculate flowers, which ended at the white wash concrete wall obscuring the scene beyond.

It hit me. Every room in the house was all white. No other colors at all.

"You'll be comfortable here, Mom," Pam said. "Our room is next door."

"This is a huge house, Angel. Where is everyone?"

"Well, Uncle Luis had to go deal with a harvest of grapefruit. It's going to my parents' stores in Chicago."

I interrupted him. "Your parents own a grocery store, the one you worked at? That Pam worked at?"

"Yes, ma'am. Actually, my parents own three stores in the Chicago area."

"Sorry, go on," I said. I was in disbelief.

"The rest of the family is in the fields all around the area. We grow all kinds of produce, which we sell to grocery stores all over the country. Being so close to Thanksgiving it's very busy for us. But by the weekend, this house and the other two, will be overflowing with people. Our extended family will come from all over the country to be together on this day. There could be a hundred people all totaled."

"Staying here?"

"Oh, not everyone. Many will stay in hotels in Florida City."

"I have to say it's not as warm as I hoped, being Florida."

"Yeah, my uncle says it's one of the coldest winters he's ever seen. Hopefully it won't impact our crops."

The air was cool, but the sun was warm on the face. We spent the rest of the afternoon by the pool, sipping any number of intoxicating drinks. But they were so good. Better than the rum and coke I usually have. I could get used to this.

At dinnertime the table was full of people who gorged themselves on local produce and locally grown chickens done up in a number of ways. And more people were arriving. They ate by the pool not far away.

Luis and Zamira sat beside each other at the head, being equals. I sat further down with Pam and Angel. Beside Angel were his parents, Eliecer and Evelyn.

Eliecer looked like a younger version of his brother Luis.

The meal was preceded by everyone holding the hands of the person beside them as Luis spoke a prayer.

The Sotolongo family consisted of four brothers, and three sisters. Plus their families – each of which had at least four of their own children. One of Luis' brothers had twelve children!

Luis was the oldest, hence the head of the family. He owned the villa, and the surrounding farms.

I didn't say much over dinner. Though there was a number of inquiries as to when Pam's baby was to arrive, what they were going to call it, and so on. Newborns were a big deal in this family, quite obviously.

After dinner, Luis called me over to the bar and made me a Culto A La Vida. It's made with lime juice (fresh from the trees), cranberry juice, Havana Club 7 Añejo Rum with a teaspoon of sugar. It's served in a tall glass. It was the most tasteful cocktail I'd ever had.

"Go easy," Luis, said, "you can get mighty mareado."

I looked confused.

"You call it tipsy. Easy to do with this drink."

He made another for himself.

"I guess you have some questions for me," he said.

"I do."

"First, let me say, your Pam is a wonderful woman. Angel is madly in love with her. He wants a large familia. I hear you're an only child?"

"I'm a lone orphan now."

"I heard. I'm so sorry for your loss. My father died long ago. My madre died of cancer last year. It's a terrible time for a big familia like this. So what do you want to know?"

"You're Cuban, aren't you."

"Si, third generation here in Florida. When we were exiled when that barbarian Castro..." he spat on the floor, "...took over we lost everything. My familia did. My grandfather came here with almost nothing. He worked on one of the farms around here. Eventually, the familia pooled their resources and bought our first plot. Then it just grew. This villa was first built in 1965, and has grown since. We're still adding more. We built the wall just two years ago.

"It was a sad decision to make. It took away our view of the countryside. But we were concerned over the bad things happening of late. The world's going to mierda, shit. America is not the America I grew up in. We are losing too much of our freedom. Freedom was the reason my grandfather risked death to bring his familia here.

"I'm babbling on about politics. I'm being maleducado," he ended.

I had no idea what that word was, but I suspected its meaning was rude or impolite. "No, actually, I'm interested. At least over the last couple months I've been learning more about the political end of things."

"Well, Marg, política is everything. It touches all our lives. It decides if you are going to be a prosperous country or not. Just look at what Cuba used to be, and still is to a great extent.

"You couldn't own anything. No homes, no farms, no businesses, nothing. What drives people to better themselves. Typical serfdom, you know?"

I just shrugged.

"Oh, you know. In Cuba people worked twelve hours a day for seven days a week. That cigar sucking bearded prick said it was for the collective. For the good of the país. For him it was, sitting up there like some king while the rest of the peasants fed him and his fat brother.

"Communism isn't about collectivity for the good of all, it's about a few at the top wanting everyone else to be poor all the while providing them the royalty.

"That's why it always fails in the end.

"And yet, here we are in the United States of America, where we are supposed to be free to build our own futures. Instead we are moving backwards into a communist state.

"This fucking President... Oh, I'm sorry, I shouldn't use such language in the presence of a lady..."

"I'm a cop, I've heard a lot worse."

"Guess you have. Well, as I was saying, this Democratic..." he spat on the ground, "...president, I refuse to speak his name, is destroying this country.

"You know when the decline of the United States started?"

I shook my head.

"Democratic President Bill Clinton. There, I was forced to say his name. He started this all when he let China into the World Trade Organization. That communist dictatorship then sucked just about all the manufacturing jobs in America.

"And we are all suffering for it. Even your city is bankrupt. Anyways, I've hablar on too much already."

We paused for a few moments, but his message was sinking in.

Finally, he said, "But people still have to eat. Even in this bad economy we're still doing OK. You know, I work in the fields with my people. Come harvest I'm there, picking, packing, and driving.

"I own this company, but that doesn't give me a pass to sit on my las nalgas. I do the same work as all the rest of my familia. I prosper they also prosper. That's the American dream. These socialists who want everything free handed to them. It sickens me."

"I must say I'm impressed with what you have built here." I was near the bottom of my cocktail and already my head was starting to go light.

"Built by my father's own two hands, and his father before him, rest their espíritu."

The evening was a mass of people dancing, singing, playing musical instruments. Someone came over and pulled Luis away from the bar to join the festivities.

As the night drew on, more food, more people, more dancing, filled the merriment until way into the early morning. I don't recall when Pam finally got me into bed. Man, what a night!

After missing a few passageways, I managed to make it to the dining room, it was after 1:00pm. I've never slept in that long. Everyone I passed looked like me, hung over with a massive headache.

Evelyn made sure I got coffee. It was the first time we were alone. "I love your daughter. She's so beautiful. She will have a beautiful bebé."

"Thank you," I kind of blushed.

We spoke for a few minutes. They owned three stores in the North Chicago area, the one area, which was at least normal, not as crime ridden as the other areas.

Even then, she said they were robbed at gunpoint by three masked men not that long ago. She asked me if they had been caught yet. Of course, I didn't know, but promised I'd look into it for her.

"What is this world coming to," she said as she headed back into the kitchen.

The hired hands were serving breakfast. Luis came over later in the afternoon and sat beside me at a table by the pool.

"Too cool to swim today. One of our coldest falls I can remember."

I found that funny and so must have Angel. Chicago was in deep freeze, so Florida felt like the tropics.

Still, all I could manage was a nod as my head hurt so much.

He laughed. "You had a good time last night I see."

I gave a thumbs up while sucking back some coffee.

Once my head cleared a bit I asked, "I meant to ask you last night, but we got a little distracted. What does Angel do here? He's marrying my daughter, I have a right to know how he will support his family."

He looked at me strange. I realized it was a stupid thing to say in this mansion.

He laughed. "I know what you mean, Marg. My business is growing, and I promoted someone who looked after my Cuban mission. Angel has worked for me on that mission for a number of summers. So I asked him to run it."

"Mission? Religious work?"

He laughed. "No, actually it's illegal. But even you as a cop would approve. For decades we've been sending things to Cuba by boat. Very illegal, of course. But the State Department lets us do it. We send electronics, books, and other things they can't get in Cuba. On return, we bring back dissidents to the US. They get handed over to the State Department for processing as refugees. We've been doing it for decades. Even the CIA has used our shuttle to get agents into Cuba.

"Did you know that Cuba has to import eighty percent of their food? They have three growing seasons a year. But because of communism, they aren't producing properly. Fucking Castro." He spat on the ground.

"All Angel has to do is organize what needs to be sent to Cuba. But with the opening of the border now, it may all become legal. And more profitable, I will add. Angel will have his work cut out for him."

I didn't even know this took place. Of course, one hears of rumors, but weekly trips? I guessed they had to keep it as quiet as possible for it to be effective. I was kind of proud he was part of this noble cause.

On the following Monday, Pam and Angel took me to the house they picked out. It wasn't far from the villa. It was empty, as the former owners had abandoned it. It was real cheap, $125,000. Though it needed some fixing up, it was spacious with a large lot.

"See Mom," Pam said inside the house, "it has three bedrooms, one for you."

I smiled. "Maybe one day."

"If it's OK with you, Ma'am," Angel said, "we want this house. It's the third time we've been here."

I looked at the agent who was eagerly waiting with documents in hand. "We'll take it. I'll be paying cash."

Angel had to leave once the documents were signed. A trip to Cuba had to take place at the end of the week. That left Pam and myself to finish the details. The agent took us to a lawyer to get the last legal documents signed, then he drove us back to the villa.

I was confident that all was going to work for Pam and her new family. It was time for me to head back to Chicago.

I called all twenty-seven people, mostly businesses, about the loans De Luca made to them. Three were weird calls, so I visited them.

It wasn't so weird when I talked to the three of them at different locations. They were just happy "the fucking prick" was, they assumed, dead. When I inquired why they came to that conclusion, one just said "fate." They all gave rock solid alibis on the day De Luca went missing.

I looked over the rest of the list of people who had borrowed money from De Luca. One caught my eye. I called Becky.

She answered, "Hey, I'm supposed to be on vacation."

"I know, but what was the name of the used car dealership? Remember the guy that was shot down several weeks ago? You interviewed the uncle."

"Yep, I remember. He was starting that car dealership."

"That's him. What was his name?"

"Damn you would. Oh, I remember, Clark Hall. He was going to call it Uncle Halls Used Cars. Why?"

"That's him. De Luca lent him money for the dealership."

"And his nephew is now dead."

"I don't like coincidences."

I hung up. In the morning I'd pay Uncle Clark a visit.

Of the seventeen properties De Luca owned, ten were small apartments, three were vacant lots, and four were homes. I talked to all the tenants. Of course, none of them had heard from De Luca in months, they just either sent regular checks, or had direct withdrawals.

Midweek I went to the banks and talked with their managers. None of them knew if De Luca had been in lately. All his accounts had automatic transfers to his main account.

Dead end after dead end.

Next was Clark Hall. I waited for Becky to come back before we tackled him.

Hall was nowhere to be found. The family didn't know where he was.

I ended the weekend no further ahead than I did on my first day of this case. I dropped myself on the couch in front of the TV, rum and coke in hand. I missed the cocktails from the villa.

Someone from NASA was on about eight previously unknown near Earth asteroids with possible catastrophic impact potential had been discovered. They also found a host of smaller bodies that had the potential to wipe out a city.

He went on that they were somewhere between 100 and 300 meters in size. Hitting in the oceans, he said, would send tidal waves big enough to wipe out hundreds of millions of people.

What bullshit, I thought. I was getting tired of the endless fear mongering. If not so called global warming, it was this. I guessed we really couldn't ignore it. But then again, what can one do? If we're going to be struck in the head by a large rock, all one can do is bend over and kiss our own ass goodbye. Swell.

The next segment was on the one hundred people who were going to start a permanent settlement on Mars. I shook my head, turned the TV off and said, "Best give them all a Darwin Award now."

I was brushing my teeth for bed when my phone rang. "Hey, Marg," Becky said. "They found a body along the lake. It could be De Luca."

I took down the location, looked it up on Mapquest, and headed to Lakeshore Drive in a community south of Kenosha in Wisconsin, just over an hour away.

It was near 1:00AM by the time I got there. Blue and red flashing lights illuminated the expensive homes in this secluded neighborhood along Lake Michigan.

People lined the streets, even in this cold, to get a glimpse of some dead cadaver, half-rotted I figured.

Becky met me as I came up to the "Do Not Cross" yellow tape strung between two trees. Lights on poles turned the night into midday. Sparse snow falling twinkled as they reflected in the rays.

"He's over here," she said.

"What makes you think it's De Luca?"

"He's fat."

Was everyone infected by some kind of stupid tonight? Anyway, I needed to have a look.

The body was covered in a blue tarp.

I met the local State Police officer in charge.

"Looks like he washed up on the ice out there," he pointed out to the lake. The lake ice had formed out to about a hundred yards from shore. "Those people over there found him about two hours ago. That's their house there," the State Trooper said pointing at the house outside of the yellow tape. "They were out for a late night stroll, I guess. We had to borrow a snowmobile to drag his fat ass here. We're just waiting for the coroner to show up."

"Can I have a look at the body?"

"Sure."

We went over and he pulled the tarp off completely. It wasn't De Luca. The face was close, and the body size was similar in volume, but the clothes were all wrong. Besides, he had running shoes on. Running shoes in winter. Not De Luca's style.

"With our currents here, it looks like he was dumped into the lake off shore, maybe even the other side."

"The far shore?" I asked.

"Possible. It would take a couple months to get here."

Months. Way too long. I went up to Becky. "It's not him. But we can confirm that with DNA. I'm going home to bed. See you in the morning."

"Ok, I'll stay here a bit first."

DNA came back two weeks later. It wasn't De Luca. Some drunken idiot went out on the ice in Milwaukee, fell in and drowned. Swell.

I did get a break, Clark Hall called me. We arranged a visit for Becky and myself to talk to him at his home.

"Have you found my nephew's killer yet?" were the first words at the door.

"No, we need to talk."

Reluctantly he invited us in.

"You borrowed some thirty thousand dollars from Roberto De Luca?"

"Yeah. The bank wouldn't lend me any money for the dealership Ronnie and I wanted to start. What does this have to do with Ronnie's murder?"

"Did you know De Luca is missing?"

"No. But I haven't seen him in about a month, when I took the loan out."

"And not since?"

He snapped, "That's what I said."

"Are you having a problem paying De Luca?" I asked politely.

"No, not really. He wasn't expecting anything until we started to sell cars. Then on top of the loan payments, he was going to take five percent of each sale until the loan was paid off."

"Just selling cars?" Becky asked. "I thought you also had a garage."

"I do. I've had that for a while. But it's a struggle by myself now." He thought, "You don't think my nephew's killing was related to our loan, do you?"

"I don't like coincidences, Mr. Hall. Thank you for your time. We'll be in contact," I said.

"I don't understand," he complained. "How could I pay my loan if my nephew was dead? It doesn't make any sense."

I didn't have an answer for that. It could have just been another senseless gang thing.

We left, but this time maybe not empty-handed. There had to be some connection here between the murder of his nephew and him borrowing money from a Mob-linked De Luca. But paradoxically, with Ronnie Sawyer dead, it would be more difficult for Clark to make his business work. Hence more difficult to make his payments.

Detective Carlton James stopped me as we entered the squad room. "You had a murder of Darnell Flournoy a couple weeks ago?"

"Yes," I said. Becky stopped to listen.

"A Gail Gordon picked out the shooter, a Randal Daryl?"

"Yes, Daryl was arrested in Grand Rapids."

"Well, he's not going to be convicted now. Last night we found Gordon dead in an alley not far from her home."

Shit. Fuck me.

"Daryl was on bail. He's bolted. And no one else is willing to testify now. One added to the 'ex-cleared' list," Carlton said.

And so the 'no-snitch code' of Chicago's streets continues to hamper our abilities bring justice to the victims.

Carlton started to walk away when he turned and said, "Oh, and watch the news tonight on WGN, they're doing a segment on the department's budget cuts. This isn't going to get any better."

When I got home, I poured a glass of my friend, and turned on the news at 11pm.

After twenty minutes of various bad things happening around the world, mostly about terrorist attacks, like Yemen collapsing into anarchy, they got to the segment on our force.

I knew it was bad, but not this bad.

Last year, only 132 of the 507 murder cases in the city were solved and resulted in a conviction. The recent restructuring of how detectives were distributed, making them accountable for more cases, over larger areas, was responsible for the growing list of unsolvable cases, or so some so-called expert said.

The city, in an attempt to save money, had closed down two districts, one in the highly violent west side, merging them with other districts.

"It's a perfect storm of shit," one detective from Area Two on the south side was anonymously quoted. I wondered who that was. The voice sounded like Brian Olmstead.

The Superintendent, Dan Dillane, said they were hiring more detectives, but they had "a responsibility to taxpayers to make every dime count."

That was political double speak, in my opinion. He had a tough job trying to keep the department functional, while at the same time, keeping the politicians happy in a deteriorating economic situation.

A University of Chicago criminal professor said that the department was putting fresh people right into detective college because the city didn't want to take officers off the street. This was causing a rift with beat cops who wanted to get promoted as detectives.

I guessed my job was going to get a whole lot harder.

The beginning of the week brought something extraordinarily new to every detective on the force. Each area held a meeting with all their detectives together. It didn't matter if you were missing persons, homicide, special victims, the organized crime unit, or even the intelligence unit. We were all together in one room rented at a local hotel.

Our Area Commander took the microphone as we all wondered what was going on.

Some uniformed officers started to hand out brown envelops to everyone. I opened mine to see a photo of a number of rioters who were in the process of overturning a cop car. It was footage from Becky and my search for videos of the garbage riot. Along with the photo was the arrest warrant for the person circled in the picture – George Radcliff.

The call to order came.

"You have all been given arrest warrants," Commander Moore started. "You will pair up and execute these warrants today. This is citywide sweep, people, ordered by the Mayor. Go to it."

Someone else got up and explained how we were to pair up, by the numbers on our envelopes. They lined us up according to the three-digit number into columns and rows, just like little school children, according to the first and second digit. Then within our small group, we were to find our matching third number.

That's how they randomly pair us up so no one from the same squad would be working together. I wasn't sure the logic of that.

My counterpart found me, Sergeant Will Koteas from Intelligence. "You're Don Cunningham's daughter aren't you?"

I nodded.

"I knew your ol' man. We were in different areas, but I met him a few times. Great cop. Let's go and get this bullshit over with."

On the road Koteas complained about having to do this job. But at the same time he was pissed at the people we had to arrest.

We went to mine first on South Avenue J. It was a nice looking neighborhood of small bungalows. The house had a for sale sign, with a 'REDUCED' sticker on it. It wasn't the only one on the street.

A middle-aged man answered the door. His wife and two middle school aged kids were with her.

"Mister Radcliff?" I said.

"Yes. What's this about?"

Koteas forcefully said, "Step outside, you're under arrest for the destruction of public property."

"You've got to be fucking kidding me. For what?"

"Please don't make this any worse for you. Step outside," Koteas ordered.

"You do this in front of my kids? You arrest me in front of my kids and neighbors?"

"You should have thought about that before you torched one of our cop cars. Now step outside. Don't make me come in and get you."

The pissed off looking Radcliff came into the cold. I cuffed him as his wife handed Koteas a coat for her husband. The kids were crying.

I felt awful having to do this. The guy lost his job. It looked like he was losing his house.

On the way to the next arrest we had to make, one of Radcliff's former co-workers, Radcliff laid into us about how wrong it was that he lost his job.

Koteas looked into the mirror at Radcliff. "The new company hired you guys. You could have worked for them."

"Yeah, right, at minimum wage."

Koteas pulled over, slammed on the brakes, and parked the car. He turned around and looked at Radcliff.

"You're a god dammed garbage man. You're not saving the world or risking your life like we are. You're a garbage man. How much were you guys making? Twenty-five, thirty dollars an hour? For what, working only five or six hours a day, and getting paid for eight? Plus overtime?

"So you think you should get paid the same as us? Let me ask you. How many people have you had to kill? Oh, none of course. Absolutely none.

"I, on the other hand, have had to kill five people. Do you know what it's like to be forced to kill a twenty-two year old kid who has a knife on your partner's throat?

"Have you had to deal with a kid's brains splattered all over the sidewalk because he stepped into the wrong gang region?

"No, you haven't. Yet for some bizarre reason you seem to think that somehow someone who picks up our trash is worth the same as us?

"Your demands for more pay has caused our job to get harder and more dangerous. It's greedy shitheads like you who would turn this city into another Detroit."

He paused for a moment.

"How many years were you a garbage man?"

Radcliff didn't look at Koteas. "Look into my eyes, you garbage man." Radcliff didn't. "Hey, asshole! Look at me when I'm fucking talking to you!"

Reluctantly Radcliff surrendered.

"Let me ask you," Koteas continued his lecture. "When you were in high school, did you want to be a garbage man all your life? No, you didn't. You couldn't make it in the real world, so you took the job because of the pay and benefits didn't you. You hated the job. Likely bitched about it to the wife every day, didn't you.

"We, the two of us in the front seat here, we wanted to be cops. We always wanted to be cops. Not because of the pay, but because we wanted to make our streets safer. Safer for idiots like you and for your kids. You want your kids joining a gang, Radcliff?"

He shook his head.

"Of course you don't. Look, none one of us in this car want to be here doing this right now. Marg and I would much rather be catching real criminals, instead of hauling your sorry ass into court.

"This is what you're going to do." He looked at me, "What was that phrase that Bruce Willis said?"

I shrugged, as I had no idea what he was referring to.

"Oh, I remember." Koteas turned back to the shaking Radcliff. "You're going to cowboy the fuck up and be a man..." I chuckled inside. "When we get there, standing in front of that judge, you and your friend we're going to pick up next. You and your friend are going to plead guilty for what you did. You're going to pay the fine. Then you're going to take you sorry butt home, and on your knees apologize to your family for embarrassing them in front of your neighbors.

"Then you're going to find an honest job. I don't care if you have to go stock shelves at the grocery store in the middle of the night. But you're going to find that job, and make your family proud of you for keeping a roof over their heads and their bellies full.

"Because if you don't, and you destroy your family, Marg or I may have to one day pick up one of your kids off the street with their head blown off.

"Do I make myself clear?"

He nodded.

"Good." Koteas turned around, put the car in gear and drove to the next address.

Wow, now that was one tough love speech. I felt sorry for the poor guy. But I bet he'd do it right for his family.

CHAPTER 5

GOLDEN SHIT

One Saturday morning, after I made my breakfast, I decided I needed to do something different. I had so many notes on my father's arrests, there were so many people, that my head was spinning trying to figure it out.

The night before, as I lay in bed trying to drift off, it dawned on me what to do. I needed to make a chart.

I got my tools out, and took the flat screen off the wall. I moved the small dresser I had under the TV. I actually had to completely rearrange my living room to free up the only long wall I had available.

I started in the morning, and I just kept going. I didn't even venture out to get a coffee.

Pam called, but I made the conversation short.

By Sunday night I was done, well, as to how far I had gotten in my research.

On the wall was a spider web of lines connecting to boxes. Each box was a name of someone my father was in contact with from his notes. Each line was a connection of who gave my father the next contact, and so on.

What I needed to do was to see who was still alive, who was still in prison, and who was free on the streets.

Then I could go and visit those I could to get the information I needed.

Becky and I went to another shooting. A fifteen-year-old kid was in the hospital hanging on for dear life. We found the mother in the waiting room while her son was in surgery.

They were very distraught, but we needed to get what we could. I started with the victim's mother, Iris Ramirez.

"This code of silence and 'don't talk' and 'snitches get stitches' is bull crap," she said.

"I know somebody knows something," she pleaded. "All closed eyes aren't sleep." She wept.

"Can you tell me what happened?" I said.

"I spoke to Nicolás on Friday by phone and told him I was going to the school to pick up his report card. He decided to stay with a friend for the night," she said.

The police officer in the room said, "Nicolás was walking with a friend in the 10400 block of South Bensley Avenue around 10:45 p.m. The friend said the driver of a dark minivan opened fire and then sped off.

"The friend said Nicolás had spent Thursday night at a friend's house and didn't come home last night."

The mother said, "I knew something was wrong when I noticed missed calls on my cellphone.

"I looked at my phone and had seven missed calls from Nicolás' phone and four missed calls from his friend's mom's phone. Nicolás don't call me back to back to back like that seven times. I called him back to back seven times," Iris said all teary eyed.

She said she couldn't remember if it was her son's friend or the friend's mother who broke the horrible news that Nicolás had been shot.

"The doctor was just here," the cop said. "The boy had been shot in his abdomen and his heart stopped. They cut him open to restart his heart to try to keep him alive. The doctor told the mother that it didn't look good."

"Ma'am," I said. "Who would want to shoot your son?"

She explained her son was a sophomore, and had gotten into a fight earlier in the week after leaving his high school.

The cop said the shooting could have been in retaliation for the fight.

"Fucking kids shooting kids because of a fight?" I said.

"I know, it's sad. If I got in a fight, that was that. My father would go see his father, and they would have words, end of story. Today, kids shoot each other." The cop shook his head.

"Any ideas who?"

"The friend got a plate number. We'll have them soon enough."

Iris continued, "Nicolás was one of the school's strongest students. He loved math. He dreamed of going to Florida A&M University to major in architectural engineering. He was on Butler's first football team. Now nothing." She sobbed again.

The doctor came in about an hour later with the news. Nicolás didn't survive the surgery.

The next day we got a hit on the vehicle, spotted at Trumbill Park, not far from the shooting.

Becky and I went to meet Brian and Carleton. We got to the area, and parked behind their unmarked car.

I walked over to their vehicle. "So, where's the van?"

"On Oglesby in the back behind the complex. We were waiting for you," Carleton said.

"What's the plan?"

"You come in from the north. We'll come in from the south. There's no other way out. Then we wait for them to pick the vehicle up."

As we came along Oglesby, we saw the minivan parked under some trees. It was quiet.

The other guys radioed they were in position.

We waited...

We waited...

Becky dozed off.

We waited all night in the cold. It started to snow.

The next morning a fresh layer of snow was on the ground, and the sun was starting to peak over the horizon.

Two black men came over to the vehicle. I jabbed Becky in the ribs to wake her up.

One unlocked the door, and got in. The other looked around, then got in on the passenger side.

"Go, go!" Brian yelled into the radio.

We sped up to behind the vehicle, while our other car cut them off from moving forward. The passenger side man bolted over the fence and into the bushes.

Carleton stopped the driver at gunpoint.

Becky and I ran off in pursuit. I got on the radio to get backup.

We emerged a few hundred feet into an open area. We were in a large railway yard, at one of its ends. In the distance we could see the perp running towards the roundhouse. A line of footprints in the snow followed him.

He ran over the tracks, tripping to the ground as he looked back at us.

We ran as fast as we could. I radioed for backup to meet us at the west side of the yard.

He made it all the way to the roundhouse where a crew was working on a locomotive.

"Stop him, we're police!" I yelled.

One of the men picked up some big tool, and threw it at our runner as he passed by. He went down and didn't get up.

We caught up to him. He was rolling in the snow, moaning. The huge wrench, which caught him in the head, lay beside him. He was bleeding profusely from his right side.

Completely out of breath, and spent, I thanked the workman, as Becky cuffed him.

I read the perp his rights.

Back at the Division we put him in a lineup. Nicolás' friend, Tony, reluctant at first, picked the running man as the shooter.

The county lawyer assigned to the perp complained that his client was the only one in the lineup with his head bashed in and covered in blood soaked gauze.

Didn't matter to me. We caught the murderer. Now, the question was why.

I took the perp, eighteen-year-old Aaron Jefferson, into an interrogation room. We got a semi confession. Seemed the fight was between Nicolás and Jefferson's younger brother. Jefferson wanted to show his brother that he didn't take "no shit from anyone," in his words.

I shook my head in disbelief.

Hollenger was outside watching through the mirror. "Welcome to homicide," he said sarcastically as I came out of the room.

I'd had enough. I was beginning to wonder if I made the right move. After going through most of my father's early notes, there was nowhere near the number of murders as this, especially murders for no reason other than a show of who's the boss.

Five AM on a Friday morning, Becky called me. We had a break-in on West Parker Avenue, with a man shot. Our assistance was urgently needed.

We came into the small two-story house, but was stopped at the front door by an officer. "She won't come out."

I could see part of a body on the floor behind the cop.

"Who won't come out?" I asked.

"A little girl. She's cowering in the kitchen broom closet with a sawed-off double-barreled. I think it still has a cartridge in it. Maybe a female voice will get her to come out."

"How old is she?"

"I can't tell. Soon as I peer around the corner she points the gun at me."

"Where's the mother?" Becky asked.

"Dead upstairs. OD'ed. There's a couple lines of cocaine on the bathroom vanity."

"I'll check it out," Becky said.

"Hey," the cop put his hand out to stop Becky, "It really stinks in there. The rigor shit himself bad, you may want to wait for the fire department to come with their air bottles." Becky looked strange at the cop.

"Suit yourself," he said to her.

She took two steps into the main hall and immediately came back outside. She looked like she was going to puke. "He's... not... kidding. Oh, that's acrid." She took a deep breath and quickly went upstairs.

"Thanks for leaving me with the gun wielding kid, and the stench," I said annoyed.

I took my coat off, and got my badge out. "Know her name yet?"

The cop shook his head.

The fire eaters showed up and put one of the air systems on me. After a check it all worked I gave the thumbs up.

I crept up to the body which was half in the kitchen. A large pool of blood was congealing on the vinyl floor. The corpse's ass end was oozing brown fluid through the pants.

Swell.

I looked back at the cop. "When did this happen?"

"I don't know. The neighbor outside heard the shot. But didn't call right away." He said it was around 3AM. The cop moved away from the door to get some fresh air. Popping back to the doorway he said, "Child Services is coming. They should be here any minute."

"Hello, little girl?" I said loudly. I turned to the cop and said, "It is a little girl, right?"

"We think so judging by her room upstairs."

I said hello again into the kitchen. "I'm detective Margory. What's your name, honey?"

There was silence. I did a quick peering around the corner, and caught the glimpse of a very young black girl. She was holding the shotgun towards the dead man.

"What's your name?" I said again. "You look scared. But the police are here now, there is nothing to be scared about."

With each breath of the Scuba gear I sounded like Darth Vader. There was no way she was going to trust me with the mask on. I took a deep breath and took the face shield off.

The stench was so bad I could smell it even holding my breath. What the fuck did this guy eat before being shot? How did the little girl not bolt with the smell? I peered around the entrance to the kitchen, looked at her and asked again for her name.

After a few moments the child quietly said, "Elizabeth."

"Oh, that's a beautiful name. I like that name. Can I call you Lizzy?"

I had no choice I had to take a breath of foul air. It was all I could do not to puke myself.

"That's what my mommy calls me. Is she still sleeping?"

Swell. She doesn't understand, or doesn't know. "She's still sleeping, Honey. We're here now. Can you come out of the kitchen now?"

"My mommy told me when she was sleeping to shoot any strangers in the house."

This kid sounded like five or six. What sick fuck would tell a little girl that? "We aren't strangers, Honey. We're the police. Look."

I exposed my right hand to her, with my badge showing. "Can I come in, Honey?"

There was a pause. "Lizzy, can I come in, Honey?"

"Ok. But just you."

I slowly came into the kitchen. She was wearing a dirty nightie. Her hair was done up in lots of tight braids mixed with beads. I looked at the body. He was a black man, in his twenties, wearing a black hoodie and shit stained grey jogging pants.

"Looks to me, Honey, you did what your mamma told you to do. Very good job. Now give me the gun, Honey." I extended my right hand.

After a bit of thinking she said, "OK." Then handed the gun to me barrel first. I quickly turned it around, and broke it open. A spent and live cartridge were in the tubes. I handed the shotgun to the cop, who was turning blue holding his breath. I guessed he figured if I could stand it, he could too. I then put out both my hands to pick her up.

I took her past the living room, which was a terrible mess. Dirty dishes were everywhere. A jar of peanut butter and a jar of raspberry jam were open beside an almost exhausted loaf of white bread. We went outside where Child Services were waiting.

I went to the cop as Becky came outside. "She's dead. Been a couple days by the looks of it."

Fuck me, the poor kid was all alone in the house for days with her dead mother upstairs. How can people be so irresponsible? But that's what drugs do.

Back at the Division, we were writing our report on the event previous, when Carlton and Brian came in arguing.

"I'm just sayin' if one of those bystanders had a gun, that priest will still be alive, and instead it would be two towelheads dead," Brian said.

"Unless they shot someone else by accident. Hey, Marg. I heard about the kid. Nasty. But at least you missed ours."

"What happened?" I asked.

"A bunch of people were waiting for a bus on West North Avenue. Some priest was there, waiting for the bus. Well, some car comes up, two guys get out with machetes. They grab the priest, took him over to the building and proceeded to chop his head off. In broad fucking daylight!"

"They were screaming 'Alli Akbar', or so the other people said," Carlton added.

"Yeah, that was the weird thing. They all stood there like mannequins watching. No one helped the priest. A priest getting killed before their eyes and they did nothing."

"Did you get the perps?" I asked.

"No, they took off in the car. We found it a few blocks west burnt to a crisp," Carlton said.

"Damn Jihadists have now struck here. Right here in our town. In broad fucking daylight! Mark my words, it's a perfect storm of shit," Brian said.

Bloody hell, it was him quoted on TV!

Boy, was I glad that week was over. But Saturday was to become an eye opening experience. I was going to Sheridan Correctional Center, in Sheridan, Illinois.

I watched the news with my end-of-the-day friend – his name was rum'n coke – like I did every night. There was a segment on the beheading of the priest. I stopped in disbelief.

"A priest was beheaded by a lone crazy man today as bystanders did nothing. He managed to get away. Police are still looking for a bearded man with long black hair wearing a khaki colored coat."

What the fuck was that?! This political correctness bullshit of the media was starting to piss me off. I had to wonder about anything they reported.

I had already made the arrangements a week ago with the warden of the Sheridan Correctional Center to see an inmate. It was with one of Dad's contacts who was spending life in prison for a triple homicide.

I waited at the glass partition for Emilio Lincoln to arrive. He was an old white haired black man. The thirty years behind bars had taken its toll.

"What't you want woman?" he said picking up the phone.

"Do you remember being arrested by a Don Cunningham?"

"What't it to you if I was or wasn't?"

"He was my father, and I'm tying up some lose ends from his old cases. It would have been in 1986."

"I remember your ol' man. You look like him. He ripped me off. He's a dirty pig cop. Your ol' man was a dirty cop."

"How so?"

"How many times do I have to say, you bitch. He ripped me off."

"How?"

"He stole my money, about forty G's. He promised if I gave him the money, I wouldn't go to jail. Does this look like I'm not in jail?"

"You murdered three people in 1995. I looked at your file. My father had nothing to do with that arrest. You fucked yourself."

"Your ol' man still ripped me off. I gave him some names for my freedom, and he ripped me off. I told the pol-eece 'bout what he did, but they no believe me."

"Do you know if he did the same thing to others?"

"Hell, yeah. I know a few dudes he ripped off."

"You got their names?"

"I'm done giving up names. You get me out'a here and I'll give you names. Are we done here?"

"Yeah, we're done here." He got up and left before I could thank him.

On my drive home I wondered how deep my father's corruption went. My gut ached because of this.

On Monday morning I was at my desk dealing with some of my new cases. I was finishing up my weekly report when the phone rang.

"Detective Cunningham?"

"That's me."

"This is Special Agent Alex Kiley from the FBI."

Great, they want to take another case from me. I bet they want the De Luca file if he was involved with the Mob. The FBI always had to take my cases away.

"How can I help you?"

"I understand you're looking for a Roberto De Luca?"

Yep. Here we go. Swell. "You found him?"

"Hmm," he paused. "Some of him. Can you come here?"

"Where is here?"

"Just outside Solon. Just a second, I'll text you the directions."

Solon was in Iowa, a four-hour drive for me.

I arrived at a pig farm just west of town by late afternoon. Becky stayed behind in Chicago as she was checking some more leads on the three people who borrowed money from De Luca.

There were Iowa State Police and FBI everywhere, mostly clustered around one of the long barns.

I was met by a man in a gray suit, with a blue tie. He had an FBI vest over it. He was around my age, with short well-cut brown hair, with a few strands of gray. Just a little taller than me.

"You must be Marg Cunningham," he said shaking my hand.

"Yes."

"I'm Alex. I spoke with you on the phone. Glad you could make it."

"So why am I here?"

He showed me a nugget of gold in the shape of a crown of tooth.

"De Luca's?" I asked.

"Yep. Some kid found it cleaning out the pig paddock. Just over there on the other side of that barn. He showed it to his dad, who called the State Troopers. They sent in a team to go through the pig shit and they found a human toe in a corner in the barn. We're waiting on the DNA, but I'll bet a week's worth of donuts, it's De Luca's."

"How do you know the gold was De Luca's?"

"We emailed a photo of the tooth to every dentist in the Midwest. We got a hit. A dentist in Chicago IDed the crown as his work."

"That's all you found of De Luca?"

"So far. Not holding my breath for any more, though."

"Tell me he wasn't fed to pigs."

"Looks that way."

I had bacon with my eggs this morning. I felt sick.

"The Mob did this, right?" I asked, knowing the answer.

"Looks like it. We've been staking out this farm for months now. We think they're money laundering funds through here. Jackpot, now we know they've been disposing of bodies as well. Hopefully we'll find more than just De Luca."

We toured the area. After about an hour, Alex said, "Let's go into town for some lunch."

"I'm a little grossed out for lunch, aren't you?"

"I'm famished. Haven't eaten anything since this morning. Maybe we can find a restaurant with ham sandwiches."

He smiled at me in a joking fashion. Funny guy...

Alex laughed at my expression. "Actually, Food and Health have already sent notices around here about not serving any pork products. They're also tracking down the hogs for the last few months. A lot of people are going to lose a lot of money.

"Hey, there's an Arby's in Iowa City, on your way home anyway. My treat."

We both had roast beef sandwiches. At least cows don't eat meat. We chatted about personal stuff. He was, like me, single, never married, except to his work. Unlike me he had a family: A brother and sister each with two kids. His parents were living in Chicago. His siblings also lived near the surrounding suburbs of the Chicago area.

We talked about work. Alex was stationed in Chicago in their building on Roosevelt Avenue. We exchanged cases. He seemed genuinely sorry the FBI took my cases, and that I never got credit.

He didn't know about the Easton case, but he promised me he would look into what the FBI was doing about it and report back.

We parted ways at the parking lot. Alex had to stay for a few more days. Before he drove off, he said he would make sure all information about De Luca would be made available to me as a courtesy. I headed home.

Seemed a nice enough fellow. He was willing to let me take credit for De Luca, even though I had not had any break on the case. Clearly, now that his body, well, part of it anyway, was out of State, the case would belong to the FBI. I was done with it, or so I thought.

About three weeks later, Alex called me on my cell.

"How did you get my number, anyway?" I said.

"I'm the FBI, I know everything." He laughed. "Can we meet? I've got some info for you and a proposition."

That afternoon we had lunch again at a local restaurant not far from the Division.

"So, here's the situation with Easton. As of last week, they closed the book on the case. They agreed with the theory that he was in Brazil. The trail went cold, as it looks like he's changed his name."

"Damn it."

"Something's wrong?"

"That's not what I think happened." I explained my theory of Whitman killing Easton.

"Interesting idea. But I can see why it was rejected. Anyway, nothing more you can do about it now."

"No, I'm preoccupied with other things."

"Like De Luca?"

"No, I'm off the case, we closed it." My eye's squinted. "Since it's now the FBI's case. But also I'm busy with my father's history." I didn't explain too much. Just that I wanted to learn about his military history, his time in Viet Nam, and how he solved so many cases. I didn't say anything about the money.

"My mother's brother was in Viet Nam. Roger O'Keeffe. He was a Warrant officer. Intelligence and such. He has some interesting stories. I can hook you up with him. Maybe he can show you how to get more information. He lives in L.A. though."

We ate quietly for a few moments. He took a slurp from his Coke, cleaned his mouth off with the napkin and said, "So, what do you think about all these killings?"

"With the cops?"

"Yes, and others. But let's start with the cops. You agree with the protesters?"

"I think the police need to do the proper investigation. And let the courts decide. That's how our system works."

"I'm not referring to that. I'm asking, what would you do in the cop's place? Would you have shot the kid?"

"No one knows that answer until the time comes. I'd like to think the day will never come when I would be forced to put someone down. As far as I know my father never used his weapon in anger to tarnish his career. I'd like to be proud of that."

"Of course."

"Have you been in that situation before?" I asked.

"No. Not really. I was on a raid once, in Alabama. But I didn't have to shoot anyone. There was a shootout. Our snipers took care of them. None of our guys were shot. Thank God for our surgical sniper teams. I don't care what other people say, snipers are not cowards by any means. They are instrumental in saving lives."

I had to agree with that. Even our SWAT team has had to use deadly precise shots to take out a situation that was rapidly getting out of hand.

"But over all, you think the protestors are right?" he asked.

I was wondering why these types of questions were coming my way. Was he probing my integrity to be unprejudiced in cases? If so, why?

"It's a free society. Whether I agree with them or not, is not the issue. They are free to protest," I replied.

"Even to call death to cops? That's what they're doing in New York."

"No, I don't, obviously, agree with that. To me that's just intent to murder. Or at least entice people to murder. That itself is a crime."

"Good, that's the answer I wanted to hear. Of course, freedom to express one's views, however offensive it is to others, is a must allow in our Union. Any free society for that matter. Something these radical Muslims don't seem to understand."

Hmm, he was going to go off on some anti-Islamic tirade?

"I know that might sound Islamiphobic, but think about it. The people who are really afraid of these Muslims are the ones who are afraid to offend them. Look around the country. We are pandering to their ways, which they are entitled to have, but at the same time we are not entitled to our views? I think the liberal politically correct class are the ones who are Islamiphobic, not the rest of us who have every right to protest, or be critical.

"As you said, if those people can protest the police in a free society, we should also be free to protest the encroachment of Islam into our public lives. Or am I wrong here?"

I didn't understand why he would bring up this political hot potato. However, I had to think about that. He did have a valid point. This was a man of true integrity, willing to openly express what he felt was right. He reminded me of my father. Swell, that's all I needed: to get a father complex on this guy.

We finished our lunch, and it seemed we were done with our meeting.

"You said you had a proposition," I asked.

"I do. I've been cleared for this because of our short handedness. I've also cleared it with your CO. I'd like it if you could help me with my investigation into the Outfit. Share resources, and such. We'd be working together almost every day. You in?"

Now how did this come about so fast? I had to think about it. Me. Working with the FBI. How ironic.

CHAPTER 6

THE FBI ARRIVES

I arrived at my desk in the morning to a surprise. Boxes and boxes piled around my desk. Becky wore a huge smile as she sat on one of the piles.

Alex and three other FBI agents were waiting for me.

"What's with this?" I said.

"To show our cooperation," Alex said. "We're sharing some recent cases with your department. This is all the Outfit and gang activity we have in your jurisdiction."

"Don't you guys already share this with us?"

The three of them chuckled. "Well," Alex said sheepishly. "Some things we share. Some things we don't. This is what we don't share."

Captain Hollenger came in. He queried where it all came from, which Alex had to explain again. Hollenger called a few detectives over and asked them to disseminate this information. "Marg, you should marry this guy. We could use his close relationship. Thank you, sir."

They laughed. I blushed. Alex just looked at me with a slight grin.

"I'll call the Gang Unit in so they can get up to speed," Hollenger said. He left to make the call.

"I can stay, but these guys have to leave," Alex said.

The other two FBI agents left, Becky went into the washroom. The two of us were alone in the squad room. Well, not alone, alone, as everyone went about their business.

It was an awkward few seconds as we stood there. Alex was playing with the top of one of the boxes.

"So," I said, "You did all this just for us?"

"Well. Yeah. With all the anti-cop sentiment going around. With so much animosity built up over the years." He looked right into my eyes. "I think it's right that we start to work more closely together. Don't you think?"

"We? As in you and me?"

He held my right hand gently and said, "Of course. Come and have dinner with me tonight. Let's take some time off from the world and just be together. What do you say?"

I was deeply flattered. But why me? I'm not that great. Hell, the only guy who recently was interested in me was Abinormal. Which reminded me, since I got to homicide I hadn't seen Norman at all. What a relief.

"So?" he queried.

I reluctantly said, "OK."

Becky came back. "So what's the story? Are we going to get briefed on all this?"

Hollenger came back. "Tomorrow. They're all busy. Can you be here tomorrow, Alex?"

"Sure can. I'll see if Byron can come too. He's our gang expert. Let me call him." Alex went off.

He came back a few minutes later, "Yep, what time, Cap?"

"Ten."

"10am bud. That OK?" Alex said in the phone. "Great, see you then."

He hung up.

That night, as I got dressed up... Dressed up? The only outfit that could remotely look like a dress for on the town was at least ten years old. The last time I wore it was at a CPD official party event, some four years ago. It still fit, which I found surprising.

Hell, I even put a bit of makeup on. Not much, just enough to look, well, sexy I guess.

As I waited, I was getting a little nervous. This was my first date, since, damn, it was Pam's father and our one-night-stand.

Alex picked me up at six and we took a taxi to The Loop district. That's where the transit system all came together at the downtown.

We went to the Girl and the Goat restaurant. First we ordered pre-meal drinks before our seat was ready. We both had their "Best of Three" cocktail, made from ketel one vodka, pimms #1 (whatever that was), cucumber and lime. It was the best drink I'd ever had. Better than the one's at the villa.

It dawned on me as we chatted. "This place is always packed. It's a month waiting list. You planned this a month ahead? Rather presumptuous aren't you?"

"No. Not really," Alex confessed. "I know the owners. Sort of, my father knows them well. It's a long story. But they told me any time I needed to come to eat, just call and they'd slot me in. This is actually the first time I've used the favor."

Dinner was called just fifteen minutes later. As we made our way through the maze of people enjoying their meals, I thought I saw a couple of celebrities.

We had a great table. We could watch them create their masterpiece meals for the patrons.

We got plates you could share together. That was a deliberate tactic by Alex, I was sure. He was trying to get closer to me. But would I let him? I wasn't sure yet.

We had their famous crisp braised pork shank, shishito peppers and roasted cauliflower. We washed it down with their Omegang beer.

It was a wonderful romantic evening. Something I hadn't enjoyed since before Pam was conceived. Actually the last time was when Pam was conceived, I remembered with a bit of delight.

The thought made me think that Alex would want to have sex with me. It wasn't a thought I was thinking of rejecting.

"So, tell me about your family." Alex broke my thoughts. "Christmas is coming. Are you going to Florida to be with your daughter and her new family?"

"No, actually I'm not. With the new relations we have with Cuba, her boyfriend wants to have Christmas there with the rest of their extended family. Some huge reunion."

"And you weren't invited?"

"I was. But I've decided not to go."

"Why? Why would you give up the chance to be with a large family?"

"I'm not used to large families, well, not that large. I was there for Thanksgiving, and to be honest, I was overwhelmed with so many people.

"Besides, the last time I spent Christmas with Pam was when she was seventeen. It was just the two of us. I made the mistake of telling her a bit about her father. She was furious I kept it from her. She moved out the next day. She went to New York with some friends. But she tracked her father down, and went to stay with him in San Diego."

"In all those years, you've spent your Christmas alone?"

"No. Before my father died, I'd spend it with my parents. Just the three of us. After he was gone, it was just my mom and I."

"But now she's gone. So you're planning to spend this Christmas alone?"

"I guess."

"No, you're not." He got his phone out, picked a number and waited for the call to go through. "Hi, Mom?"

I could hear a woman's voice, but not what she said.

"Mom, make sure you set another place at the table. I'm bringing someone for Christmas."

I could hear the voice go into excitement.

"Mom, you'll like her. She's just like you."

Oh, shit. He wants his momma for a wife. Geeze, and I was getting attracted to my father. Swell.

After a few more words, he hung up.

"No, you're not like my mother, don't worry. I just say that because she likes it. You're similar in your mannerisms, but you are very different in the ways that count."

That relieved my apprehension. I thought that was a compliment.

After dinner we walked through the diamond district along Wabash. That's where people go to buy wedding rings. I got the feeling he was fishing.

Then we made our way down by the waterfront. It was cold and crisp, but the air was calm. Light fluffy flakes of snow reflected off the lights as they floated to the ground around us. Alex held my hand.

"Have you been married, Alex?"

"No. Umm, sort of. Some say, my mom actually, say I'm married to my job. I just haven't had the time. Nor have I found someone who I could connect with."

And there it was. His eyes made the connection. I felt nineteen again, when I wanted to be loved.

"I'm getting cold," I said. "Let's go back to my place for a night cap." I wanted him to make love to me. This man swept me off my feet. I didn't think it was ever possible I could find love. But this man appeared to be it.

First thing going inside my apartment, Alex went right to my wall chart.

"What's this?"

"Every one of my father's arrests. Well, it will be when I'm done."

"Wow, that's a lot. These are people arrested I assume, but what are the lines?"

"Every line is a reference in my father's notes to another person he got from that person."

"Ah, I see. And this is a progression in time from left to right."

"Yes."

"Interesting. This is a lot of work."

"I'm not done yet. I'm only into the 80's."

"You're going to need another wall," he laughed.

"Look who's the primer," I said pointing to the first one.

"Fuck me. De Luca. Your father arrested De Luca, back in 1975?"

"This all started with him."

"What's with the different colors for each name?"

"Yellow is still in prison. White are still on the street. Red is dead, of course."

"Lots of red ones. Hey, De Luca is still white, you haven't updated him yet," Alex chuckled.

"Yeah, I'll change it."

"This is a lot of work. What do you hope to get from all this?"

"A pattern."

Alex looked confused.

"My father had almost double the number of arrests and convictions than any other detective in Chicago. I want to know why. It has to do with all these connections. Each one precipitating the rest." There was no way Alex was going to learn about how my father made all these connections. Hell, I didn't even know all of it myself.

"See that many of them are dead ends. Literally, in some cases." I chuckled.

"Same name over several times."

"Yes, looks like one gave up another, which eventually came back to the same person again in a loop."

"That must have been frustrating for your father. Par for the course, unfortunately."

He looked at it in detail, nodding his head a few times.

"I assume these are different endings you've noted at the end of the lines."

"Yes, some as petty as car theft. Some robberies. A few murders. Lots of drug cases cracked."

"Yeah, in those cases someone else just fills the void."

"You can see that in this chart, when new people pop up as major players when my father bagged someone. Never ending war against crime."

"Or another gang takes them out."

"Yep, see here," I pointed to some notes. "I've indicated that."

"You must be very proud of him."

"I am." That was a lie. I couldn't tell him that I was worried my father was dirty and taking bribes.

"Looks to me you're trying to find his secret and emulate him."

If only I could tell him how true that was, but not in the way he thought.

"Hmm, if I had free time maybe I could find some pattern you haven't thought of yet."

I kind of looked hard at him. I'd found a pattern. There was no way I wanted anyone else to find it. Seemed he picked up my silent rejection of his offer. He quickly said, "But this is your project. I shouldn't interfere."

Alex finished with, "I'm sure your father would be immensely proud of you. Now, Marg, what've you got to drink around here?"

I poured him a rum and coke, plus one for myself. I sat on the couch beside him.

"So, those questions at the Arby's, your interrogation, was that to see if we were compatible, or professional?"

"Hmm, they were rather narrow in subject. A bit of both. To see if you fit in. To be more personally compatible I would need to investigate you more."

We laughed over a few more drinks, then we went to bed, very late.

In the morning I work up completely satisfied. His performance was wonderful. But he wasn't in the bed when I opened my eyes. Did he leave? Did he have second thoughts? Was this just another one-night stand? How would we work together after that?

But I could hear rustling in the kitchen. I could smell cooking. Then he appeared with a tray in his hands, and nothing else.

"When was the last time you got served breakfast in bed by a naked waiter?" he said with a wink and smile.

"Never," I mewed. "You can do this any time you want."

No, there was no pork in the breakfast. He made a four egg omelet with chopped green onions, chopped green peppers, diced mushrooms, and grated cheese. It was divine.

He even made coffee, which I rarely do at home because I just can't get it to savor the same. But this was just like from the drive through.

Maybe this is why it all tasted so good. Someone else made it for me.

After breakfast, and another round of sending me to the height of orgasm, we decided we better do what we got paid to do: police work.

While I was getting dressed, Alex was looking at my chart again. I came out of my room pulling down a sweater.

"I know one of these names," he said tapping on one of the last squares on the wall.

"Who?"

"Paul Cerone. If I'm not mistaken, this is John Cerone's father. If that's the case your father was onto the Outfit."

"Interesting."

"Will be when you fill the rest of this in. We've been trying to nail the

Outfit since the Capone days. They're the only Mob family in Chicago."

I looked at the clock on the microwave. It was almost 11am. "Shit, isn't your friend coming today to brief us?"

Alex nodded, and laughed. "For ten. We need to get going."

Soon as I locked my door, he grabbed me and kissed me on the lips with passion. "I'll be back here tonight, and every night."

"Don't you have your own place?" I said sheepishly.

"I do. But I'll have everything moved to storage, and move in with you. I'll be anticipating tonight all day." He kissed me again.

Hollenger was real pissed. "Your man has been waiting for more than an hour. Where the hell were you two?"

"Something urgent came up we needed to check out," Alex lied, giving me a quick glance.

Well, it wasn't a lie, just a different interpretation of events. I blushed a little.

Byron got to the head of the table, with his PowerPoint on the screen behind him. He gave us a brief outline of the Mob to give us content.

"The last decade, the Outfit has traditionally stayed away from the hard core crimes, like murder, drug trafficking. The heat on them was too much. Too many of their crew were ending up in prison.

"It all came to a head when we arrested, and convicted, the family boss, Frank Torrio senior. He's serving life for, amongst other things, racketeering. Since then the family has been diminished. Many members moved on to other families in New York, and elsewhere. We don't know who controls the Outfit today.

"Torrio has only one son, Frank junior, but he's only nineteen. He won't get to be running the Outfit any time soon, if ever, if someone else has taken control.

"So to keep their hold on power and keep the funds flowing, they've moved into things like loan-sharking, online gambling, even selling stocks of fake corporations.

"They have flowed that money into legitimate businesses, and even funding unions. The more union members they have, the more union dues they receive.

"They own a lot of properties around the city area. Small shopping malls, small to medium sized business malls, a few car dealerships. Apartment buildings. Stuff like that.

"Incidentally, they have, over the last few years, bought up more and more funeral homes. With homicide on the increase, they have capitalized on that influx of money for funerals. No opportunity left untapped, it seems."

"Plus making their own customers," someone added.

"Yeah, no kidding. They also own the Capone Spaghetti House over in Elmwood Park. It used to be in Little Italy, but when the city demolished the public housing, and tore down a number of other buildings, the Outfit moved their icon business.

"It's where the old timers go to reminisce about the good old days. Well, those who have managed to stay out of prison."

Everyone chuckled.

"But profit margins are thin for their legitimate businesses. Not enough for them. So they have recently expanded: Casinos in Florida, Las Vegas, and New Orleans. But they are in competition with the New York Mob families.

"A number of these guys in prison will soon be getting out. They will be under pressure to start making money for the Outfit again. We need reasons to keep them locked up.

"We are already seeing that. In April of 2005, the U.S. Department of Justice launched Operation Family Secrets. That managed to indict a number of these guys, some fourteen of them. They were all tried at the same time, and convicted to various sentences in prison.

"So, as of 2011, we figured there's about thirty active Outfit family members. There may be as many as one hundred associated members. How many they have now is a mystery.

"This is a big job going after these guys. But the question is, why have they resorted to killing again? De Luca wasn't the only one we found at the pig farm. We found DNA for at least two dozen other people so far.

"The interesting thing is they are almost all gang members. Most of those were from the three main gangs in the Chicago area: the Latin Kings, the Black Gangster Disciples, and the Vice Lords.

"We think the Outfit is laundering drug money for these gangs, as a service, taking a skim off the top."

"You have evidence of this?" Hollenger asked. "'Cause we haven't. Seems to me the Outfit would be in competition with the gangs."

"They are. As with everything, things are more complex. We have surveillance photos of Outfit members meeting with gang leaders."

"How long has this been going on?" I asked.

"Oh, at least three, maybe four years. What we think is happening is the Outfit is using these deals to increase their own territory. To get back into the drug money. By taking out some key gang headpins, making it look like rivalry with other gangs, they can fill the void themselves.

"As I said, margins are damn thin on the ligit business. Margins are very high on drugs."

"What about gun trafficking?" Alex said.

"Oh, yes. Thanks for reminding me. We think the Outfit is bringing in weapons – AK47s, and other high-powered guns, in from New York via the Bonanno family. The Bonanno family was kicked out of their council. Let me back up a bit.

"The New York Commission is the council of the five families. They keep the peace between the families, divvy up the resources between them. Anyway, the Bonanno family was kicked out because they started to get back into drugs. But also because they were bringing in weapons from the Middle East and West Africa by container ship.

"NYPD has managed to shut some of that down. But we expect many of those weapons have been disseminated around the country.

"Homeland Security thinks Muslim groups have bought many of these weapons in preparation for their coming Jihad against us."

Alex turned to me, "See."

Byron continued. "Jihadist attacks in the States have started to increase. You guys here just had that priest decapitated in broad daylight. Plus that female LEO run down in Atlanta..."

Geeze, the media said it was anti-cop rioting who ran down that Law Enforcement Officer.

"...plus there's chatter that they are planning major attacks around the world.

"It's turning into a nightmare. We know the local gangs in several cities around here have been buying these weapons, mostly handguns, from the Outfit.

"It's a war zone out there, ladies and gents. With weapons like these on our streets, vests are optional."

Swell. We took a brief break. I had to get a coffee, and pee, anyway.

In the washroom, Becky came up and congratulated me for my catch. "I know why you were late. Any woman could see it. You're glowing. Don't let him go, now," she said going out the door.

I smiled. I then looked into the mirror. Was this my life change? Was Alex really going to be my soul mate? I wasn't even sure that was possible. I had surrendered myself into thinking there was no soul mate out there I would ever meet.

But I had to admit. Alex was indeed a good catch.

"Ok, so let me add one more thing before we get into specifics," Byron continued. "With the economy tanking, and we have this civil unrest around the country, we're worried the Outfit will make some moves to gain some more control. They may be forced to take more risk…"

A low rumble reverberated in the building. Glasses of water on the table shook. The windows rattled a bit. We looked at each other. The entire squad room stopped.

Alex's phone rang. "Hello?" There was a long pause. His face grew grim. "Fuck me. We'll be right there. We gotta go, Byron."

At that moment someone came into the room. "There's been an explosion on The Loop. We need all hands on deck right now."

Alex looked at me as he got up and started to the door. "I'll call you when I can."

CHAPTER 7

DEATH AT MADISON STATION

I arrived at the corner of Randolf and Michigan to a mass of confusion. Smoke and gray haze was pouring eastward from between the buildings. People were flowing like a tidal wave from every building. Sirens wailed and echoed in the downtown.

Where I stood it was a bottleneck as a dam of vehicles stopped others in the middle of the roads.

Of course the media added to the chaos and congestion.

I walked along Michigan to see where I could be deployed to help. But most people were just heading out into the winter towards the lake.

I walked up East Washington towards the corner with Wabash. I had to navigate a sea of people heading east. As I got closer to Wabash, more and more of the people were injured, with blood and thick gray dust covering them.

I looked at a few. Their faces seemed blank and confused. "It all just blew up." One kept saying over and over. Some didn't even acknowledge

I was there. In Zombie fashion they stumbled their way east.

The air got thicker and thicker with smoke and dust the closer I got to Wabash. Through the haze I could see red, yellow and blue flashing lights. It was starting to get difficult to breathe. Coughing, I turned around and headed back to Michigan.

At Garland Court a homeless man with two little kids came up to me. He had long straggly dirty hair, with a full beard. His clothes were a patchwork of coats and sweaters, mostly torn and covered in grime. What was he doing with kids?

"You a cop?" he said.

I nodded.

"I found these two in my alley. Where should I take them?"

I didn't know if I should just leave them with him, or take them. "I'll take them," I figured was best. He headed off in the direction of the destruction.

"Hey. You! Where are you going? You should get out of here."

"I may be able to help some more people get out. I was deployed in Afghanistan. It's my duty to help those in need."

I was flabbergasted. Even the homeless were helping. Even after his country had abandoned him to the streets, he still had a sense of duty to assist.

A paramedic team pulled up in their vehicle from Michigan. I stopped them and told them to take the kids. I ran up to the homeless man. "Show me where you found them. Their mom must be looking for them."

I followed him along Garland. Funny, Garland had very little smoke. Almost an island of clear air. I couldn't see the buildings at the end of the court, however, it was just gray plumes heading to the lake.

Garland was the back door to all the buildings on Wabash and Michigan. It was lined with dumpsters and fire escape stairs. People were climbing down them onto Garland.

"In here," he said as we entered a loading bay on the west side. "I found the kids coming out of here."

I went into the loading dock on the back of one of the stores. The homeless man followed me. I had to turn on my flashlight as we walked into a room. I shone around at the destruction. Ceiling tiles were all over the floor.

We got to another door and opened it. Light from the world poured in. But it wasn't a room, it was a void in space. Rubble filled the floor to over my head. Huge beams were contorted and bent hanging down with strands of wire.

Snow was adding to the layers.

There was no way we'd find any one. But as I turned, I could see a bloody leg protruding from under some beams.

I headed back to Washington, taking the homeless man with me.

Fire trucks were crammed along the street. Firefighters, cops and even civilians, were getting gear out to take to the fire. Civilians were helping our front line emergency personnel. I was impressed with the patriotism. I was proud of our city.

Millennium Park, on the lake side of downtown, was being set up as a staging area.

No one seemed to know what to do. Cops were hustling people out of the buildings. Some said one of the towers was going to collapse. They had to evacuate every building in the surrounding blocks.

What struck me was the help perfect strangers were freely giving to others in need. For months now, the city, hell, the entire country, was at war with itself over racial lines. But not today.

I saw black people helping whites, and vice-versa. Asian's helping blacks. Latinos helping injured cops. It didn't matter your race today, this was an attack on everyone.

My phone rang. "Cunningham." I had to bold my finger in my other ear to denude the sounds of sirens, screaming, and roaring of the fire.

"Marg, it's Alex..."

The line dropped. I tried to call him back, but a message said the system was overloaded.

All of Chicago was trying to contact their loved ones, but couldn't get through. They would be worrying that their family was dead, was all I could think.

To top it off, I overheard a cop on the radio getting a message that the entire transit system was shut down. "L" trains were to go to their next station, and evacuate everyone. Busses were to pull over wherever they were and disembark all passengers.

Roads into the downtown core were being blocked off by cop cars arriving from all over the city.

That meant all those people who couldn't contact their spouses wouldn't have the ability go home any time soon. Everyone in the downtown was trapped. Not even walking out was an option. The Mayor was in the process of locking the entire city down. Those in buildings not affected were being stopped from leaving, and told to return to their offices or apartments until further notice.

Conflicting orders were common.

My phone beeped that I got a text message. It was from Alex:

ISIL admts attaks in NY DC Chic Atnta also Tornto Mtrl more 2 come

Then another message:

Air shut down flghts grndd gvnr ordrd NG shuld be thr soon wont be hom 2nyt

Then another:

Luv U C U soon

We were under attack with only five days until Christmas.

I was heading back to help some more when my phone beeped with another text. It was Alex again. It only said:

Going to LA emergency ther

I texted back: Be safe. Luv you.

By mid afternoon, I was in the triage area helping sort the not so wounded from the severely wounded. North West Memorial Hospital was over flowing. The call went out to send all city busses down to the waterfront. They were loaded up with wounded and sent to other area hospitals.

I spent a few hours helping people into those busses until I got a call on my cell. Service was working again.

"Cunningham."

"Marg, where are you?" It was Hollenger.

"How did you get through?"

"The phone companies have suspended everyone's accounts except emergency services. Where are you?"

"At the waterfront loading busses with wounded."

"Ok, I figured you were somewhere around there. Look, they're getting the fire under control. I need you to meet the rest of the squad at the Federal Emergency Management Agency. It's on Jackson."

"I know where it is."

"Great, make your way there. We're going to head up the investigation as to what happened. You'll need to gather all the evidence you can. Later, well, just do that for now. I'll see you there."

It took me a long time to make my way to the FEMA building. Most of the people had been evacuated, but it was the vehicles blocking the roads. Some cars were even on the sidewalks. I had to show my badge at the National Guard roadblock on Jackson.

As I passed Wabash, I tried to get a look at the bombed area, but it was still too smoky to see anything.

At 4PM we all met in a lecture hall at the Federal Emergency Management Agency building. Every conceivable organization was represented there, FEMA, Homeland Security, FBI, local police, state police, National Guard, were just the major players.

Alex was there at the front. I figured he must have been grounded. I was at the back against a wall. Alex saw me, smiled and waved. Others around looked back towards me. I looked back, but it was just a wall. I gave a small wave back.

A spokesman for FEMA gave a lecture. It wasn't a speech. The President of the United States closed every airport in the country.

She explained a number of measures they were doing to help the people displaced into the cold. The hotels in the area agreed to take them all in, including feeding them. That effort was underway.

McDonalds also stepped up to the plate, offering free food to all emergency workers. A Costco representative was there, and they offered the same help they always had in times of emergencies.

With all the roads closed into the city, and most of the people being processed at the waterfront, boats were organized to bring in supplies off the lake.

Alex gave what he had been told. It appeared to be an Islamic attack, he said. ISIL was taking credit. He also explained what had happened in other cities.

New York City was hit with a suicide bomber at Grand Central Station. L'Enfant Plaza station in DC was also hit with a suicide bomber.

Someone beside me said, "We need to kill all those goat-fuckers." It was loud enough for the mayor's spokesperson to hear.

"You want to share your views with everyone?" she said.

People looked at the man beside me. He seemed to blush a bit, then got angry. "Yes, I do. It's clear we are under attack by radical Islamists. We need to hunt these fuckers down before they leave the country."

"We don't know they're Islamic. This could be part of the rioting we have seen around the country," the female spokesperson said.

"Are you nuts!? The FBI there just said that ISIL has taken credit for this. What more evidence do you want?"

"Just because they took credit doesn't mean they did this, or that it's a coordinated attack," she said.

I had a hard time believing she believed herself.

Under his breath the man said, "Mother fucking political correctness." Then aloud he said, "You people are going to get more innocent people killed. Enough of this political correctness bullshit. It's time to wake up to the reality that we are under attack."

"The president isn't calling this an Islamic attack..."

Someone else piped up from across the room, "This President is destroying this country. This is not the America I grew up in. We used to take the fight to our enemies. Now we appease them? We no longer call a spade a spade?"

The room clapped, well, not all.

"Everyone stop right now. We are not jumping to any conclusions until we have more evidence," the spokesperson said.

"Fucking evidence is all blown up, asshole," the man beside me said under his breath.

Alex continued to explain what they knew. He ended with, "I'm heading to Los Angeles. We have a lead from one of the mosques there." He looked hard at the mayor's spokesperson. She didn't look too happy.

After the meeting, which I really didn't need to be at, we were to break into our respective groups. On my way out the door I cornered Alex. He pulled me off to the side.

"I thought you were gone already. With airports closed how are you getting west?"

"They shut the airport down before I could get a flight. I'm getting on a chopper for Grissom Air Force Base where a plane is waiting for me. Look, I'm not going to be back for a few days. But we're still on for Christmas at my parents. I promise I'll be back before then. I gotta go."

He gave me a quick kiss on the lips, as others going by popped a peak. He mouthed 'love you' and disappeared into the elevator.

I was elated he said those words. I had someone who really cared about me. But I worried about his mission. A military aircraft was not likely to be bombed, but I still worried.

Hollenger caught up to me with Becky. "Good, finally found you. I need you and Becky to head to ground zero. I want you two to get into as many buildings you can, safely of course, and find any and all surveillance footage you can. Something has to have been caught on tape. Two National Guardsmen will go as protection."

I was confused.

He continued, "Look, we don't know how many more crazies are out there. As I said, they're there for your protection, end of story."

We came down Madison towards Wabash. It was dark, most of the power in the area was out. The snowfall was picking up.

The chaos at Madison transit station on The Loop in the downtown was horrendous. Smoke and dust filled the area, even after those hours. The elevated station at the intersection of Madison and Wabash was gone.

Cars from two trains were tail up in the massive hole where the intersection used to be.

One subway car had been tossed into the TFC Bank building, where it slid down the outside, then dropped on top of a bus. Firefighters and National Guardsmen were extracting bodies and loading them into trucks.

Across Madison, a school bus was stuffed into the Dunkin' Deli storefront, only its rear end protruded onto the sidewalk.

Its back door was open, so I looked inside shining my flashlight around. There were no bodies.

Cars had been thrown up the street. Many were upside down.

Fire was still burning in the middle of the hole. Its orange-yellow glow sparkled off the falling snowflakes.

The fire department was trying to put it out, but had difficulty getting close. Rubble was everywhere, not just from the station, but also from the surrounding skyscrapers. Windows were shattered for as far up as I could see.

Bodies were hurled up into fifth and fourth floors, part of them draping over the gaping chasms that were once building fronts. Trails of blood dripped down below them.

The explosion had sent hundreds of bodies into chunks of shrapnel. They were everywhere. The station was loaded with Christmas shoppers. The surrounding stores would have been filled with people buying presents.

But none of them were going home. There would be an empty seat at their table on Christmas. There would be no joy in those homes, not ever again on Christmas.

Tears formed in my eyes. A solid lump welled inside me, making it difficult to breathe. I wanted to scream.

Building owners had given us the plans where their video cameras stored the images, mostly in the basements of the buildings.

Becky and I went through the rotating doors of the TCF Bank building into complete black. By flashlight we made our way to the room in the basement to get the tapes.

It was like that all night, frog hopping from building to building, trying to ignore the carnage as we transected the roads to the next building.

It took us well into the next morning to make the loop around ground zero to get a dozen tapes and drives. Hungry and exhausted, we headed back to FEMA with our National Guards trailing us. Of course, we used them to carry as much of the electronics as we could pile on.

The fun, as in boring plus, was when Becky and I had to watch all the tapes. The first one was as gruesome as it could get. The image was from over the Prudential Gem and Jewelry shop on Wabash. Vehicles stopped at the lights to let Madison traffic through.

You could tell when an 'L' train stopped, as a lot of people came down the steps onto Wabash.

Coming into view on Madison, a US Postal Service van turned onto Wabash away from the camera and stopped at the side of the road.

No one got out. It waited there for ten minutes as traffic and pedestrians made their way. A young couple, arm in arm, scanned the gems and rings in the windows of the stores. I thought of the night before when Alex and I stood in front of that very shop.

A mother with a stroller and toddler walked behind them.

The image instantly went all white, then the screen turned into static as the connection to the recorder was severed.

Becky found the same thing from another angle. This one was further north on Wabash. It was mounted on the Stevens Building main entrance and had a clear view up that side of the street. The post office van was clearly visible as it waited before the explosion.

From this vantage point the camera was far enough back to not be damaged and kept recording. But after the flash of light, the rest was gray. What was visible was a number of cars, which were thrown into the direction of the camera.

Miraculously, someone got out of their flipped car, stumbled to their feet and ran off.

More videos showed the same scene. We called in the FBI to have a look.

The regional coordinator for the disaster was Lewis Kincade. He watched all the videos.

"So they used a postal van. Get a number and call them."

After calls to the three central distribution centers we got a hit. One of their vehicles never came back from repairs. Becky and I headed to the North Kedzie Avenue location.

The building was surrounded with postal vehicles, not just in their tiny parking lot, with the gate open, but lined along the street, well past the building.

We met the area supervisor and the fleet manager.

"Van 3520176 was definitely the one sent for repairs, about a week ago," the fleet manager, Terry Lang, said. "It was supposed to be here three days ago."

"Anyone not show up for work today?" Becky asked.

"Several," the supervisor, Sharon Popwell, said.

"Can we have their names please?" Becky said.

"I'll get them, just a second."

She came back a few minutes later with the list. Twenty-three people either called in sick, or called in for the day off. There was one on the list who didn't call in at all, "Will Donnely," I said.

"Oh, no, that's not his name any more. He said he wanted to be called Mohammed Al-Turaab. I think it was."

Bingo.

"Tell me you have photos in your records," I said.

"Of course we do, for their security passes," Sharon said. She got up.

"And his employment records, please," I added.

She gave a slight nod, then left.

"Did you not call the shop to find out why the vehicle was taking so long?" Becky asked.

"I did, twice, including yesterday morning," Terry said. "They said they were waiting for parts for the transmission. Mohammed found the problem, or so he claimed."

Becky and I looked at each other.

I turned back to Lang. "Where's the shop?"

"Not far. 4439 North Kedzie Avenue. We've had a contract with them for years. They've always been great with our vehicles. There's two more there now for engine work."

Becky wrote it down.

"Mr. Lang, tell me about Mr. Donnely," I asked.

"Nice enough kid. On his breaks he would just sit alone reading their Bible."

"You mean the Koran," Becky said.

"Yes. I don't want to sound racist, you know."

Fucking coward. "How long has he worked here?" I asked.

"Oh, six, maybe seven years."

"And how long was he a Muslim?"

"Oh, just recently. He used to be a Christian, a Baptist, I think. He used to carry around a Bible. But then, sometime after his summer break he showed up unshaven with his Koran. He said he was liberated. He seemed so much happier."

Sharon showed up with a nice photo of a twenty-five-year-old all cleanly shaved, well groomed and handsome young man.

"He doesn't look that way now," she said. "He has a beard and his hair is much longer. We tried to get a new photo for his ID, but he said it was against his religion to have himself photographed, so we went with his wishes."

Bullshit, of course, he didn't want to be recognizable and caught.

It must have dawned on Sharon because her face completely changed to a grim realization. "He blew that bomb up didn't he?" She covered her mouth with her hand.

"Using our van? Fuck me," Lang said, sitting back in his chair.

"We don't know at this point. We'll visit his home. Thank you for your time," I said and we left.

I got on the phone to Derik. "I need warrants for two addresses, ASAP. I need a run on the owner a building." I gave him the addresses. "Put a rush on this, Derik, I think both were involved in the bombing."

"I'll pdf them to your phone," he said.

"So which first?" Becky said.

"Our Muslim friend."

Donnely's address was an apartment over on Irvine Park on West Byron Street. Soon as we pulled in the driveway my phone beeped. My warrants arrived. We knocked on his third floor apartment door. There was no answer. We got the Super to let us in.

Clearly he lived alone. It was a mess. The living room had one wall with a collage of photos of the downtown corridor on Wabash. An ISIL flag hung on another wall. Islamic artifacts filled the apartment. I called the FBI.

Next we stopped at the shop. It was a small building nestled between a fire hall and a bridal store. It occupied the left third of the property, with a parking area on the right, which contained several vehicles, including two postal vans which were parked up against a wall of snow.

The front had two bays on either side of the office and waiting area. Down the side were three more bays.

We pulled in and got out. It looked deserted. The front door was locked, as were the bay doors. Peering inside through the door windows, we could see a few vehicles in the shop. One was on a hoist. But there was no movement, no employees.

There was a fence to the service road behind the shop. The gate was padlocked. Between the fence and the building were two brand new plastic 45gal drums. Both were empty. Beyond them were two large tanks, one had 'WASTE OIL' on it, the other had 'HEATING OIL'. Beyond those were bins with scrap metal.

We went to the fire department property and followed the fence to the service road. We walked along the back fence, which had been draped in blue tarp, to hide the oil tanks, I figured. At the far back corner was a door to the parking area of the adjacent shops.

I tried it, but it was locked. I looked closely at the latch. There was no cover over it, and the deadbolt didn't appear to have been set.

"I think I can jimmy the latch," I said.

"Glad you got that warrant," Becky said. "Though, should we not wait for backup? SWAT or the bomb guys?"

"That'll take too long. Besides, they're all too busy downtown."

"But if they built the bomb in there..."

"We'll be cautious."

I reached into one of the bins through the fence and selected a length of contorted steel. I inserted a sharp end into the latch area and jiggled it around. "Got it." The door opened.

Becky drew her sidearm.

I gave her a WTF look.

"You never know."

Swell. I drew my Glock.

Instead of warmth as one would expect, it was as cold as the frosty day outside. No lights were on.

"Chicago Police!" I said as loud as I could as I entered with my gun preceding me. There was no reply.

We walked past the vehicles; several of them had their hoods up, with tools lying on the fenders.

We walked into the waiting and office area. There was no one.

"It's like they all just vanished," Becky said.

"Or bolted."

The shop phone rang. We looked at each other. It kept ringing. "I'll get it," Becky said. "Hello?"

I could hear a male's voice at the other end.

"Sorry, no one is here. This is the Chicago Police."

"Police!?" came through clearly.

"Yes, we've secured this place as a possible crime scene."

There was more talk. I went into the shop area to look around, specifically the work area for one of the empty bays. There was a lot of wiring, several rolls of duct and electrical tape, all partly used.

The place was well swept, and cleaned, unlike some of the other stations. I heard a crunching noise as my foot stepped on the grate in the middle of the bay.

Between the metal grate and the surrounding concrete were small green and tan colored beads. I used my car keys to pluck one free and look at it.

I checked the other bays. I couldn't see the same particles anywhere else.

Becky came in. "Man, he's pissed. One of these cars must be his."

"Evidence now."

"That's what I said to him. What's that?" she said looking at the beads in my hand.

"I don't know. But I don't like it. We need the forensic guys here."

I called Hollenger.

After I hung up I said, "Let's talk to the fire eaters. They're there twenty-four-seven. Maybe they know something."

We left through the front door, leaving it unlocked behind us, and went to the firehouse next door.

We talked with the crew of six men and two women. They had been brought in on overtime as the regular shift was helping downtown.

Some had used the shop, letting their vehicles get fixed while they were on shift.

No one had a bad word about the place, nor the people who worked for it.

They all agreed the service was better than when the old Greek guy used to run it. The changeover to new management was during the summer.

"Hell," one said, "they must have gotten real busy because for the last few months they were working all night."

Interesting. Bet it wasn't on cars, I thought.

Within ten minutes, the forensic sniffers were all over the building.

The rest of the week was spent identifying the bodies and contacting families. Becky and I had that latter grim task.

The devastation from the explosion was far reaching. We did about a dozen house calls for each of the next days. And that was just the two of us. There were whole teams of detectives doing that horrible task, right up to and including Christmas Eve.

No one was being arrested by our people those days. What crime that was going on was being caught by the roaming National Guardsmen in their Humvees. Because of some looting, which had started in the absence of cops, and the potential of more, martial law and curfew had been invoked by the Governor.

Each night I got home totally spent from the emotional toll on having to deliver the news. The worst part was that we had to give the grieving families instructions on how to go about identifying their loved ones. Tents had been set up along the waterfront. With the cold of winter, they had a natural freezer for the corpses.

Of course, I crashed into my chair, staring at a blank TV while nursing on my nightly rum and coke. I couldn't help it. My mind just kept rehashing the past days' events.

Having to walk into a living room with a decorated tree, loaded with presents under it, kids on the couch cuddled by either the father or the mother and tell them their loved one was dead, just wouldn't leave my mind.

The worst one was this father, alone sitting in front of a decorated tree, clutching a family photo album, who found out that his entire family of a young wife, one toddler and one baby were gone. I wondered if it was them in the street cam photo. I made a note to myself to get a copy of that to give to him. The last photo of them alive.

Christmas Eve morning Derik called. He gave me the name of the seller, Nikola Kalohristianakis. I had to get Derik to read the letters to me several times.

The buyer was Nizar Orfali. The sale price on the documents was $250,000. There was no realtor, just the lawyer. It was James Rudd. Bloody hell, De Luca's lawyer!

I asked Derik to track the two of them down. He protested a little, he wanted to head home for the holidays, so I had to insist.

I called Rudd's number, but his answering service said he was gone for the holidays.

Alex called just as I hung up. He was on his way home. He would be there by the morning. An elephant left my shoulders I was so relieved. But at the same time I felt somewhat guilty that I still had someone.

CHAPTER 8

CHRISTMAS WITH A NEW FAMILY

Alex's parent's home was in a luxury neighborhood of Oak Park. A very nice, and that meant expensive, home on a tree'd lot. Everything was covered in snow, but I could imagine what it would be like in the summer – lavish, quiet, and contented.

It was a wood clad home painted in a light beige with white trim. The porch covered the entire front of the house. The steps up to the veranda had a peaked roof held up by four pillars. On top of the apex was an American flag. Every home on that, and other streets I could see, had an American flag displayed.

The house was decorated in multi-colored lights, with some flashing. A Christmas tree, all lit up, was visible through a bay window on the left.

Actually, the entire area was lit up, almost deliberately over doing it. It was so beautiful for not only the color in the fading light, all blanketed in fresh snow, but for the "fuck you" message this said against those who wished to disrupt our way of life.

Five days after the bombings around the country, and people had rallied.

Alex's mom greeted us at the front door.

"So this is Marg. Alex, she's beautiful."

I never thought of myself as beautiful, handsome maybe, a five or six out of ten. But it was a nice gesture.

Who also greeted us at the door was a huge black dog, with a white face and patches of tan between the eyes. He came right at me planting his muzzle between my legs, with his white socked paws wrapped around my knees. The white tipped tail flashing vigorously.

"Bailey buddies!" Alex said laughing, "Stop, you'll push Marg off the porch."

The dog went to Alex and did the same thing. Alex dropped to his knees and the two went face to face while Alex rubbed the thick black coat. The tail didn't stop fanning.

"He's a beautiful dog. What's his breed?"

"Bernese Mountain Dog," Laurie said. "They love everyone."

She pulled the dog back into the doorway. "Now let these people come in."

Bailey danced off into the living room.

"Come in out of the cold and give me your coats. Scott! Our guests have arrived! He's just getting firewood."

She took our coats upstairs.

The living room was on the left, entered through an arched double doorway. A fire roared on the far wall. High back leather chairs and two sofas were organized around the fireplace.

Another arched double doorway on the right of the living room led to the dining room.

We took our boots off, and entered into the living room. It was painted in a light green, with white trim. It even had a cornice around the entire perimeter of the ceiling.

The fireplace was fieldstone with a long wooden mantel, from which hung a half dozen stockings. On its surface was a series of scented candles, adding light and fragrance to the atmosphere with the dancing flames reflecting off the mirror behind.

Presents under the tree supplemented the color arrangement.

"There you are," Scott said as he emerged from the dining room, arms loaded with firewood.

"Hey, Dad, let me take that for you."

Bailey tried to help by pulling a log out of Scott's arms and ran into the kitchen with it.

"Come back with that, you goof," Scott said as he tried to rescue the log from Bailey's jaws.

Alex set the freshly chopped logs in their holder.

"So this is Marg," his father said. We shook hands.

"Pleasure to meet you, Mr. Kiley."

"Oh, please. Call me Scott, and that's Laurie upstairs. Would you two like a drink? Bourbon?"

"That will be fine, Dad."

Scott went off to the dining room.

Laurie came down. "Oh, please sit and get warm by the fire. It's awfully cold out there."

"Coldest December in memory, I was told," I said, trying to lose my shyness. I felt like a sixteen year old meeting my boyfriend's parents for the first time.

"The rest should be here any moment. They're running late."

"Not surprising, Mom, with the city still in chaos. The airports only just opened yesterday."

"I know. It's so awful. Oh, your uncle Roger is coming in from California. I hope he gets here today. He was supposed to land yesterday. With all this mess he got delayed."

"Excellent, I haven't seen him in years," Alex said. He looked at me. "That's mom's brother. He's the Vietnam veteran I told you about."

We chatted together for about an hour before the rest of Alex's siblings arrived. I was introduced to his brother, Derrick, and his wife, Jaime, and their two boys, five year old Ryan and toddler Brad. Then his sister, Ellie, was next, with her husband, Charles Cobb, and their two kids, nine year old Eddie and seven year old Erin.

Bailey was even more excited to see the kids, knocking the youngest over. Laurie rescued the child saying, "He really loves kids too, right Alex?" She stared at Alex as she emphasized "right Alex?". I took that as a hint.

They opened presents. The kids were elated at the volume of toys from the grandparents. Alex handed me a small wrapped box. It was a winter hat and gloves.

"It's too damn cold out there with those flimsy gloves you have."

"But, I don't have anything for you. With all the chaos, I didn't get a chance."

"You're the best gift I have ever had."

I was flattered, and humbled. I smiled.

Grandma managed to get the boys down stairs where there apparently was a room full of Legos. The dog went with them.

We all gathered around the dining room table. There was more than enough space for us, as the table would hold twelve people with the extra leaves in it. Scott was at the head, with Laurie on his left. She beckoned me to sit beside her. Alex sat beside his father opposite me.

One large window, with a sliding door, led to the back yard. The room was in a light blue, with white trim, and again with a cornice. A medallion suspended a huge crystal chandelier. A glass and dark walnut china cabinet filled the wall behind Alex.

Bourbon, and rum 'n eggnog for some, were poured out.

A knock at the door prompted Laurie to answer it. "Oh my God. It's so wonderful to see you!" filled the house.

"Must be Roger," Scott said.

Sure enough, a large tall man with very gray hair came in, shook hands and exchanged greetings, with everyone. As he shook my hand he said, "You're new."

I introduced myself.

"Mother, let's eat. We're all starving here," Scott said.

Roger sat at the other head end of the table.

The food was enormous. All the usual for Christmas dinner: fresh baked rolls, cream corn, scallop potatoes, green beans, squash, mushroom gravy, stuffing and of course the turkey with cranberries. Enough to feed a small army.

There was also a large shank of ham. I let it pass me as I remembered De Luca. I think Alex caught it because he gave a quick short chuckle, but I noticed he didn't have a slice of it either.

We dove into the food like we were famished. Home cooked food. Wow. I never ate anything so exquisite. Thanksgiving, and now this, I was going to add twenty pounds.

I decided to be brave and ask a question. "Roger, what years were you in Nam?"

"Sixty-two to sixty-seven."

"My father was there at that time, sixty three to sixty six."

"So were a hundred thousand other guys."

"Oh, I didn't expect you'd know him, just wondering if you can help me to find out how to get more info on my father. He won a Bronze Star."

"You can go online. They'll be able to give you your father's entire history. What was his name?"

"Sergeant Don Cunningham."

"I don't recognize the name, sorry."

"I have a picture." I rummaged through my purse, and pulled out the copy the photo with the three other buddies with my dad. It was passed down to Roger.

"I'm sorry. It's been too long, and I trained so many GIs. I don't recognize them."

He passed the picture back. I was a bit disappointed.

I explained things to him. How I'd been trying to learn about my father's history in the service.

"Well, looks like you've done your best to find out about your Pop's medal. These things take time to process. Six months I've heard. Don't worry, it'll come."

"How's Nathan?" Laurie asked. "He should be here. He's never come to a Christmas with us."

"I called him before I came, Sis. " Roger looked at me. "He's with his family in Fort McMurray. He's a materials engineer at the oil sands now. Making the big bucks. You know, Sis, he'll never come to the States again. He was a draft dodger. Went up to Canada when his number came up. Our family was a little pissed."

"I wasn't," Laurie said. "I encouraged him."

Roger paused. "My sister, the anti-war flower child."

The table was silent.

"Yes, I was. I admit now I was wrong." Laurie leaned over to me, "I was at Woodstock. Went topless for a week."

"We don't need to hear about your escapades at dinner," Scott said, half chuckling, half wanting the subject to end.

"That was long before I met you, dear," Laurie said grabbing his hand. She turned back to Roger. "And your boys?"

"With what's going on, both are on duty. Ron is on the George Washington in the Sea of Japan. A show of force over those disputed islands. Fred is somewhere in the Mediterranean. Submarine duty is all top secret, you know.

"Their families are together today in San Diego. So they don't get to have Christmas with their dads. I'm going to see them New Year's."

Like so many of our armed forces families. Like so many right here in Chicago, who lost loved one's five days ago, I thought.

"Well, it looks like we're at war again," Charles said.

Off on that tangent we went with the discussion of differing opinions.

Then it came to me with the questions. They asked about my work, and my cases. They asked if we had any conspiracy suspects for the bombings. That was privileged information Alex reminded them.

"I heard you guys found the repair shop where the bomb was built," Charles said.

"Maybe. We did find a shop with suspicious circumstances. It's being processed as we speak," I explained.

Many of the legal questions came from Scott. Alex interrupted, "Dad's a corporate lawyer. He used to be a defense lawyer."

"That's how I met him," Laurie said. She leaned over to me. "He defended me for a marijuana charge. He got me off." She held his hand again. "And we fell in love."

The family talked some more, about old times, how their jobs were doing as well as other stuff I didn't get involved in. I just sat there, eating, and admiring the family. So this is what I missed. This is what a medium sized family, a close-knit family, looked like. Joy filled the room as much as the aroma of food.

I remembered: 1,329 families were in deep grief today. Another four thousand were suffering as loved ones recovered from injuries and permanent disfigurement, both physical and emotional. And that was just Chicago. Last I heard there was no definitive death count for the rest of the bombings, likely doubling what we knew here.

Yet here I was in this house of happiness, as if the world was a Utopia. It wasn't fake. It was very real and very powerful.

All my life, our family Christmas was just the three of us. Then when

Pam was born, the four of us. Occasionally, my Aunt May and her family would come, but that was rare.

Compared to the Thanksgiving dinner at the villa, this was, I thought, quieter and closer in a different way. Certainly smaller, and was more intimate. I felt a little overwhelmed at the villa, far too many people. But this was, well, comfortably cozy.

The table was cleared. Ellie, Jaime and Laurie brought in the desert. Swell. I needed to release a button on my pants. There was no way I could eat another bite. They kept pushing more servings of the main course to me. I didn't know there was going to be sweets.

Home baked apple pie, green tomato minced meat pie, and a large glass bowl with multicolored layers. I had to ask what it was.

"English trifle. You'll love it," Laurie said with a great sense of pride. "Takes three days to make it."

"And wolfed down in a few minutes," Alex added.

Adventurous, I tried it. It was the tastiest mix of jello, fruit, custard, bananas and whipped cream.

Scott took Bailey and his food outside, coming back in with another load of logs. "He loves the snow," Scott said to me. "The fire will make the room too hot for him."

After dinner, the room broke up into groups. I helped the women in the kitchen putting things away and cleaning up, while the men went off back in front of the fire, sucking on brandies.

The kitchen was at the back right of the dining room. It had a breakfast island with two chairs. The granite counter was in an L shape on the right. On the left was a bay window overlooking the backyard.

I asked Laurie about the trifle. "Oh, that's my mother's recipe. She was a war bride. That's double-yeah-double-yeah two, Honey. My father was a Navy Commander in D-Day. He was injured, and spent some time in a British hospital, where he met my mother."

She paused a few seconds, then talked with the other women.

Once everything was cleaned up, I sat at the island. Laurie served us all tea. It reminded me of my interview with Easton's wife. I had to decline the tea. So Ellie poured me a coffee.

"Let me be bold, Marg," Laurie said after the other two women had left the kitchen. She sat beside me. "What's your plan with my Alex?"

I was taken aback by the question. Seemed out of line.

"Oh, don't get me wrong, Honey. I like you. I think you are perfect for my son. He's getting on in age. I really was hoping he'd give me some more grandchildren by now."

I blushed.

"Oh, I'm sorry, Honey. Am I too forward? Look, Honey, life's too short to live it alone."

That was actually reassuring. "Well, so far we're doing OK. It's a little early to be thinking something permanent."

"Oh, Honey, the way my Alex looks at you, you are permanent."

That I took as a compliment.

"You two can have the room at the top right, at the back of the house. Roger will have the front bedroom."

That was unexpected.

"Well, um, I was, um, going home later."

"Not on your life. It's winter out there. You will stay the night. In the morning we'll have a nice breakfast. Now, I won't take no for an answer."

We got up, she wrapped her arm around my shoulder, and we went in to join the rest of the family. Boy, did I miss a lot in my life. Here's someone who could replace my mother, as much as that could be.

We all sat paired up in front of the fire. A box of Pot of Gold was passed around. Are you kidding me!? Geeze, the food never ended. I felt like that fat guy in the Monty Python film – a wafer thin...

Roger then said, "Scott, let's sing some Christmas songs, like we do every year."

"Of course."

Scott sat at the upright piano that was on the opposite wall from the fireplace, just beside the living room entrance.

"Come and join us, Marg," Laurie said pulling me up from the coach.

"But I can't sing," I tried to protest. I had never sung that I could remember, not even to radio music. It never dawned on me as to why.

"Oh, Marg, Honey, everyone can sing. We're family now. You must join with us."

They started with the simple songs: Jingle Bells, White Christmas, and such we hear every year. I tried Jingle Bells as I knew the lyrics, but the rest I kind of just hummed along.

Alex was kind, he didn't press me to sing, but just to be beside him as the rest filled the home with warmth, song and jubilation as all sang beautifully. I was mighty impressed, as well as humbled.

Some ruckus with the children downstairs interrupted us, forcing the women to go and sort it out.

After a couple of hours of more song, we'd had enough. Singing was getting off track once the booze was taking effect. They became a bit incoherent, especially when people interjected their own sexually suggestive words. They were getting rather giddy. So we took a break and sat by the fire.

Roger, beside his sister and brother-in-law, looked somber as the rest of us cuddled. Until, that is, another ruckus in the basement erupted and the two mothers had to go to referee. Something about the toddler destroying what the others built with the Legos, again.

"Uncle Roger," Derrick broke the silence, "is your book finished yet?"

He smiled. "No, sometimes I don't think I'll ever get it finished. Too many stories."

"Uncle Roger," Alex said to me, "is gathering stories of Nam vets from all over the country. It's his hobby since he retired. How many years has it been now, Uncle?"

"Fifteen. I'm up to thirty thousand pages."

"Damn," Scott said, "that's an encyclopedia. You'll never get a publisher who will even touch that."

"You should just publish it online, Roger," Charles said.

"I just might."

"I'm in web design, I can help you set that all up," Charles added. "That way people can submit their stories online, and it would become a living document."

"Well, I thank you for the offer. I just might do that. Not too many years in these old bones. I need to get it out there. These stories need to be told." He paused thinking. "Marg, let me look at that photo again, please."

I got it out and handed it to him.

"I recall four guys who got me shitfaced drunk after one of my training sessions. I think these are the boys."

He looked carefully at the photo. "That sure looks like a Walther P38 that sergeant had. That's your Pop, right?"

"I found a P38 in my father's drawer," I replied.

"That could be him." He looked closer. "Well, I'll be a darn tootin'. I did meet your father. I was there when he bought it. I was at one of my informant's place of business. I bought a Luger from him. Your Pop came in and asked if I was going to buy the Luger. It was for my kid brother, Nathan. So your Pop bought that Walther instead. Jesus, the daughter of one of my students. Who would have guessed?"

"One in a million," Alex said.

Well, that was one mystery solved.

Finally, the festivities broke up just after midnight. The kids were all asleep anyway. Each family said their goodbyes. It was just Alex, his parents, Roger and me remaining.

Scott brought Bailey in and the three of them went into their bedroom.

Roger said his good nights, and went upstairs. Alex and I followed.

The bedroom was like a museum. Old furniture adorned the room. It was finished in a light yellow with white trim. The four post canopy bed had a solid wood headboard. An intricate quilt lay over the bed. A walnut dresser was beside the window.

Alex closed the door and said, "I need to shower. Come join me."

Another first for us. The bathroom was off the bedroom. It had a bath, with a separate shower. We stripped, and squeezed in once the water was just right. We got very intimate as we slowly washed each other down.

What a perfect time to end a perfect day. This is what a normal American family was about. I was in heaven.

We emerged into the dining room after ten in the morning. Roger was already eating bacon and eggs. He just raised his orange juice and smiled as he chewed.

Scott came in through the back door with more wood. "Good morning, sleep well?" he said as he passed by us, arms full.

Bailey was outside, ignoring the calls to come in. He was prancing around in the fresh fallen show. His thick coat was covered in white masking the black fur. Planting his face into the snow he ran as fast as he could until he hit the fence and fell over. He got up, shook his body until it disappeared in a gale of snow, then continued to dance. I had to laugh aloud.

Soon as we got into view Laurie said, "There's the love birds. Sleep well? Here, come and sit. It's all ready for you. I'm sure you worked up an appetite after last night."

"Kept me awake for an hour," Roger said between mouthfuls.

"Mom!" Alex said in a high-pitched voice.

I blushed. I was sure we weren't that loud.

"What? Making love is perfectly normal for two people in love. Now sit. Marg, I have your coffee ready."

She could be my surrogate mother. Hell, my mother was prudish compared to Laurie. We rarely openly talked about my sex life. Laurie was, well, still a flower child, just near seventy years old. I'd bet they'd be dancing to the Rolling Stones when they're eighty.

After breakfast, Scott invited us into his sitting room. It was off the opposite side of the living room. That's where the wall sized flat screen TV was hung. The right window faced out the front. Fresh snow fell from the gray sky. To the left was a full wall library of legal books. A large dark walnut desk was in front of the shelves.

The wall with the door was filled with family photos going all the way back in time. Few were color, the rest black and white. One was a US Navy officer standing with a white robed bride beside him in front of a church.

Looking at others, and yep, there was Laurie, the flower child. The sheer volume of 1960s photos seemed to indicate they missed those days very much. Life must have been far simpler. There were certainly no terrorism attacks in the US. Just anti-war protests.

"Let's see what's on CNN. They were predicting bad holiday sales." Scott pushed a few buttons on the remote. He sat back in his chair and put the footrest up.

Alex and I sat on the love seat kitty-corner to Scott, our backs to the window.

Most of the show was on the bombings. They were interviewing the usual series of experts giving their opinions. Scott just said, "Idiots" after every one. Then they got to the shopping. One reporter was at a major mall in Boston. The view was sparse. Few people were shopping. Already, as she interviewed one shopkeeper, prices were slashed to the bone. Yet few were buying.

Then they got into the economy. Scott raised the volume a bit. Another series of experts explained that the bombings, with the subsequent shut down of the transit routes and flights, would be devastating. The next day the markets would open, and one expert predicted a major sell off.

One analyst said that negative interest rates in the US was a real possibility. I wondered if Scott could explain what they meant, as I had no clue how that would work.

What was also interesting was that Scott never said "idiots" after each one. He mumbled something about selling off his portfolio. I couldn't help but wonder about my own stash of my father's stocks. I didn't ask for any advice, as I didn't want to spark a discussion, which would expose my father's questionable behavior.

I was relieved that I bought Pam that house using some of my cash to pay it in full. If the economy went for a shit, at least they had a home.

CNN did an update on the dead, wounded and missing from the three bombings. Chicago's death count was up to 1,356, with 20 still missing. Two were Chicago police. New York's death toll was much less than I figured, less than one hundred. But several hundred injured. No one was missing. Washington's fatalities "just" 123, with one still missing, and three hundred injured.

One engineer interviewed said it would cost a billion dollars to clean up and fix all the stations, and months before they were operational again.

Loss to business was going to be in the tens of billions. The airlines alone, being shut down country-wide for three days, was going to be devastating, one analyst said.

CNN glossed over the notion it was an Islamic attack. We were all frustrated that this political correctness could be so blind.

Scott said it best, I think. "It's not us who understand the truth who are being Islamophobic, but the liberals and Democrats. They're too afraid of offending the religious zealots. That makes them Islamophobic, not us."

I could see where Alex got his opinions from.

They then reported on rioting happening in Europe. Especially the anti-Muslim crowds building in Germany and the UK. A number of mosques had been torched. Cars burned. Factions were attacking each other on the streets. It was all getting out of control.

Laurie came in and said it was ruining the day, and to turn it off.

We didn't do much that day. We played a few rounds of hearts. I'd never played it before. It was fun. We had a lot of laughs as someone got nailed with the queen of spades. Adding some alcohol certainly helped.

Alex got all the point cards in one game. How the hell he did that half-drunk was beyond me. I think it was because the rest of us really weren't paying attention.

We finished a couple games as the day faded outside. New snow was falling, with each flake catching the lights. We sat in front of the fire finishing off the last of the spiked eggnog. It was a nice quiet time with the five of us.

No one needed to cook. We just nuked some leftovers whenever someone got hungry. I was disappointed there was no trifle left from the night before, but the apple pie with ice cream was heavenly.

Roger had to leave, as he was heading into the city to meet with some veterans, so he said his goodbyes.

"Ok," Scott said. "Now we're down to four, let's play some bridge."

What was bridge? Alex explained it to me. "You'll like it," he said. "It's intellectual and strategic, right up your alley."

Little did I know at the time that playing this game would prove important later on.

We played one round for me to get familiar with the rules. It was involved, but one part intrigued me very much. My hand was laid down for Alex to play. The bid was four diamonds. But we didn't have the biggest diamond cards.

Alex played a number of tricks, one of which he took with my ace of clubs. Then he pulled a small heart from my hand. Scott paused, then played the jack over it. Alex played the queen of hearts, while Laurie played the six of hearts.

Alex took the trick. Then he played an off suit for which I had the top card in spades. Next he played another small heart from my hand. Scott played the king, and Alex took it with his ace. Laurie played a small heart again. There were moans from our opponents.

"How did you know how to do that?" I said confused. It looked like Alex knew what was in his father's hands. But how?

After we played the last hand, Alex explained that his father must have had the king, because Scott had bid one heart at the beginning. "Since I had the queen and ace of his bid suit, and mom didn't reply to the heart bid of my dad, I knew he had the king. The jack was a gift. That left my ten as the high heart. Three tricks won, when I didn't have the three highest hearts. It's called a finesse."

So Alex finessed his father's king allowing the queen to win the first time. Had the father played the king, Alex would have taken it with the ace, leaving his queen to take the jack anyway. But it only worked if I or Laurie played the first heart of the trick.

Finesse – a way to make a lower card win a trick, over opponent's larger cards. Interesting.

We played a real match next. Now that I saw how the game was played, I picked it right up. I even did a number of my own finesses. Well, a few didn't work. That was frustrating.

We played more rounds until well after midnight. I was really getting into the game.

Overall, we didn't win. Scott and Laurie were just too good at it. I guessed decades of weekly playing in a group did that.

I was intrigued by the strategy and thinking involved, an experience which would mold my thoughts and plans in the future.

Alex and I stayed until Monday morning. Up at six, we had a quick breakfast, then prepared to leave. Laurie brought our coats for us. She gave me a big tight hug, then kissed me on the forehead. "Now Alex, you bring Marg here as often as you want. I think we're going to become good friends."

"Maybe we can do bridge Sunday nights," I said.

"Well, that would be wonderful, wouldn't it Scott."

"Delightful."

I wasn't entirely sure what that meant by the low tone of the comment. But he did say he was pleased to meet, and would like us to come by any time. Alex said his father was likely put off with the economy, and the threat to our country.

As daylight broke, we drove from the fairytale into the real world. I didn't want to leave.

CHAPTER 9

GETTING TOO CLOSE

I went into work on the day after Boxing Day to get caught up on what was going on. Soon as I came in the squad room Hollenger called me in.

"Good catch on that garage. Good police work. The lab boys found evidence of industrial fertilizer."

"Those pellets?"

"Yep. Twenty empty sacks were found in the dumpsters of the apartment buildings just up the road. Seems they used the heating oil mixed with it to make the explosives. So, it looks like that's where they assembled the bomb, in a postal van.

"The place was cleaned up. There were no records of who worked there.

"Derik left you a note before he took off for the holidays. The previous owner, the Greek, he left for Greece in the summer for good. Orfali has disappeared. He's not at his residence, and those at his mosque haven't seen him since before the bombing. We don't think he's left the country yet.

"According to the FBI he's Syrian, a well-known radical in ISIL. They have him on their terror cell watch list. Have you contacted Rudd yet?"

"No, I tried this morning but still got his answering service. I left a message to call me. How bad is it down there?"

"A disaster. Billions in cut diamonds scattered all over the place. The damn crater filled with sewage and water from the mains, and has since frozen. Bodies are still being found. Frozen parts mostly. I'm not sure what the count is up to."

My phone rang. It was Rudd.

"You're at your office?" I said.

"Yes."

"I'll be right there, don't go anywhere."

Becky went with me.

I asked Rudd about the garage sale. He admitted he did the paperwork. It hadn't been made public yet about the place being the bomb-making site. So Rudd was likely unaware of the roll he played in the bombing downtown.

"Why no realtor?" I asked.

"I mean, I didn't need one. I rarely use a realtor for these kinds of transactions, you know."

"Do you know who bought the place?"

"A recent immigrant from Turkey. His family wanted to open a shop, you know. They asked me to look around to see if someone was willing to sell."

"Who referred you to them?" Becky said.

"I didn't ask. What's this about?"

The question appeared genuine. He was to get the shock of his life, which we can use as leverage.

"The garage was a front. It was used by an Islamic terrorist cell to make the bomb. You know, the one that killed all those people downtown," I said.

His eyes lit right up. He started to fidget.

"If you know something, now's the time to tell us. Because if you don't, I'll have the FBI down here in a phone call and you'll be arrested for terrorist activities. You'll be charged with the murder of several thousand people."

His mouth dropped. His eyes almost popped out of their sockets. He put his hands into the air.

"No. No. I mean, I knew nothing of what they were doing. I swear. But I can tell you this. Those documents, with the sale price, it wasn't $250,000, you know. It was 2.3 million."

"They paid two and a half million for that little garage, and you didn't think to ask why?"

"I received ten percent, you know. Why would I question that?"

Becky and I shook our heads.

"Look, for now I'm going to keep this between us. I'm going to believe you had nothing to do with this. Just a profiteer looking for a quick buck."

He gave a big sigh of relief.

"Whatever I can do for you," he pleaded. "I mean, you want a deal on selling your place? I'll do the paper work for free, you know. I can't be involved with terrorists. I mean, it's bad for business."

"Maybe you can help then." I moved closer to his desk, almost leaning over it. "You do deals with the Outfit, don't you? Don't bother to deny it."

He looked at the two of us. Beads of sweat started to form on his forehead.

Eventually he said, "All legal. Nothing illegal, you know."

"Right," I said with a snicker. "Like forging a legal document is legal."

He didn't say anything, the sweat beads got bigger.

"Ok, so you're going to turn informant. You're going to provide me with every sale of every property you have done for the Outfit."

He looked at both of us in turn. "All of them?"

"All of them."

"That's going to take time, you know. I mean, you do realize I'm putting my life on the line here. They find out I'm talking to you guys and I'll end up like De Luca, you know."

"That or a Federal prison. Take your pick, you prick," I affirmed.

I had one more errand to do before I went home for the day. Robert Dillon was the father who lost his whole family. We sat at his kitchen table. He said he hadn't heard anything about identifying his family's remains.

"I may have a photo, which might be them. Do you want to see it?" He gave a hesitant nod.

I showed him a photo from the videotapes of the woman with a baby carriage and toddler.

He started to shake. "That's them," he said with great difficulty. "Where did you get this?"

I told him.

"Their last moment alive." Tears fell from his eyes. He clutched the photo in a hug. "We weren't doing so well. We were on the verge of divorce.

"She teaches... She taught at Abraham Lincoln Elementary. Grades five and six. They're going to miss her very much over there. The kids just adored her, and she loved her job.

"I've been out of work for three years now. I can't find any welding jobs. We've gotten into a lot of fights over that."

He sat there silent for a few moments looking at the picture.

"Can I keep this?"

"Of course."

"I'm leaving. I'm going back to live with my parents in Virginia. A thirty-year-old bachelor living with his parents. According to this, she, they, were... I can't have a funeral because there aren't any bodies." He sobbed.

"How do I tell this to her parents?" He sobbed some more.

I held his hand. "I'm so sorry this happened."

He held his breath, with his cheeks bulging. Letting it out, his face turned red as his grief turned into anger.

"You find these mother-fuckers and you kill them all. Nuke those fucking cock-suckers back into the fucking stone age. You hear me?"

I had a double rum 'n coke when I got home. Alex came in late and found me asleep in my chair, with the TV on, or so he said in the morning.

Alex and I spent the first Saturday in January of the New Year at his parent's for dinner. I thought we'd play a round of hearts or bridge, but instead we had four tickets to the movies. They said they wanted to get their minds off their dwindling financial situation as the markets had a precipitous week. The 22% drop in the Dow wiped off hundreds of billions of wealth.

"This is right up your alley, Marg," Scott said. "The Imitation Game. True story."

After the film, once we got back to Alex's parent's home, we discussed the film. But first, we had a glass of wine and sat cuddled by the fire. The deepest cold January in memory was gripping more of the northern U.S.

The movie was a sad story at the end, but what was interesting was what Scott said.

"Deceit and finesse. Notice that's what they did? They figured out the German enigma code, but they couldn't act to stop the Germans. If they did the Germans would be on to them and change their machines. So they had to use deceit and finesse to beat the Germans."

"I suspect after D-Day they used more info from the messages, as more Germans were captured." Alex said, as Scott nodded.

They continued to discuss their theories, but I was thinking of the basic premise. You win wars with deceit and finesse. The real world is nothing more than a card game. How you play your hand is how you win.

I knew that was the case, I just hadn't put it together in those terms.

One morning Alex came into the squad room and put a small box on my desk. "My late Christmas present to you."

"What is it?" I opened it. In the box was a tiny microchip. "What's this for?"

"You. We're going to the FBI building where they'll implant this under your skin."

"What? Why?"

"Precaution. I'll know where you are every second on my phone."

"Sounds like an engagement ring to me."

He smiled. "It's to keep you safe. Works for finding lost puppies."

"Oh, so now I'm a lost puppy?" I tittered.

He chuckled. "No, it's just a precaution."

I was expecting it to go into my arm. But the doctor at the FBI office said criminals often scan people for them. The best place to insert it was in the bottom of the foot between some bones. He said they rarely scanned below at the feet because the rebar in the floor sets off the scanner.

It sounded painful.

"You think I'll get abducted?"

"Most of us in the FBI have it. Personally, I think the management just wants to know where we are," Alex said.

"We've rescued four of our agents with these things the last five years. They work," the doctor added.

I was given a local in the bottom of my left foot, then without even knowing it, the chip was part of me. Alex tested the connection on his iPhone. All worked.

"Ok, next order of business," Alex said. "We're going into the basement to see how well you shoot."

"What? I qualify every year."

He chuckled. "A couple rounds a year isn't qualifying. Let's see how good, or not, you are," he smiled.

"I don't have a weapon on me."

"Not to worry, we can use my Cz85."

"I thought the FBI issued you guys with Sigs?"

"They do. This is my personal weapon. I always wear it, especially now."

I sucked. Alex just laughed at my target's lack of hits.

"Ok, smarty pants," I said, "let's see how good you are."

"Oh, I make no bones that I suck too. Just not as bad as you," he laughed.

He fired off his ten rounds at fifteen yards. He got them all in on the twelve inches, but they were all over.

"See, I told you I wasn't that good. But you definitely could improve."

We spent several hours of shooting, and practicing. On our way out he said, "Well, that's better. But you should seriously look at hiring someone who can give you better lessons than I can provide. I did. And, hum, I think I can save myself if I needed to. I'm sure I could protect others as best I can. But there's always room for improvement."

Rudd called me few days after our meeting. "Today, McDonalds on Clark. 2PM." He hung up.

With Becky driving, me in the passenger seat, and Alex in the back we arrived at the fast food restaurant just before two. We waited in the parking lot.

A blue Nissan showed up, driving around the lot a few times, then passed in front of us. It was Rudd. He pulled in beside us, and, with a brown envelope in hand, slid into the back of our car beside Alex.

"Hey, you said nothing about the FBI being involved," he protested.

"Live with it," Alex said. "Give me the envelope."

"Look, you never got this from me, you know. Understand?"

Alex opened it and looked through the documents, a CD accompanied the contents. "What are we looking at here?"

"They're copies of purchase agreements where I did the legal work for the past two years. I mean, mostly real estate sales. The Outfit has been buying up property big time the last four years, you know, since the economy started to tank and people need to be bought out.

"They've been concentrating on four locations, West Englewood, Lower Westside, Bridgeport, Englewood, and Southside."

"That's five," Alex said.

"Oh, right. I meant five."

Rudd was visibly shaking.

"That's all near the Latin Kings and the Disciples territory," Alex said.

"That's no coincidence, you know," Rudd continued. "Look, they're deliberately encroaching into the King's area. I mean, the Outfit has made a pact, a non-aggression pact, with the Black Gangsters Disciples, Vice Lords and a few others. The Outfit launders their drug money, you know."

"How are they doing that?" I asked.

"I'm not one hundred percent sure, you know, but look, they have a bank in the Southside—"

"They own a bank?" Alex interrupted.

"Yeah, they bought it, I mean, at least ten years ago."

Alex said, "Geeze" and shook his head. "Didn't know that."

"Plus they own at least three payday loan stores, you know. You can bet that's how they're funneling the money."

"You have evidence of this?" Alex asked.

"I don't. I mean, I've just been doing their real estate sales. Fudging the numbers, you know. Part of the laundering is to pay more for property with a kickback to people like me."

Alex was looking though the list of properties. "These are legit businesses in these buildings?"

"Yes, I mean, they get the rent from those stores. I know they have people come in and buy..." he made quotes with his fingers, "...things, well over-priced. That way they funnel dirty money through legit business accounts, you know. That in turn returns to the Outfit through rent surcharges."

"What's that?" I said.

"Oh. I mean, as well as rent on the property, the Outfit takes a percent of the profit, or so it is written off as. When, in fact, it is this dirty money, you know.

"On top of that, you know, they send fake invoices to these companies, which they pay with the dirty money."

Alex looked through the list some more.

"Can I go now?" Rudd asked anxious to get out.

"Not yet," Alex ordered. "These businesses, like container rentals, what's that about?"

"The money has to go into tangible things, you know, something which will give them an income. So they buy shipping containers around the world, and rent them out, you know. These things go all over the world. They layer this money so well it is impossible to figure it out."

"And these loans to businesses?"

"Oh, and that is the great part. I mean, they own the businesses they lend money to. The dirty money is used to pay the interest on these loans, you know.

"Some of the loans, to small businesses, are legit to help cover it up. Mostly to businesses who can't secure loans at a bank, you know."

"Loan sharking," I said.

"Not really. I mean, these are on the level, loans at reasonable rates. Their loan sharking is completely different, you know. They make loans to those gangs so they can buy drugs. The drug money is used to pay off the loans as a means to launder it."

"Sounds complicated," Becky said.

"Oh, you know, this is just a tiny portion of what they're up to. I mean, here in Chicago, this is puny compared to their international holdings.

"This is just what I know about. I mean, these guys have their tentacles all over the country and even in Europe. I heard they've been buying carbon offset credits in Europe, you know."

"That system is rife with corruption," Alex said. "I was relieved when the Chicago Climate Exchange closed down."

"Oh, I mean, they had a large play in that too. They bilked that system for millions. Even I... I mean... Look at their influences in the union movement. The Mob owns most of the big unions, you know."

Clearly he was trying to skip past his involvement in that carbon scam.

"We've put a dent in that," Alex said.

Rudd shrugged. "If you say so. Can I go now?"

"We thank you for this," I said.

"We never met, you know. I mean, you didn't get this from me. But

I'm off the hook for that terrorism, right?"

"That's why I'm here," Alex said.

"Good. Good. Look, I might be a crooked lawyer, you know, but I'm a patriot. I hope you find those goat-fuckers and kill them all."

Rudd got out, then hastily drove off.

As we drove back, Becky asked, "Ok. I don't understand how this money laundering works. Can you explain it to me please?" She was looking in the mirror at Alex.

I had to agree I wasn't sure how it worked either.

"I guess you didn't see the Lethal Weapon where that was explained."

Becky looked confused.

"The one with Joe Pesci, where he came out of the drive-through saying 'they fuck you at the drive-through.' I loved that line."

Alex looked at Becky waiting for a reply. She just cocked her head.

"You're too young, I guess." Alex explained it: "It's a three-step process. The first step is to get the cash into the financial system. There's a number of ways they can do that. Because that is the most vulnerable stage, because it can set off alarms with such large amounts of cash, they use a number of techniques. This includes using the money to pay off loans, buying gambling chips at a casino, blending of the money with legitimate purchases, say at a store, or the use of Smurfs..."

I laughed, "Smurfs?"

"Yep, they split the funds into smaller amounts and have a number of people deposit the cash separately. Less likely to raise a flag.

"Once the money is in some form of financial system—"

It dawned on me, "Like that bank the Outfit owns."

"Yes, and the payday loan places. Anyway, once into the system they then have to do the next stage. That's called the layering stage. Moving the money around makes a complex audit trail. Often the money is moved out of the country, wired to other banks off shore."

"So how do the owners of the money get it back then?" Becky asked.

"That's the integration stage," Alex continued. "Once the money is in some account, the owners can access it through wire transfers, or a credit card, or turn it into gold, or other savings vehicles. They can then use the funds to buy cars, or in our case here, these properties Rudd gave us. It would look like some foreign company was buying the properties, but in fact it is the Outfit right here using their foreign accounts."

"Sounds very complex," Becky said.

"That's the idea. The more complex it is the harder it is for us to trace, especially when its gone offshore. That means we have to deal with foreign, often corrupt, governments."

It dawned on me. "Hey, with so many people now using debit cards, there's less cash going in and out of banks. Wouldn't that be a problem with them trying to cover up the first step?"

"It would. But it will also make their ability to extract the money that much easier. They just get a card and can extract from it any time they want. So it works both good and bad for them.

"Don't underestimate these guys, they have some smart well paid accountants to figure this all out."

I remembered Alan Song, the financial investigator. He'd love this stuff.

Back at the Division, Alex looked over the material, and the CD. "He made pdfs of it all," he said. "I'll take the CD, you guys copy all of this to your gang unit." He got up from the table and came over to me. "I've got to take this to our people so they can also check this out. I assume you two will start to look into these places?"

"First thing," I said smiling.

"Ok, I'll see you at your place. I'll bring Chinese and a bottle of wine to celebrate."

He left after giving me a quick kiss.

I turned to Becky who wore a big grin.

"What?" I said.

"Oh, nothing." She chuckled.

Alex called as I was heading to my apartment.

"I'm not coming home. We have a lead on Orfali. He tried to cross the border into Quebec. There was a firefight with border guards. I have to go there."

"When will you be back?"

"I don't know, a couple days." He hung up.

The next morning, Becky and I went through the list deciding where to go first. Hollenger came over.

"Why are you doing this?" he asked me. "This should all be the gang unit's job."

Swell, I get the scoop and someone wants to take it away from me. "It has to do with the De Luca murder."

"But I thought the FBI was handling that?"

"They are. They're investigating those out of our jurisdiction. Here in the city it's our job."

He looked at some of the papers, "Ok. But you have other cases. When we need you for a murder, I expect you two to be on the ball with them too."

"Of course."

Becky and I hit the road. Our first stop was a freezer storage facility on West 21st Street. It was a fairly large building, and we had to navigate a number of trucks on the street.

We talked to the manager. The business stored frozen foods for the restaurant industry in the city. He said the company was owned by another numbered company. About once a week someone would come by to check things were operating properly.

As we left Becky said, "Exactly what are we looking for?"

"To be honest, I have no fucking clue. Something out of place I guess."

"That didn't look out of place to me."

"Well, that's assuming we'd recognize something is out place, doesn't it."

"Talk about being blind."

We visited a number of places that day. The last one, as the sun faded, was a building on Blue Island Ave. It used to be some kind of store, but the entire front had the windows bricked up. In the middle was a steel door. Over the door in rough painted letters it said "Church of the Holy Mary."

We got out and looked around. "To me, this is out of place," Becky said.

On the left of the front of the building was a door. I suspected it was the stairs to the upper two floors over the store. There were no names on the buzzer. I pressed it, but there was no sound.

We walked along 19th Street to the back alley behind the row of buildings. The back of the church had nothing. No dumpster, no garbage cans. Nothing. Just a steel back door.

As we came to the front, someone was walking along the sidewalk. I asked if he'd seen anyone go into the church. He hadn't.

The building next door was a chiropractic office. We entered to get out of the cold, and ask about their neighbors. The receptionist said the same thing. They'd never seen anyone come or go, but they were not open on Sundays, she said.

The building on the right side was for sale. It was locked.

We got back into the car and left.

The following Sunday morning Becky and I returned to the church to see if anyone would show up. We parked across the road at 8am. It was too cold to not have the engine running.

Two hours and no one showed up. We got out and walked around again. Fresh snow had fallen, so I checked the back to see if there were any footprints. But there was nothing.

Back in the car I said, "We'll give it 'till noon."

Just then a knock at the passenger side startled us. A man gestured to get into the back.

Two men got in.

"What Division are you with?" one said.

I told him.

"Why are you staking out this building?" he asked.

"Who are you first?" I demanded.

One showed me his badge – The Bureau of Alcohol, Tobacco, Firearms and Explosives. The Feds. Swell.

"Again, why are you staking this building?"

"We think it's a front for the Outfit," I said.

"You think, or you know?"

"Well, since you're asking about the place, I'd say we now know."

He paused as if wondering what to say.

"Look," he said eventually, "We've got the church under 24-7 surveillance. We're set up in that building diagonally across the intersection. On the second floor."

He paused some more.

The other fellow piped up, "We've got a tip that the Outfit is using the church to sell illegal weapons. So far, they only had a few people come and go on Sunday a few weeks back."

"There's certainly no congregation," the first man said.

"Look," the second man said, "in no uncertain terms, you two are not to come back. We've been on this case for two years..."

"Almost three."

"Ok, for almost three years now. So if you please, we would appreciate it if you didn't stand outside like this. Just leave the building to us. What we don't need is local PD fucking up this investigation."

"So you must not have gotten the memo," the other man said.

I gave the man a "what memo?" look.

"The memo from your department letting you all— Look. Just go before you're spotted."

As they got out, the second man peered through the open door. "Why are you here anyway? Who tipped you off?"

"We were told by an informant the building was owned by the Outfit. And we're investigating possible money laundering." I didn't share what else we were looking into.

He just closed the door and they walked off.

As we drove away I said to Becky, "We're on the right track."

Alex called me that night to say he was in Boston, and they were hot on the trail of Orfali. Alex said he was going to be a while yet, maybe even a couple weeks, which turned into a month.

The rest of February Becky and I continued to check on all the locations, and talk to people on Rudd's list. This was intermingled with our normal once a day senseless murders, coincidentally many of which were happening in the same area where we were checking the buildings.

What was interesting was when we confronted the shop owners about the counterfeit invoices submitted to them. They all denied they were fake. But when we looked at the invoices, they were all for "cosmetic construction." Right. The questioning certainly made the shop owners nervous.

We got the same reaction from those businesses who borrowed money from a "numbered company" instead of a bank.

It was the first week of March and the winter looked like it was finally over. Angel called me and said that Pam was in labor at the villa. A doctor and nurse were brought in for the delivery. He would call me back when things progressed.

Swell. I was disappointed I couldn't get there. I would like to have witnessed the birth. Maybe the next one.

I arrived at the Division later than usual that morning. I looked around the room. "Has anyone seen Becky?" I asked. It was not like her to not meet me in the mornings.

"Not yet," someone said.

I called her cell. I just got her answering service. I called Hollenger.

"Call her parents, they're in DC."

I got their number from Becky's files. They hadn't heard from her in a few days.

I called Hollenger back. "When are you getting here?"

"Couple hours, we aren't finished here. No luck finding her?"

"No. I'm getting worried."

"Does she have GPS on her vehicle?"

"No idea."

"Check it. I'll be there as soon as I can."

Becky drove a cheap older model car, someone in the Division said. It didn't have a GPS. Swell.

The second day of her missing I went to her apartment. The super let me in. Everything seemed in its place. The car keys weren't anywhere to be seen. Her clothing was still in the closet. Dirty laundry was in a basket in her room. The fridge was half full of food and leftovers. A few dishes, from her last meal, were soaking in cold water.

Nothing. No disruption to the apartment. She just disappeared.

That night, sitting alone in front of the TV, sucking on my friend, Angel called. My first thought was that I was now a grandmother. Me, a grandmother.

"Pam gave birth to a girl, three hours ago. Eight pounds, two ounces. Both are doing great, Mom."

We congratulated each other. He sent photos to my phone. Pam looked great, and the baby was just pricelessly cute. I couldn't help but remember the day Pam was born. And that I did alone. No father to help.

"And her name is?"

"Maggie," Angel said. "Pam wanted to name her after the character in The Walking Dead."

I'd never seen the series, so it didn't mean anything to me. But it was a nice name since it was also similar to my own.

Almost hourly, Pam or Angel sent me new photos. They were clearly immensely proud parents. And I was proud of my daughter. Come to think about it, that was likely the first time I was proud of her for a long time. I hated myself for those lost years without my daughter. Years I will never get back.

I promised Pam in a text message I'd get out to see them sometime end of March, when Alex was back and he could come with me.

By week's end Becky Clarke was officially declared a MisPer. I was worried big time.

The following few days I was on my own, trying to find people to contact for my investigations into De Luca, the Outfit and my regular murder cases. Becky's empty desk haunted me every day. Where the hell could she be?

I called hospitals. I called the morgue. Nothing.

Then it dawned on me. Does this have to do with our investigation into the Outfit? Have they retaliated and kidnapped her? My heart sunk and I broke out into a cold sweat. I wondered if I would be next.

I got scared. But what would my father have done? He must have been a target too from all the backstabbing he seemed to have done to perps. They must have put some kind of contract out on him. But he kept going. So I'll keep going.

Hollenger came in and sat at Becky's desk. "I talked to your old Captain, Doroszuk. He said your previous partner, Derik, is looking after Becky's file."

"He's good. He'll figure it out."

Alex came in and greeted Hollenger.

"You're back!" I exclaimed.

"Yes, fucker Orfali slipped our tail. He's gone."

"That sucks," Hollenger said. "Last time it took us ten years to finally track them down. Well, I'll let you two get back to work."

"Come with me," I said to Alex.

We went into the men's washroom. "What's this?" Alex said chuckling.

I locked the door, then grabbed him and we locked lips passionately.

I had to get some breath. "A month. I missed you. You not there... You not being with me... It reminded me how alone I was all those years before I met you. I don't want that again."

"I missed you too. At least the time went fast."

"How was France?"

"I wished I had time to take it in."

"I'd love to go to Paris, the city of love," I said in a dream like voice.

"I guess the media here isn't covering the riots."

Someone tried to get in. They knocked at the door. I said, "We're busy. We'll be out in a minute."

"I need to piss bad." came the reply.

"Try another washroom," I retorted. "I've see some TV coverage of rioting in Europe."

"Not this. Almost every day there are riots in Paris between Muslims and police. Looking for Orfali... The French government told us to stay out of the Muslim parts of the city. It wasn't safe."

"So no luck finding Orfali there, I guess?" I said.

"We thought he was in Paris. But it looks like he disappeared into the Muslim enclave in Belgium. He's gone."

"Sorry your trip was for nothing. But, am I glad you're back." I kissed him hard again. "I can't wait to get you home. We have so much to catch up on. Like, I'm now a grandmother!"

"Wonderful. They're doing well?"

"Perfect, every day Pam sends me some pictures. Here, look."

I showed him the photos on my phone.

"End of the month we're going to see them."

I couldn't sleep. I quietly got up, picked up my robe and closed the door to my room so as not to wake Alex. I turned the light on and powered up my laptop.

I was into about an hour of reading my father's notes and making more contact boxes when Alex emerged.

"I'm sorry. I didn't mean to wake you," I said.

"I rolled over and you were gone. Your father's notes?"

"Yeah. I've done nothing for weeks, since the bombings. Look, I got them all done. Every contact is now on the wall."

"So, have you figured it out yet?"

I sighed. "No. I've interviewed about twenty more while you were gone. I didn't get much from them." I paused. I hated having to lie to him. "Well, that's not entirely true. I've not told you the whole story. Since we've been together I've neglected to get back at this because I was afraid you would find out."

"Find out what, Babe?"

I paused. It was very difficult to admit. "I think my father was dirty."

"No. Why would you think that?"

I showed him some of the tagged notes. "I've been able to speak to thirty six of his contacts. They said my father ripped them off for thousands of dollars. Most of it drug money. They said he forced them to talk, or he would arrest them.

"One of the perps said my Dad said he could walk if my Dad gave him five grand. But only if the perp give up someone he was buying drugs from."

"That's not unusual. Cops have been doing that for decades. You haven't finished them all yet have you?"

"I have all the names as you can see. I'm only part way through the interviews."

"Do you see any pattern yet?"

"No. There's too many lines and too many names."

"What about your Dad's partners?"

"The only one still alive from then is Deputy Strong. There's no way I'm going to ask him if he and my Dad were involved in bribery and theft of evidence."

Alex scratched his stubble. "Hum, I don't believe it. There must be a logical explanation. Your father sounds like a smart guy. You're his daughter. If you did that what would have been your plan?"

"I don't know." A tear started to form in my eye. Alex kissed me on the shoulder.

"Come to bed. You're not going to figure this out tonight. Let's get some sleep."

The next morning I got up to find Alex was entering the names of my father's contacts into his computer.

"What are you doing?"

"Look, I understand this is your project, but what you're doing on that wall isn't going to work. You need software to see these connections.

This program is called Social Fabric. We use it in the FBI. It's a social network program. It does the connections in multiple dimensions, not two-D. Don't be mad, but if you want to find his secret, this software will do it. We caught the Boston bomber using this."

We spent the entire weekend entering the data. Late Sunday after dinner we were done, we celebrated with a bottle of wine.

"OK, so what does this show us?" I eagerly asked, finishing my glass.

Alex laughed. "Relax, Marg. It's going to take a couple hours to work the data to see any pattern." He looked at his watch. "It's after midnight. We both need to get up in eight hours for work. So, let's get some sleep. Then tomorrow night we can play with this. Besides, I want to take it to our guys and let them have a look. See if we have any matches in our database."

Reluctantly I agreed. We went to bed but we didn't get to sleep for long.

My phone played the Dragnet theme. I groggily woke up and looked at the clock: 2:45am. Alex stirred as it played the tune a third time. It was Rudd calling in a panic.

He was stumbling over his words. "They're onto me—to kill me. Shit. Mothers. I mean, you've got to protect me."

"Calm down, who wants to kill you, the Outfit?"

"Of course, the fucking Outfit, you know? I shouldn't have given you those documents. They're outside my house. My house, goddamn it. I snuck out the back. You've got to bring me in. Now."

"Where are you? We'll come and get you."

Alex and I pulled into the parking lot of a factory on McDermott Drive in Elmhurst. We stopped in the middle of the side lot.

"Where the fuck is he?" I said.

Alex got out, letting the night's frigid air pour into the car, and looked around a bit. Then got back in. "Nothing."

"Fuck, we're too late," I said.

A thump at my window scared the shit out of me. It was Rudd. Alex unlocked the doors, and Rudd slid into the back seat. "Drive," he said.

We turned around and headed out. "Where are we going?" Alex said.

"I don't care, just get me the fuck out of here. It's fucking cold out there, you know. I almost froze my balls off waiting for you." He took his toque and gloves off. He cupped his hands and blew into them. Alex turned up the heat full blast.

"What's going on?" I asked Rudd.

"Look, those documents I gave you? Well, the Outfit found out I gave them to you, you know. How the fuck did they find out? That's what I'd like to know. Look, I know a lot more. You know, enough to put a lot of them away for a very long time. But I want immunity, you know. I mean, I don't want to end up as pig shit like De Luca."

"How do you know about that?" Alex said looking at Rudd in the rear view mirror.

"Of course I know, you know. I knew the first day you came to interview me. That's because I helped them do the legal work to buy the farms, that's how I know. I know who was fed to the pigs and when. I got it all in a safety deposit box. I haven't eaten any pork for the last two years, you know."

He shuddered. "Fuck me..."

"We aren't going to get at a bank safety deposit box tonight," I said to Alex.

"You get nothin' until I know you'll protect me," Rudd protested. "I mean, I want a new identity. I want a new place to live, preferably not on this side of the continent, you know."

He looked out the side window into the passing darkness and lights. "Life is a series of disappointments punctuated with the occasional tolerable event. I got too close. Too close..." He paused then said, "I don't want to be anywhere near this fuckin' place, ever again. You know?"

He was shaking vigorously, and not from the cold.

We got onto US 294, then east on US 290. "Don't take me to the FBI building if that's where you're heading. I mean, they'll be there waiting. Waiting for me to get out so they can pepper this car with automatic fire."

Alex and I looked at each other. "Where then?" I said to Alex.

"I'll need to get there. If he's going to open up to us, he needs to get in front of a Grand Jury. I'll need to set that up."

I called Hollenger. He was a little pissed at being woken up at near four in the morning. But he agreed this was urgent. He said to meet him at the medical center at Harriston and Damen, just off the highway.

Hollenger was waiting there along with a marked cruiser and an un-marked car.

We switched around vehicles. Alex got our next destination, the Stardust Motel in Naperville, from Hollenger then he headed to the FBI building.

I was in the back of the unmarked car with Rudd, while two beat cops in plain-clothes drove. It was snowing heavily as a cold front moved into the area. It made the drive slow.

It was going down to zero that night. So much for a mild winter-ending March.

The normal forty-minute drive was double that with the deepening unplowed snow on the road, and the deteriorating visibility. Thus we arrived at the motel around 7am. Chicago Police had used that location a number of times to house people before they had to appear in court. It was close enough, but also far enough out of the city.

We stopped at the entrance. The passenger cop got out and went into the office.

He came back a few moments later, "Room twenty four. First floor at the back."

In the deep snowfall we loaded Rudd into the room. The two cops left.

"You're not staying with me are you?" Rudd asked.

"I am just until Alex gets here to pick me up. I just want to make sure you're all set and settled in."

"You're sure I'm safe here? These guys have long arms, you know."

"We've used this before."

"That's the problem. I mean, they know of this place, you know."

"No one knows but myself, Alex—"

"And those two cops. You sure you can trust them?"

"Yes."

"Well, you're too trusting for me, you know. I don't like this place."

"What's not to like? You have internet, cable TV."

He looked in the small fridge. "No booze."

"No, and you won't."

"How long do I have to be in here?"

"I told you already. Soon as the Grand Jury hearing has been booked. A couple days maybe."

"I don't like this, you know. When's the FBI agent going to get here?"

"He texted me. About seven hours."

"Fuck. Seven hours. I mean, I could get a hooker in here in that time."

"You get nothing. And don't ask, we'll feed you. You aren't to leave this room, for any reason. Best you get some sleep."

He drifted off pretty quick. I left and walked the short distance to the Wendy's. It was tough slogging with the snow, which had started to blow hard. It stung my face. It made Alex's Christmas gift a God-send.

I sat there drinking my coffee when Alex texted me to reaffirm he would be up to get me in the evening. The Grand Jury was on in two days.

I came back about an hour later, and Rudd was still asleep. I crashed on the other double bed.

It was dark when I woke to the sound of a toilet flushing. Rudd had been up only a few minutes.

"I'm starving," he said.

"There's a Wendy's just up the road," I said, rubbing my eyes and getting off the bed.

"Oh, I love Wendy's, you know. I'll have an Old Fashion Hamburger with onion rings and root beer. Please, that is."

I made the second trek in the deepening snow.

It didn't take long for him to devour the meal, topped off with a loud burp after the soda. I just had one of their chicken salads, and another coffee.

He turned the TV on.

We watched segments on the violent protests in the Mid U.S. This time it was over grazing rights of some free ranger's cattle on federal lands. Apparently, even though his family had been doing it for generations, it was illegal. The government wanted to rustle up all the cattle to confiscate them. But people from all over Utah had rallied setting up an armed perimeter.

They interviewed some yahoo who belonged to the Oath Keepers, about how the government was "trotting on the Constitution."

After that they showed bombings in a number of countries by ISIL or ISIS, or the Islamic State, or what ever their name is now, and Al Qaeda. 147 people killed by a bomb blast in a mosque in Yemen. They were killing each other now? I didn't understand this shit at all.

"Geeze, will this ever end?" I said.

"If it wasn't for those fucking towel-heads I wouldn't be in this mess right now, you know." He paused and changed the channel to sports news. He seemed frustrated his favorite hockey team lost last night.

There was a rapid triple knuckle knock at the door.

"Must be Alex."

I opened it just a bit when it was shoved into my face knocking me on the floor. A flashbang went off blinding me. I covered my eyes, only to be forcefully picked up by the arms. Someone punched me in the gut, sending me into incapacitating pain. They then stuffed a cloth in my mouth, and put a bag over my head.

Rudd was screeching, "No! No! No!"

They took me out the door as I heard muffled gunshots, three of them. Rudd was gone.

They zip-tied my hands and feet, then threw me into the trunk of some vehicle. My stomach still radiating pain everywhere, but I couldn't scream.

We drove off into the winter storm.

CHAPTER 10

Blasted Away

Two men grabbed my arms and dragged me out of the trunk of the vehicle by force, scraping my left leg on the latch. I couldn't scream out because of the gag stuffed in my mouth. I couldn't see anything but black because of the bag over my head.

I was petrified.

They had to drag me because my arms and legs were zip-tied.

My lower stomach was still throbbing and radiating pain from the punch.

After a long march, which included a short elevator ride down, I was told to stand and not move. They cut away my clothes. All of them. I was naked, and freezing.

I was totally vulnerable, embarrassed and indignant.

Were they going to rape me?

I started to shiver in the below freezing temperature.

One voice said, "Scan her."

Someone cut my bonds. Another voice ordered, "Put your arms out to your side and spread your legs wide."

They were looking for any chips. Shit, would the doctor be right? Would they stop before my feet?

I felt nothing but the cold as I could hear a light beep from some device. I jumped as it touched my privates as they scanned the insides of my thighs.

I was scared they'd find the chip. I was also embarrassed at being totally exposed.

But a voice said, "She's clean."

"Put your arms down," the first voice said. I also closed my legs tight. I was relieved they missed the tracker. It was a race for time now for Alex to find me.

I stood there, shivering in the frozen void for what seemed like minutes.

This was part of their tactic. It wasn't to rape me. It was to thrust as much agony and humiliation as possible on me. I was alive because they needed to know what I knew. I also knew this was the first step of what was to come.

They pushed me into a chair. The cold wooden seat on my bare butt spiked up my spine. They then zipped my arms to the arms of the chair. Followed by zipping my legs to the legs of the chair.

My shoes and socks came off last. My bare feet felt the sting of the frozen concrete.

They took the hood off. Then pulled the gag out. I was shivering in fear, as well as the cold. Try as I might, I couldn't stop shaking. I was breathing quickly, with each exhalation producing a white mist. My heart was pounding.

The only light came from two naptha lamps on tables on either side of me. I could feel the weak warmth from their flame. The room was black. Three heavyset men were around me, one on either side, one in front.

I had to say something. "I'm a cop you assholes! You're going down for this."

"I think not," a voice came from the black. A red glow appeared in the distance, then disappeared. A man emerged from the void with a large stogie in his mouth. He pulled a chair up to me, and sat right in front, just arm's length away.

I was shivering even more. I was scared shitless.

He looked my naked body over.

"Getting your rocks off?" I said. "Why don't you boys go away and jerk each other off."

He didn't say anything. His smile turned into a set of pinned eyes below bushy brows. He took a long drag of his phallic symbol, the embers glowed a bright red.

He slowly blew the smoke into my face. I closed my eyes, turned my head, and tried to hold my breath. But a searing pain jabbed into my right thigh. I screamed. He was rotating the cigar trying to put it out on my leg. I could smell my flesh burning.

He pulled the Cuban up to look at the end. He seemed disappointed it was almost out. He took several long drags as it re-ignited to his pleasure.

I broke out into a cold sweat as the throbbing pain radiated from my leg. The sting brought tears to my eyes, which dripped down onto my exposed breasts.

I looked down at the wound which still had a few glowing embers that slowly faded.

I was breathing heavily and shivering.

"You're cold, I see," the man said.

I just looked hard at him.

"It'll all be over soon. I need to know what you know about us. Where you are in the investigation, and where can I find your partner? That FBI lover of yours."

I was surprised. How did he know about us? The Outfit must have been spying on us for months.

He laughed, then leaned close to my face. "I know everything about you. Including your wall chart trying to figure us out from your ol' man's notes. He got very close to us too, you know. Too close. He had a lot of our people put away.

"Now, tell me what you know."

"Well, I know the Chicago Black Hawks lost their game last night."

He smiled. "Funny. Smart-ass aren't you. I want to know—"

I interrupted him. "I know you murdered De Luca And I also know that you are a sadistic fat pig—"

He slapped me across my face with the back of his right hand. It swung my head violently.

He yelled, "Tell me the names of everyone you've told about us."

I said nothing except a slow, "Fuck. You."

The man sighed. "Your other partner, that pretty young blonde, was in that same chair. My friend here," he pointed to the man beside him, "didn't have to do much to persuade her to talk. She blubbered everything she knew. Too bad she was so small. She wasn't much of a meal for the hogs. Now, if you don't want to end up as pig shit, you better start talking."

Oh my God, they did take her. They tortured that poor girl. They killed her. And I was next.

So here I was at the end of my life, and it wasn't going to be a quick quiet end. They were going to torture me, brutally. It didn't matter if I told them everything or not, I was going to be dead soon. If I told them, they would have just killed me quicker. If I didn't they would have their fun with me first. In the end I'd be dead anyway.

"Fuck you!" I spat in his face.

He sighed, and got up wiping his face with his hand. "My friend here is a heavy weight boxing champion. He's very good at what he does best

– making people talk. The Boxer here will..." He stopped. "Well, you'll talk before long."

He disappeared with a cloud of blue-white smoke following him.

The Boxer wrapped his right hand in strips of cloth. He came up to me with his left hand on my head, right hand as far back as he could. Then I felt a pain like never before in my left face. Stars and flashes of light filled my eyes. I screeched out.

He grabbed my hair this time, so tight it pulled my head up. Again he struck me. Again the pain was intolerable. Pam's birth was nothing compared to this. I could feel some teeth moving.

He struck again. A tooth dislodged into my mouth. I spat it out along with a volume of blood. The warmth flowed down my bare cold chest. I then threw up all over myself, into my lap.

He struck again and I blacked out.

I came to when they threw ice-cold water on my face, stinging my eyes. I couldn't see out of my left eye, it was swollen shut. Blood flowed down into my right eye, then dripped onto my chest. I was covered in sweat, snot, vomit and blood. Steam from my own vapors rose up all around me.

The punching had stopped. My entire body was in pain. My heart was skipping beats. Occasionally thumping back to life when it felt like it stopped.

It hurt to breathe, a sharp piercing pain was in my ribs, in more than one place.

I couldn't even cry I was swollen so much on my face. I just moaned, "fuck you," over and over.

One of the other men replaced the Boxer. As best as I could see he had a fat hammer in his hand. He knelt down in front of me.

The big man emerged from the darkness again. "This can all end, Marg, if you just tell us what I want to know."

A weak "'uck 'ou" was all I could muster while spitting up blood.

"The Mallet here is going to crush your toes, one at a time. Then he will crush your feet, several times. Now, tell me the fuck what I want to know!"

If they crush my foot, they could destroy the chip and I'd never been found. I needed to buy some time.

I moved my mouth a little, trying to get words out. The big man moved the mallet wielding man out of the way. I tried to look up with my right eye, again moving my lips. He got closer, inches from my face. I spat a huge volume of blood and saliva in his fat mug. "Fuck you!"

He backed up. He seemed quite disappointed, which was delightful to me. He picked up a towel from the table, and cleaned his face off. He beckoned the mallet man to return.

The Mallet knelt again, just back from my feet. He lifted the mallet high above his head and swung it down with all his might.

The previous pummeling of the Boxer's fist was nothing compared to the pain this inflicted. I screeched out so loud the Boxer covered his ears, laughing at the same time.

I uncontrollably excreted a large volume of urine into the chair that flowed onto the floor, where the pungent vapors rose into the air surrounding me.

The mallet found another pristine toe. Again I screamed.

He raised his weapon up for a third blow. But in the distance I could hear pops, in rapped succession. The men all stopped, and turned. A radio piped up, "FBI, FBI!!"

A sense of joy trumped all my pain.

"Get him out of here," the Boxer said.

The two men left into the dark with the big man in tow.

I was alone with the Boxer. He pulled his Sig from his pants, and pointed it right at my head. Here it comes, the end of my life. In that moment I thought about my daughter. I thought that my granddaughter would never know me. My heart raced even more. But then...

Shots rang out even closer. The Boxer looked around, then he disappeared into the blackness. He panicked and had fled. I was going to live. The relief was a new flush of energy.

There was what seemed a long pause of nothing, no sound except the hiss of the lamps.

Out of the nothingness I could see a figure coming towards me. He came back to finish me off. Here comes the end. I mentally prepared myself for my death.

But then a familiar voice said, "Marg, it's me."

Alex! My love found me. Thank God for that GPS chip.

I looked as best I could up at him. Distant pops echoed in the hollow void.

"Don't talk." Alex pulled his multi tool from his belt and cut the zip from my right arm. Two loud gunshots filled the room. Alex stumbled, then pulled out his Cz, and turned to fire. Three more flashes from the dark impacted Alex in the chest. He went down. The Cz slid out of his hand a short distance.

The Boxer emerged from the darkness, his handgun pointing at Alex.

I leaned over to my right, and fell on the floor behind Alex. I grabbed the Cz, and squeezed off the trigger as fast as I could in the Boxer's direction. The sound deafened me, sending pain into my ears, the only place which was free of pain. I blasted away until the trigger didn't move any more, and the slide was locked back.

In spite of the ringing in my ears I heard a thump in front of me.

I tried to get up to glimpse past my love's dying body to see the Boxer on the floor. A pool of blood formed beneath his body and flowed outwards on the cold concrete.

I moved as best I could to get my body under Alex's head. Short wisps of condensation came from his mouth. He was still alive.

"I'm sorry, Marg. I fucked up." He winced in pain. My left arm was still tied to the chair, so I couldn't use it. With my right hand, and my body crying out in pain and cold, I undid his coat and shirt. He was wearing his vest. Three 40 cal impacts were dead center. But didn't penetrate the Kevlar.

He probably had a number of broken ribs, but he was going to live.

"Help! Officer 'own! I 'eed 'elp!" I screamed as loud as I could. The effort, the motion of my diaphragm on my ribs, sent debilitating paid through my chest. I couldn't yell again.

I looked around for his radio, but it was out of reach near his feet. I tried to lean over him to grab it, but he screamed in pain. So did my own body. The pain made me woozy.

I just lay back holding his head between my breasts.

"I love you, Marg Cunningham."

"Shhh, don't talk, my love. You're going to be just fine."

"No, I'm..." His life evaporated from his open eyes.

"Alex?"

Nothing. No breath came from his mouth.

"Alex!!"

I shook him.

"No, no, no! Please! No, no... Don't go. Please..." I screamed a long, "Nooo!"

Lights shone on us from the distance. Many beams focused on us. Someone yelled, "Man down, man down!"

Three cops rushed up to us. One checked the Boxer and kicked the Sig away.

Another checked Alex for a carotid pulse. "I'm sorry, Detective, he's gone."

I dropped my head onto his and cried. Tears even came through my swollen eyes.

How? He had a vest on!

"Code fifteen! Medic in here now. And some blankets!" the cop yelled into his radio.

One of the cops took his tunic off, and covered me with it. I didn't even really notice. He cut the rest of my bonds, and moved the broken chair out from under me.

"She's beat real bad," one said.

The other two covered me with their tunics. They huddled around me to try to keep me warm. I embraced my man.

"Get two stretchers in here," one yelled into the radio.

I lay there, hugging my dead soul mate for what seemed hours. I kissed his forehead.

Paramedics arrived. They had to pry my arms from around Alex. I sobbed when they separated us and put me on a stretcher. One of the medics put an IV into my arm, and they whisked me into the darkness.

I would never hug my lover ever again.

I don't remember the ambulance ride except the bumps, which sent off the scale pain through me. I think I just moaned as the medic stuck me with a number of needles.

"Push it or we'll lose her!" I faintly heard her say a few times.

CHAPTER 11

BLACK, BLUE, ORANGE AND YELLOW

I woke in the hospital. Pam and Angel were both there waiting for me. My granddaughter was sleeping in Pam's arms.

"She's awake!" Pam said. "Nurse! She's awake."

A nurse hustled in. "Miss Cunningham, can you hear me?" She said looking at the monitor.

I hurt like hell, but I managed to squeak out a "yes."

"OK. Great. Don't talk. The doctor will be right in."

Pam held my hand. I looked at her through one eye. The baby started to make some fuss. It was such a wonderful sound. I tried to smile, but that hurt too. My tongue went into the void where three teeth used to be on my left lower jaw.

I was exhausted. A small amount of vertigo made the room move back and forth. I had to close my only open eye.

When the doctor came in later he told me I had a broken left cheek, broken nose, three cracked ribs, and two crushed toes. Not including the severe bruising around both eyes, the left side of my face, and the contusions around my chest and stomach.

They must have continued to pummel me after I blacked out.

"You also miscarried," the doctor said.

"She what?" Pam said.

I what?

The doctor picked up on the confusion. "You didn't know you were pregnant? Nine weeks. I'm sorry."

Tears filled my eyes. I was carrying Alex's child. I lost him, and I lost our baby. I sobbed, crying "no" over and over.

The doctor kept talking, but I didn't hear much except that they put me into an induced coma because of the pain. They had to operate on one of the ribs as it had punctured my lung. They also had to remove my pinky toe it was so badly destroyed. They managed to brace the other toe.

He was just finishing up my chart when my boss, Captain Hollenger, came in.

"How you feeling, Marg?"

Stupid question. I felt like shit in a drowsy stupor and in pain, and I was in grief.

He briefed me on the situation. They got everyone captive in the factory, save a few they put down. The exception was the Don. He managed to escape through a tunnel in the factory basement to an adjacent building.

"I don't understand." I said. "Alex had a vest on. How did he die?"

"Seems one of the shots got in under his armpit. It then bounced off his sternum and lodged near his heart, perforating an artery. Damn, unlucky shot."

He asked who shot the Boxer, Alex or me.

"I did," I managed to get out without it hurting too much.

"Well, you hit him six times. Leg, lower hip, lower torso, upper torso, chest, and just below his right eye." Mighty fine shooting. Six out of sixteen, not bad."

"Since I didn't even aim," I said. Practicing with Alex in the basement of the FBI building came to mind. As did his accusation that I couldn't hit anything.

I stopped. My next words were hard to get out. Not because of the physical pain, but because of another pain – deep grief.

"When's Alex's funeral?" I was scared I'd missed it.

"Tomorrow, Marg. But you're not going anywhere in your state."

"Like fuck I'm not. I don't care if you have to wheel me there stuck with all these tubes. You get me there, or I'll just walk out of here."

They had placed a guard at my door. Hollenger felt I was still a target. Pam and Angel took shifts for the rest of the day. No one else visited.

Late in the evening I was actually getting hungry. But I didn't want hospital food. Angel went and got me a hamburger from Express Grill. It was fantastic. Though I had to chew only on my right side, I devoured it before the nurse could catch me.

A man walked past my room looking in. He went by at least three times. The cop at the door stopped him and asked questions. I couldn't hear the conversation.

The man disappeared.

I asked the cop to come in. He said the man was just looking for his mother. Bullshit. He could have found that out at the nursing desk. "They're looking for a way to get at me."

I called Hollenger at home. "We don't have the budget to post another guard."

"Then get me my sidearm so I can defend myself."

"You're in no shape. Besides, we can't have bullets flying around a hospital."

I hung up in frustration.

Angel looked like he wanted to say something. "What is it?" I asked.

"Let me make a call." He left the room.

He came back a few minutes later. "You're getting additional protection. They'll be here in an hour."

Around 8:30pm two men arrived, stopped by the cop. Angel went over to allow them to enter. They were big heavyset men.

"Mom, these are my cousins."

"How many cousins do you have?"

"Lots. Look, Mom, they're armed. But we can't let the cop know."

"Yes, we can." I called the cop into the room. I read him the riot act. I reminded him that this extra security would also save his life if I were a target.

Reluctantly, he agreed. The two men took turns scouting the hallway for the rest of my stay.

The following morning was Alex's funeral.

As best they could, two female cops dressed me in my blues on route from the hospital. It was excruciatingly painful. The worst was when one of the cops tried to put a bra on me, I felt like I couldn't breathe, as she struggled to do up the back hooks. "Forget it!" I ordered, "Just put my shirt on and my tunic. Hurts too much."

As they opened the back of the ambulance doors, a number of formal dressed uniforms were waiting.

"We will carry you," one said.

The ambulance driver came around and said, "No way. She goes in a wheelchair."

Some wanted to complain about that, but the driver was stern as she got the wheelchair out from the back and unfolded it.

Derik was one of them in the group, he helped me from the ambulance into a wheelchair. The driver made sure all my IV's were hooked up. Derik rolled me into the funeral parlor.

I could hear a scuffle off behind me. I looked beyond the convoy of parked vehicles to see the media was swarming past the gate of the cemetery. A large squad of police was thwarting their attempt to get a photo.

Two long rows of dressed cops flanked the stairs. Their white gloved right hands in salute. I was so moved. Tears welled in my eyes and ran down my cheeks.

Derik had to turn my wheelchair around to pull me up the steps. Every jump sent pain stabbing into my back and chest. Twelve steps seemed like hundreds. I blew a sigh of relief when he turned me around to go through the oak doors.

The celebration of Alex's life was very touching. His family gave a few words, their voices cracking with emotion. His mother couldn't say anything, and was aided by Alex's father back to her seat. Scott managed to speak a few words. So did the Director of the FBI and all the top stars of the CPD and the FBI.

As each finished they came to me and shook my hand. The officers saluted me, as well as saluting Alex's family. The Director of the FBI handed his mother a folded American flag.

Roger was there, and so was Nathan with his family.

The road from the funeral home to the gravesite was only a few hundred yards, but the entire route was packed with thousands of law enforcement officers from every state in the Union. There was even a platoon of Canadian officers – RCMP, OPP, QPP, Toronto and Ottawa police services. It was such a turnout to pay their respects.

M4 wielding SWAT, facing outward, ringed the gathering at the open grave. A chopper circled above us.

A bagpipe played as six FBI men took Alex from the back of the hearse. They carefully laid the casket over his final resting place. That's when it hit me – a trench that no one ever leaves.

A priest gave a few final words. Alex's older nephew and niece laid flowers on his coffin. At the request of the family there was no twenty-one-gun salute.

The uncontrolled sobbing is all that could be heard as they lowered Alex into the ground.

Rage and grief is all I felt. As Alex disappeared, I vowed to him I would track every last one of those mother-fuckers down, and kill them all.

Each family member grabbed a handful of earth, and let it crumble through their fingers into the grave.

Derik had to get a handful for me. I dropped my cold dirt last.

Laurie and Scott came over to me as we prepared to leave. She held the folded American flag.

She wanted to say something, but couldn't get out the words. We just held our hands together.

Scott got her away, and bent down to my ear. "I'll make any resources available to you to kill every one of them."

My look gave him the reassurance he wanted.

Once I was back in the ambulance, with a great relief from the pain, Deputy Superintendent James Strong came in, closed the back doors, and sat beside me.

Why would the second in command for the entire force want to talk privately with me?

"I just want you to know you have the full support of the entire force to find these scum."

"Thank you, sir."

"I mean it. Look, I knew your old man. I know you've been looking into his cases trying to make sense of his success. I know how he succeeded. I'm likely the only one alive who knows. We were partners for a while, but you already know that. When you recover, we'll talk and I'll explain it all."

I was stunned. I was sure I had kept my research quiet. I guessed the deputy had eyes everywhere.

He realized I was surprised he knew.

"It's OK. I made sure people allowed you to continue your research."

I knew from my father's reports they were partners for a few years, as well as his commanding officer later. But how does one go and ask the Deputy about possible illegal activities he must have known about?

"I know what you want to do. But before you do, you need to get better. I'm putting you on leave for six months."

"No. Sir. Respectfully, I—"

"Look, you're hurting. You need time to heal."

"Sir, hear me out."

The ambulance driver got into her seat. "Can you leave us a few minutes, please," Strong said. Turning back to me he said, "You were saying?"

"I got to thinking while in bed, trying to clear my mind of the pain. I want you to terminate my employment. Send me on permanent disability. Make it public so it gets in the papers."

He looked at me straight in the eyes. "You want the freedom... You're..." He paused. Then nodded, "The wrath of a woman scorned is about to be unleashed."

I just gave a painful smile.

"You're your father's daughter. You didn't know this, but I've had my eye on you for a long time. It was a promise I made to your ol' man on his deathbed. I honor my promises. Consider it done.

"I might as well tell you. Soon as your papers came through to go to homicide, I was pleased and made sure it was approved right away. Not that I was promoting you unwarranted. I knew you were ready."

He wrote on a slip of paper and handed it to me. "There's two names here. The first one is a lawyer—well, sort of. He'll help you on the resources side. The other is our head of the SWAT. He's a great guy. He'll get you trained on weapons. You're going to need the training. You made a plan yet?"

"Deceit and finesse."

He looked at me sideways. Then he said, "I don't want to know anything about it. We'll talk later. Get better." He left the ambulance, and off we went back to the hospital.

As they wheeled me back into my room I said, "I need to pee."

Two nurses helped me to my feet and walked me into the bathroom. I stopped at the door and looked in the mirror. It was the first time I saw the results of the brutality.

The left side of my face was all black, with yellow forming around the edges. I had stitches over my left eye. My nose was also black and blue, as well as part of my right face. My left ear was still swollen.

I opened my mouth to inspect the huge gap in my lower molars.

I still had my blues on. I started to quickly undo the buttons. I wanted to see the rest. The nurse stopped me.

"I want to see it all. Help me get this off," I demanded.

She ordered the men to leave. Angel took little Maggie so Pam could also help.

"We'll do it," the nurse said. "Just relax."

Relax? How can someone relax looking like this?

They stripped me completely, as I commanded.

I was horrified at the mess. Pam gasped and held her hands over her mouth.

My entire torso was black with contusions. There wasn't much natural skin color anywhere above my waist, except my boobs. A few stitches were under my left breast where they had to reset a couple of ribs.

Another scar showed where they took my spleen out. My left foot was bandaged, but there was no pinky. My upper legs were also bruised. Another set of stitches on my left calf showed where I was scraped being taken out of the trunk.

I pulled off the bandage to expose the crater in my right thigh.

All I could think of was how I could have survived such abuse.

Tears welled in my eyes. I started to shake. The room began spinning. I uncontrollably pissed on the floor as the nurses caught me before I could fall.

They cleaned me up, got me dressed and back in bed. They put a shot of something in my IV and I drifted off.

Three days later I was alone in my bed, still hooked up to tubes coming from every orifice, including new ones. I was still woozy with medication.

I was trying to watch some TV, shaking my head as CNN aired a number of pieces on the new rioting, which was breaking out all over the country. This time it was over high-energy costs. It seems a larger than normal number of people froze to death in the deepest, coldest winter on record.

One in particular broke my heart. An entire family in New England died of carbon monoxide poisoning. Mother, father, and six children ranging in ages from eight to six months – dead. They were too poor to pay for power, so had been cut off. Cut off power in the middle of winter. The father borrowed a generator from a friend and had it running in the basement hooked up to the panel. They were all found dead in the morning when none of the kids showed up for school.

As bad as I was, there were people far worse off than me. I still had my life.

This was also when the shift change for my guard took place. That was every eight hours.

Once the other cop left, his replacement didn't sit. He just looked around. Then looked at me. He walked in and pulled his sidearm out.

I became instantly lucid at the thought of not being able to fight back to stop my death. I tried to scream out when a shot fired.

The blast was deafening. The concussion reverberated in my chest. My ears rang. But I felt no new pain. I was still here. I looked up. One of Angel's cousins was standing at the door with his .50 caliber Desert Eagle still smoking. The room smelled of burnt gunpowder.

On the floor lay the dead cop. At the foot end of my bed the white sheets were crimson with streams of blood, brains, and chunks of skin with hair on them. Some red globs dripped from the ceiling, while long streams of blood streaked on the wall, under the TV. A few spots on my face became cold.

People came running in. The cousin walked to the corpse, gun pointing at it. Blood flowed from around the dead man's head. The cousin kicked the Glock away from the lifeless hand.

The officer, who was relieved just a few moments before, came running in with his sidearm drawn.

"Freeze! Drop the gun!"

I guessed the cop thought the cousin tried to shoot me. But he saw the body on the ground and lowered his pistol. He got on the radio asking for reinforcements.

Before long it was all chaos of cops in my room. They put the body on a gurney and took it away. An orderly came in and mopped up the blood before someone slipped and fell into it.

They had to change my bedding, so I sat at the edge of the other bed nearest the window. A cold breeze flowed on my bare back from behind me. I turned to look at the window. A huge hole penetrated the glass, with red spotted cracks emanating in all directions, letting the winter night in.

Hollenger came into the room. "We found one of our cops shot in the head in the parking lot. Looks like that maggot took his place."

"This is getting serious," I said.

"Tell me about it. You're going to be moved from this wing. They have an empty ward upstairs. You're going there in a few minutes. But you can't take your bodyguards with you."

"You going to charge him with murder?"

"I'm not sure yet. The gun is legal. But I have a sneaking suspicion I'm going to get a call from Deputy Strong about that, aren't I. I saw he talked with you in the ambulance. He told me after you were being let go from the force. But that's a ruse, isn't it."

I just looked at him.

"Yeah, it is. You're planning some kind of retaliation, aren't you?"

I just looked at him.

"Yeah, you are." He leaned over to me. "You have my full support. I'll make my staff at your beck and call for anything you need."

He gently took my hand, it hurt, but it was so comforting. A tear welled in my eye. I started to choke up.

"Get better first." He left the room.

They sent me up to the empty ward right away. The main doors were guarded by one cop and one of Angel's cousins. A password system was set up for shift change.

Unfortunately, I didn't make the funeral for the cop who was killed trying to protect me. I watched it on the TV. He was just a rookie. Again, a family loses their father, and little kids have to lay flowers on a casket. I was getting deadened to the grief to some extent. It just made me more livid.

The next day Pam and Maggie came to visit.

"Mom, Angel's uncle will take you in to finish your recovery. There's no way the Mob can get to you there. Oh, and look."

She handed me today's paper. A short bit on an inside page with my picture said I was recovering in hospital, and was leaving the force because of my injuries. Perfect.

A week later, I got a visit from Alex's parents. It was an emotional time. Laurie brought me apple pie, and a little bit of rum and coke in a thermos.

They came back every week until I was released.

I spent the next three weeks in the ward planning what I was going to do next.

Hollenger and four uniforms came the day I was to leave. I could walk. Most of the bruising had turned into shades of yellow and orange. I was off the narcotic pain meds, just painkillers. But I still ached all over.

We went down the service elevators into the basement. Then into a linen van, and we drove off. The van was doing a normal delivery to Rush

Medical Center where I was recovering. So as not to trigger any suspicions I was hidden in the back amongst the large bags of laundry. A cop, with a pump shotgun, was with me sitting on a bag.

We arrived into the underground parking lot of the University of Chicago Medical Center at the south end of the city. There I was transferred to a cab. The cab was driven by another cop. Two other unmarked cars followed us to the Chicago Executive Airport.

We drove into a hanger where a Learjet was waiting. Pam and family were there. Hollenger arrived before us.

"This is an FBI plane," he said. "They're going to take you to Florida. But before you head out, someone needs to talk to you. In the plane," he pointed.

CHAPTER 12

Secret Revealed

I went up the steps and entered the cabin. I was astonished to see Deputy Superintendent James Strong, in a civilian gray suit, sitting waiting for me.

He shook my hand and said, "Come in, Marg. Have a seat."

I sat across from him.

He sat and said, "I guess you're wondering why I'm here."

"In a way, yes."

First thing he did was hand me a Cz handgun. "This was Alex's."

I took it, but I started to get choked up as I handled it. Flashes of me blindly firing it filled my mind.

"How far are you in your father's notes?"

"All of them. How long have you known?"

He laughed a bit. "I knew before you began. I was just waiting for you to get at it. I figured you'd have started long before now. But I guess something happened."

"Happened? You mean this attack on me?"

"No, tell me what you know so far, then I'll explain and fill in any gaps you have."

I explained what I knew.

"Hmm," he said. "You've got a lot of gaps. You're going to find out anyways, eventually. I had thought about stopping you from finding out. But I think, in light of what's happened now, you deserve the truth. Did you find the money?"

Swell. How the hell did he know about that? I had no choice, but to explain the two cases. I guessed I was going to lose it all.

Strong laughed a bit. "Hidden in plain sight. That's your ol' man. It was actually both of our money. I assume you think your father was tainted. On the take?"

I nodded.

"Well, you're right and wrong. How much is left?"

I told him.

He sat back in the chair looking surprised. "Wow, he went through a lot. It was about three mill last I counted it."

"There's also stocks, just over two million. Maybe that's where it went."

"No, those came from your grandfather. He worked for Grumman as an aircraft designer. I met him a few times when your ol' man and I first started. How old where you when he passed on? Fourteen?"

I had to think a bit about that. "Yeah, I think so, maybe thirteen. I remember him when he was retired. So all those stocks came from him? That's a lot of money."

He poured himself a half glass of water from a plastic bottle. "He was senior engineer for a number of years before he retired. Plus the house was paid for. Once your grandmother died it all went to your old man. So, it wouldn't be surprising it would be that much.

He took a quick drink. "But your ol' man had too much integrity to put our bust greens, that's what we called it, into his own pocket. It was for work only. That I know for a fact."

I opened the second bottle of water waiting for me, and just drank from it.

He could see I was confused. "Look, I'm going to save you some time, plus not everything is in his notes. He kept separate notes. Your father got that dough from drug busts. He would make a deal with the perps. Cash for freedom, he called it. We take the cash, you go free. But the twist was the perp would have to give up someone else."

"That just sounds like normal paid CIs, or leveraging a perp with bribery of jail," I said.

"Yes and no. He would take a portion of the money and guns, kind of like a tax, before it was submitted into evidence. Let me explain."

He paused. "Actually, let me back up first," he sighed. "Your ol' man started ten years before me, so I can only go by what I was told.

"In the summer of 1979, when he was still a beat cop, he was with three other cops having lunch over on North Wells. They were sitting outside when a car came up and two men sprayed them with automatic fire.

"Three cops were killed, along with two innocent bystanders. Don was the only one who survived the attack. Not even a scratch. But his partner died..." He paused for a second. Shaking his head he said, "He died in your father's arms. I'm sorry to remind you of that with Alex."

I was stunned. I was seven at the time, but he never told me about it. "Who did it?"

"The Outfit. The other two cops had arrested one of their soldiers. It was retaliation. Your father and his partner were just collateral damage.

"It changed your dad. He realized what we all eventually realize, cops must cross the line to deal with criminals who don't follow the rules. From then on he went hard core.

"He spent the next year hunting them down. They were found eventually, floating under a railway bridge in Riverdale with two 22 bullets in their brains."

"Dad did it?"

"Internal Affairs thought so, but there was never any evidence found. They were in the drink for at least a month, so there was no way to pinpoint the day they were killed.

"Look, your ol' man, he never fired a shot in anger on the job. But, off the job, I don't know. There were times Outfit members, or some gang member, was found dead from one of the guns Don took. If he shot them, or the gun ended up with someone else, we'll never know."

"That was before he became detective?"

"Yes, your ol'man made homicide detective the following year, or in 1981, I can't remember."

"'81. Ok, so I don't understand about the money. What was he using it for? Paying CIs?"

"That's what I was trying to explain. He made deals with the perps, but what he also did was let it out on the street that the perps were talking to the cops."

"I don't understand. That would make them targets," I realized.

"That was the point. He would betray the informants so that they would be marked. That meant the gangs or the Outfit would go after them. It was a way to flush them out. When people get desperate they make mistakes. That was Don's theory. That's when they'd get arrested."

"But the marks could be killed."

"Some were. Hell, many were. Don didn't care. He figured those perps were dead anyway because of the life they chose. He said, better to put criminals away for murder than smaller crimes where they would get released in a few years."

"Many just came into a Division singing like birds because they wanted protection. That would give us even more to arrest. Your father was one smart cookie. He knew which needed to be ratted, and which would come in crying like babies.

"In a nutshell, it worked a lot. Some didn't take the bait, though. But many gave up others for their freedom. Didn't last long, though. We didn't give them immunity. They would do something stupid later and get arrested anyway. Some criminals are like a ten watt bulb, your father used to say.

"As far as the Outfit was concerned the cash went to the cops. Well, it did, but just some to your ol' man. We would then use the money to bribe others into giving up someone else. And so on we went.

"After I got promoted to division commander, I looked the other way as your ol' man just continued raking in the arrests."

"You said he would take money and guns. Why the guns?"

"For planting on perps, for more leverage later."

"You said he kept separate notes. Where are they?"

"Gone. They were in a safety deposit box. But upon his death he made me promise to destroy them. They had who he took money from and how much. It also contained the names of those who were killed because of his ratting them out. He used the notes for leverage when he needed to."

"Gone?"

"I burned them all."

I was even more confused. "I don't understand, why would he want it all destroyed?"

"To protect your career. If it ever got out, your father was worried it would come back on you."

I had to take this all in. I stood up and walked a few paces towards the back of the plane. I turned and came back. "This was all illegal, right?"

"Yes. Quite. Sit. You're obviously agitated."

I did sit. "Yeah, just a little agitated." I took another drink from the bottle.

"Well, that was the price we paid to get the criminals. They didn't play by the rules, so playing by the rules was counterproductive, according to your ol' man. Hey, he's not alone in that sentiment. There's a lot of cops out there right now keeping this city safer by bending the rules. And as things get worse, that's going to happen more often."

Swell. My father's secrets went with him to his grave. But I certainly had my perspective turned on a dime. I understood my father.

Strong stopped, then looked at me with a very serious face. "You and I never had this conversation. And I was never here. Understand?"

"I think so."

"Good. Use what you have left of the money to take these assholes down. We've tried for years. Certainly we've put a dent into them, but overall all we've done is pissed them off more.

"With you out of the department, you may do better than we did. But what's left isn't going to be enough. Did you call that lawyer I gave you yet?"

I shook my head.

"Do so when you figure out what it is you want to proceed with. What's your immediate plan? Other than getting fixed up?"

"I want to get trained in use of force. Can you hook me up with Captain Flock at SWAT, as your note said?"

"Use of force. Hmm. Well, no I can't now you're off the force."

"How about a SEAL team or Delta Force?" I asked.

"Why? What are you planning?" He paused. "Never mind. I don't want to know. Look, I don't have any connections with the military. So, I'm not sure how that can be arranged."

He looked me over. "You don't appear to be in any shape right now for that kind of training, anyway. Look, if you're going to prepare yourself it's best you don't do that in the States. I know some RCMP brass who owe me a favor. When you're ready I'll have something lined up for you."

I was a bit confused. "Why do you want me out of the country?"

"You're a marked person, Marg. Word on the street is the Outfit has put a bounty on your head. I'm sure you'll be fine at the in-laws estate, but not on the street. You need to disappear for a few months. Sending you to Canada will be safe."

He stood up, so did I.

"When you're all healed up and ready to start, call me. I'll have this plane pick you up and send you north. Any questions?"

"I don't know how to thank you."

"You can thank me by never uttering a word about this conversation."

The pilots entered. Strong shook their hands. Then he paused. "Oh, before I forget." He turned towards me. "Whitman sold everything and moved to Brazil last week. Looks like you were right all along."

"I knew it! Has Easton's body been found yet?"

"No. One day it'll show up. Have a good flight."

He paused a bit. He clearly had something more to say.

"What is it, Sir?"

He came back into the plane. "This is difficult for me to admit. But I have to tell you. It was no accident you got hooked up, professionally that is, with Alex. When they discovered what was left of De Luca's remains, they found out we were investigating his disappearance. I got the call from Alex as to where you were in your investigation.

"He said he needed some help with his side, something to do with not enough staff. Same as us. So it dawned on me that this would really boost your career. So I recommended you partner up with Alex.

"It never occurred to me you would get romantically involved. Don't get me wrong. I was so happy for you that you did. But then this. I don't know what to say, except I'm so sorry."

He turned and left the plane.

I was dumbfounded. Numb. How random acts of kindness can sometimes go so tragically wrong. I didn't blame the deputy, in fact, to have those moments with Alex, I was grateful to James.

Pam and family came aboard and we were on our way to Florida.

"We're going to your uncle's?" I asked.

"Yes, ma'am," Angel said. "He and his men will be waiting for us at the airport. Then to his villa."

"I liked the place. We had a good time at Thanksgiving."

"You'll get top notch care there."

I nodded. Maggie nursed from Pam's breast. It brought back so many fond memories. I remembered going into the shower with full mammaries, only to have them squirt out when the warm water landed on my chest. I remembered my breasts getting rock hard, and bulging from my undersized bra.

I also remembered Pam purred when she suckled. So was Maggie. I smiled.

"Miss Cunningham..."

Angel took me from my thoughts. "Please, call me mom. You did before."

"Thank you, ma'am, I mean, Mom. I was going to say. You give me the word and I can take this war to the Mob in Florida. We've been doing some digging, asking around the streets since they attacked us. And we know where they are. I can get a small army and take them all out."

"Attacked, what attack?" I said anxiously.

They looked like they had let the cat out of the bag. "Nothing, Mom," Pam said.

"Nothing, you got attacked? What happened? Angel!"

"Someone tried to shoot up the house. We're all OK. No one was hurt."

"When did this happen?"

"Just before you got abducted."

"And you just decided to tell me now?" I was furious.

"We didn't want to tell you at all, Mom," Pam said taking Maggie off her breast and covering herself up.

"Did you see who it was?"

"No," Angel said. "But we're on it."

"You're staying at the villa, I assume, until this is all over?"

"Yes, Mom," Pam said.

I was pissed, if that was even more possible. They attacked my family. These fuckers are going down.

"You need to take what you know to the cops," I said to Angel.

"Mom, with respect for your profession: fuck the police. They'll just arrest them, then before night the wops will all be back on the street. We'll find them. Then we'll inflict real justice."

"I can't be responsible for any of your family being killed or committing murder."

"Seems to me, ma'am, they declared war on all of us. Best I don't tell you anymore. You'll know when were done when it hits the news."

"We didn't want to add to your problems, Mom," Pam said. "They didn't get me, Mom. Not even close."

"Well, I'm not happy you held it back. So you're safe there? I have to say, I'm more than a bit concerned now."

"Oh, Mom. Don't worry," Angel said. "Some of our extended family have moved into the villa temporarily. There is no way they can get at us. It's an armed fortress now."

On the flight, I had time to think about my father in light of the new information. It was reassuring for sure. Guess I shouldn't have jumped to my original assumption.

I was worried somewhat when we landed at Homestead Air Force Base that the drive to the villa would open us up to risk. But it was just a short ten-minute trek.

Three months at the villa was uneventful. I never once ventured outside the compound. I was actually starting to get claustrophobic. There were only so many series on Netflix to watch.

I even got to watch all of The Walking Dead. It was better than I thought. I understood why Pam liked it so much. But one thing for sure, they definitely got human behavior right. It was kind of depressing.

I used the gym a lot. Every day I worked out. Luis got me a personal trainer to ensure I was systematic in my exercising.

I also finally got to finish the two book series, *Blinding White Flash*. Both were riveting, and intense from cover to cover. Non-stop combat scenes in the *Invasion* book were well written. I felt like I was right there. I hoped the basic theme, of China invading North America, was just fiction. But the scenes of the Islamic attacks in the book were eerily too close to real, almost prophetic.

I was inspired by the story line of civilians, ordinary people, stepping up to the plate and becoming effective warriors. Something I was determined to emulate.

I was treated like royalty by Angel's extended family. I was satisfied that Pam had made the right call with Angel.

Now that Pam had her baby, it was time we had the discussion about them getting legally married. They made a date for June. It was going to be a big event. Together, Pam and I planned it all. It certainly broke the boredom.

Some two hundred and fifty people would come. It was going to be a huge celebration, like his family does for all who marry.

Luis had a doctor, also part of his family, who oversaw Pam's birth, come and check on me on a regular basis. One of the reasons I didn't leave the villa was the doc didn't want me to do too much. I didn't tell him I was pushing my body to the limit every morning.

In April, I was sitting in a lounge chair by the pool enjoying the rays of sun on me, listening to Money by Pink Floyd, when Luis came up to me. "Next week I have a dentist who will see about getting your missing teeth replaced with implants."

It was getting annoying not being able to chew on my left side. "That's great. I've been thinking of getting it done."

"Good, we'll do it all right here. Can't risk you leaving. Some of the boys think we've been probed a number of times. The Mob knows you're here."

"Probed?"

"Si. Yesterday, they spotted one of those toy drones circling the compound. You were in the pool at the time."

My thought went back to Whitman, when he built a radio-controlled airplane with a gun in it. This concerned me that the Mob may try the same trick.

"Not to worry," Luis said. "I've stationed a number of boys around with double-barrels. They need the skeet shooting practice anyway. But I'd be sure the Mob know you're here. So we can't risk you leaving at all."

The dentist was great. The day he came he brought everything he needed. Even a portable X-Ray machine.

Two weeks later, he returned to start the first stage of my new teeth – getting the implant into the jawbone. That, the dentist said, would take a couple months to heal and bond to the bone. Then he would come back to insert the abutment, which the new teeth screw into. In the meantime, he put in a bridge to cover the gap.

I had some concerns about my health. I wasn't sore, everything seemed to be healed just fine. But I just didn't feel right. Something wasn't normal. I passed it off as just my mind playing tricks on me, or maybe my exercising was too intense.

In the first week of June my cell prompted me to answer it. It was Hollenger. A plane was ready to take me directly to Calgary in Alberta, Canada.

To ensure I didn't get picked off, or another attempt to kidnap me, Luis arranged for four vehicles to leave simultaneously, but in different routes, to Homestead Air Force Base. It must have worked as we got there, and none of the vehicles said they were followed.

There was no way the Mob was going to give up that easily.

On board, being the soul passenger, an envelope was waiting for me. In it was my new identity – Julie Winters. Dumb name. Who in the FBI thinks of these shit names?

There was a passport, a DC driver's license, an FBI Agent's badge and a few other documents allowing me entry into Canada. All under Julie's name, of course. The note said I was going up to Canada for special training for the next four months.

How ironic. For years I've complained about the FBI. Now I was playing the part of one.

CHAPTER 13

TRAINING WITH THE CANUCKS

A Canadian Forces major met me at the hanger at the Royal Canadian Air Force base at Cold Lake.

"Julie Winters..." I was going to have a hard time getting used to this "...I'm Major Randy Sommers." Great, my seasonal counterpart.

He was in plain clothes. We got into his personal vehicle, and drove into town. We chatted a bit. I had to build my new life as I went along.

Randy was in charge of a dozen JTF2 crewmen. That's the Canadian military's Joint Task Force. Deputy Strong must have pulled in some favor.

"So, you're up here to get some training in Special Forces tactics, eh? We're flattered you'd choose Canadians. But I have to wonder, why us? Your SEALs are just as good. But don't tell anyone I said that, eh?"

I couldn't tell him the truth. I wished I could. "The FBI thought it best I get some other type of training for comparison."

"Well, we're honored to have you. I hope we can give you the training you need."

"What have you been told?"

"Only that you're to be treated as one of the guys and get you up to speed on all our training methods. It's going to be a grueling four months. You in shape?"

The exercising had improved me somewhat, but I knew it wasn't enough. So, I had to lie again. I could tell him I'd just recovered from severe injuries, but decided not to. "Not as much as I should be," is all I could admit to. It wasn't a lie.

"Well, first thing then is to get you into the GoodLife Fitness in town. Hire a trainer. Go every day you can, eh?"

I was set up in an apartment, all furnished and ready to go. In the morning my training would start.

Randy picked me up at dawn, and we went to the GoodLife in town. I bought a membership and paid for a trainer to help me get into shape.

Next we went to the base and met the team. Randy's group was a dozen well-groomed soldiers. Not what our raggedy SEAL guys look like.

First order of business was to get familiar with their weapons. I was able to test fire a number of handguns, sniper rifles, assault rifles: their C7, C8 and C9 as they call them. They were the same as our versions of the M4 and SAW.

Wow. I'd never fired a fully automatic machinegun before. It was a real thrill. A feeling I didn't expect.

Randy was far more logical about it, though. "I wanted you to understand the power of a full auto. But we never use it. We have the ability, but we don't use full auto. We're a precision surgical instrument. We don't just blast away and hope to hit something. Our premise is one shot one kill. But I wanted you to have respect for what full auto is about."

"I'm impressed, that's for sure."

"Good, but you're going to learn to be cool, calm, and above all take as short as time as possible to get that precision shot."

"That includes handguns?" I pulled out Alex's Cz from the back of my pants.

"Whoa!" Randy exclaimed. "You had that on you in town?"

"Yeah, so what?"

He laughed. "This is Canada. You can't have that here. You don't even have a license to possess any gun in Canada."

"Who should I see to get that?"

They all chuckled. "The RCMP," Randy said.

"Good luck with them," another snickered.

I was missing something.

"Look, leave the Cz here, and I'll take you to the local RCMP detachment. You need to experience this."

Swell. I was totally confused, but off we went.

Once in the detachment's parking lot, I got out, but Randy didn't. I leaned into the window. "You're not coming in?"

"No. This is an experience best served alone. I'll wait."

I went in. A nice-looking young corporal was at the desk. I'd never seen their red uniforms up close in person. I had to admit, they were, well, pretty.

"Hello," he said, "How can I help you?"

"I need to get a license for a handgun. I'm an FBI agent visiting from the States."

"You have a weapon on you now?"

"No. I understand I need to get a license or some kind of conceal carry permit."

"You're not a Canadian citizen?"

"No. I mean, yes, I'm not a Canadian citizen."

"You were supposed to get a temporary license when you came across the border."

"Hmm. But I didn't come through the border. I came in by a private

FBI plane landing at the base airport."

"You didn't go through customs?"

"No. I was cleared through the FBI before I came."

He scratched his head. "You're in the country illegally then. I can arrest you right now and have you deported."

"No, just a second." I rummaged through my purse and got one of the documents I was given on flight. It was from Immigration Canada giving me clearance to be in the country for four months.

He looked at it. "Looks in order. But that doesn't change this. You can't get a license unless you take the safety course, then wait for a temporary license to arrive. Six months at best.

"But I'm only here for four months."

He just shrugged his shoulders.

"What about a permit to carry?"

"You need a license first, but assuming you get that, you can apply for conceal carry, but it will be denied."

"But I'm a cop."

"Not in Canada."

"Look, can I be honest with you?"

"Lying to the police is a criminal offence."

I sighed. "Look, I'm on a witness protection program. I'm up here for special weapons training."

"Who with?"

"Your military."

"Not applicable. You can do whatever you need to on the base. But not in public. We can't have anyone carrying a weapon in public. It's a public safety issue."

I was confused. "But I'm a sworn police officer. It's my duty to public safety."

"Not in Canada."

We were just going around in circles.

"Who's in charge here?"

"I am."

"No, who's your boss?"

"That's the Superintendent."

"Superintendent. And where is he?"

"She is in Calgary. But it won't do you any good. Your request to carry will still be denied."

Swell. This wasn't going anywhere. "I'll be back." I left the building.

At the car, Randy was just laughing.

"You fucking knew didn't you?"

He just chuckled and nodded.

"Well, we'll see." I got on my phone to Hollenger. I explained the situation. He said he would get back to me by tomorrow.

On the way back to base, Randy said I should join the local private gun club. He knew a couple guys there and they would show me additional training. He'd get me the number.

The next day, the Director of the FBI called me. He said to return to the RCMP detachment, all was fixed.

Randy took me back. He was skeptical anything had changed.

I came up to the counter. The young corporal was there again. I smiled. He did not look too happy.

"You must have some people in high places. You've been granted a permit under Section Ninety-Seven, Subsection One of the Firearms Act."

I had no clue what that was.

"Sign here." He took the document into a back room. After a few minutes he emerged with a Conceal Carry Permit in my name.

"What about a license?" I asked.

"Unless you're going to buy firearms, you don't need it. This is a special carry permit for visiting law enforcement officers."

I looked at it. Of course it had my fake name on it. Geeze, now I got a document to legally carry a weapon in public under a false name. Swell.

Randy was certainly surprised when I held up the document. "Gun laws in this country are really bizarre. But I have to ask. Why do you need to be armed in public, eh?"

"I just feel undressed without my weapon." That was a lie. When in missing persons I rarely carried.

Randy didn't say much as we returned to the base. Once stopped at our training building, he said, "Julie isn't your name is it?"

I just looked at him out the side of my eyes.

"You need to be armed. Why would you need to be armed all the time? Why did you arrive, alone, on a private jet, landing at a military base, and not on a commercial flight, eh?"

I didn't say anything. But I could hear his wheels turning.

Then he turned to look at me and said, "You're under some kind of protection aren't you. Who's after you?"

Swell. I sighed. Smart guy. "The Mob in Chicago."

"I thought that was you. You're the one who was abducted and brutally tortured aren't you."

I turned and looked at him. "How do you know that?"

"I'm good with faces. I saw it on CNN. That was in March wasn't it?"

"Yes."

He nodded his head.

His hands were on the steering wheel. "You're here getting trained because you can't be in the States in case you're found." He reached under the seat and pulled out my Cz and handed it to me.

"I can't image how that must have been for you. Fuckers. As far as the boys are concerned, you're still Julie."

He was about to get out, but stopped. He sat back down.

"Wait. You're here because you're getting training to prepare retaliation against the Mob, eh?"

One smart guy. "I need to be able to take care of myself."

He nodded his head again, thinking. Then moved his head from side to side a few times with his eyes closed. He turned to look at me, "This changes things."

"How so?"

"Well, you only need to be trained on that which will get you prepared. There's no point in training on things you don't need, eh?"

"What don't I need, for instance?"

"Well, you don't need para-jumping repelling down buildings. You need to concentrate on firearms skills, hand to hand combat. Stuff like that."

"You're the expert."

He got out, so did I. "This is just between us, right?" I said.

"Of course. As I said, as far as the boys are concerned, you're Julie. Here for FBI training, eh?"

Every Friday I made my update call to Hollenger. It'd been a while since I spoke to Alex's parents and I asked if I could chance calling them.

"They're up your way," he said.

"What?"

"Yes, we were worried they were going to be targeted, so they decided to visit their brother in Edmonton. You should go visit."

I called Scott, and he gave me their address.

Saturday morning I rented a car and headed up north to Fort McMurray.

Nathan met me at the door, but Laurie barged past him and gave me a great hug.

We spent a wonderful weekend together. We even played a few rounds of Hearts.

Sunday afternoon it was time to return for my training. Scott walked me to the car alone.

"What's your plan going forward?"

"I can't tell you. I don't want to put you in any harm's way."

"We're already in harm's way. I want them dead. All of them. That's why you're here getting weapons and tactical training, isn't it?"

"Officially, it's for personal protection."

"Yes, of course it is."

He held out both arms, and I let him hug me. I could see Laurie over his shoulder. She put her hand to her mouth and smiled. Scott hugged me hard.

Letting go he said, "You're still our daughter. Come visit us every weekend."

"I will, thank you so much."

I left with a tear in my eye, and my throat choking up, as I felt a bit on the hot side. Sweat was beading on my forehead.

The training was indeed intense.

We practiced CQB, that's Close Quarters Battle, with M4s, AK47s, and a number of other carbines. This included shooting a rifle on the move, that's walking and shooting at the same time. Man that was brutally hard.

The movies make it look so easy. But it's not. The reticle on the compact scope moved all other the place. (First time Randy said the word 'reticle' I thought he was referring to some lower body hole, instead of the name of the crosshairs in a scope.)

When exactly to shoot to even get on paper was an art I needed to practice a lot.

Even standing at twenty yards, while shooting, getting my hits into a two-by-four inch bull's eye, worth five points, was damn hard.

The targets, two for each shooter, were humanoid, what the Canadians called Herman the German. A left over target pattern from the Second World War.

Five of us fired together. Actually, it's two people per lineup. One shoots, the other is a safety for that person. The safety clears the rifles after each match.

This was all timed. You must get your shots off in a few seconds. We also had only five rounds per magazine even thought they could hold twenty. This was to force us to do mag changes under a time pressure. It also forced us to count our rounds. It's simple to fire away until the weapon is empty, but then you're stuck to not only load a fresh mag, but to release the bolt forward to ready the next round. That's lost time, and could cost you your life in the heat of battle.

But with counting rounds you count out four shots, change mags, then you have six ready to go and you don't have to release the bolt forward.

This was not only crucial with the rifle, but also with the handgun.

The four matches, consisting of three stages each, was the following. Match one, stage one, started at thirty-five yards, where, upon each whistle blast, we fired two rounds, one at each of our targets.

That bulls-eye of two inches wide by four inches tall was damn small at thirty-five yards. We did that five times for a total of ten rounds.

The second stage was a rapid fire of ten rounds, five each target, with a mag change after four rounds.

The last part of this match was a ten yard dash to the twenty yard line, fire two rounds left, two right. Once empty, we were required to show the rifle was clear to our safety guy, then pull our sidearm, rack it and get three shots onto one target: two to the body, one to the head. Then change mags, then three on the right target, again two to the body, one to the head. All in fifteen seconds.

It was impossible. I never got all my pistol shots off before the STOP command. Randy said not to worry about the time. "Get good, then get fast. Take the time to aim those pistol shots," he said.

The next match was an advance and shoot. We advanced five yards on each whistle blast, fired two left, then two on the right. Each advance required a mag change within the ten second allotment. Counting rounds was important in this match. Speed to get the next mag in was essential. That meant making sure one round was in the pipe on a mag change. That meant counting rounds and knowing when to change mags while leaving one in the chamber.

More than a couple times, I'd swap out a mag only to realize I'd miscounted and left one in my discarded mag.

The third match was called a modified prone. We lay on our side, and fired the rifle rotated ninety degrees, as if we were firing from under a car.

I couldn't get comfortable at all. My elbow was tucked under my ribs, which still hurt. But Randy was great. He showed me how to fire this left-handed. That meant laying on my right side, my right hand supported the forestock, while my left hand fired the trigger, and changed mags. That was much easier and more comfortable.

We did this shoot from the twenty-five yard line. The first stage was the same as match one. On the whistle, one left, one right for ten rounds. Then a rapid for another ten rounds.

The last part of that match was a ten yard dash to the fifteen yard line, firing two left and two right with rifle, then drew our handgun and fire three left, change mags, then three right, as in match one.

The last match was the walk and shoot. It was brutal. From the twenty-five yard line we walked and fired at the same time, four left, mag change, one left then five right.

It was crazy! I found it impossible to even hit anywhere near center because the optics was moving all over the place with each step.

The last part of the match was a five yard dash to the ten yard line. Once at the line, we fired four rounds left, change mags, one left, then five rounds right in rapid succession as fast as I could manipulate the trigger. Then we pulled out our handgun, firing four head shots right, change mag, one head shot right, then five head shots left.

We stopped mid noon for some lunch, then did it all again in the afternoon. By the end of the day we consumed some 500 rounds of ammo each.

I was not only physically exhausted, but mentally spent too. Keeping track of everything was impossible for me. Well, at first it was.

To top it off, I still had to do my physical fitness at the Goodlife before I could crash in bed. No TV and my nightly friend was absent.

At the end of each match, we counted the holes. My hits were all around the five points. Hell, few were in the four point area, which was six inches by eight inches. I thought I was at least competent with a handgun after the little bit of training Alex gave me. But this showed how absolutely shitty I was.

Compared to the rest of Randy's team, I was an embarrassment. They made fun of me, of course. But they were very helpful with tips and technique. They were also very patient.

We practiced all this over and over for a full two weeks.

At first, I couldn't even get all my shots off in the allotted time. I was nervous as hell. I would just blast away, hitting nothing. One would think in fifteen seconds one should have lots of time to get one's shots out. But with a magazine change happening, that time got eaten up pretty quick.

Many times I dropped the magazine while trying to insert it. Once I even dropped the handgun pulling it out of the holster I was so nervous.

I couldn't help but wonder if my hits on the Boxer were just a miracle. Privately I made that comment to Randy as I wanted to understand how I did that, but was having such a hard time in the training.

"It's because you're thinking about it. When you shot at that guy, you couldn't even aim, eh? You guessed where he was, and fired. It was all instinct. This is what I'm trying to train you to do. To not think, but just act on instinct. But you need a lot of practice to understand how each weapon behaves in order to do that. You shooting him may have been a lot of luck. But it was also a lot of basic instinct."

"I sure hope so," I said.

"Sure. Look, now when you bring the rifle up and look through the scope, the reticle is moving all over the target while you try to aim, eh?"

"Yes, it's frustrating."

"That's normal at this stage. Once we're done with you, your muscle memory will bring that rifle up and the reticle will be dead on center. Soon as it gets there you fire. This will all take time and practice. First get good, then get fast."

The guys were great instructors, and very patient. Slowly my groupings narrowed to the point where at twenty yards I could finally get that head shot on paper, and all my shots off on target before the end time command was given.

I was also starting to get more fives than other points.

Eventually, I could change magazines in my Cz handgun in a fraction of a second, without looking. I even practiced mag changes in my apartment.

My confidence greatly increased. Until, that is, I started IPSC at the private club.

The guys, and gals, at the club were great. They were very friendly, and always willing to help. We practiced more pistol shooting. We set up the field for IPSC, the International Practical Shooting Confederation. It's all handgun shooting.

This included shooting on the move, shooting with my left hand, shooting from behind obstacles. The interesting part, closer to police scenarios, was shooting a perp who had a hostage. Of course, we lost points shooting the hostage.

The range officer who was helping me said to look for body parts of the perp out in the open. He said under stress, perps often don't realize they have parts exposed which we can take advantage of. That means, shoot there first chance one gets.

Because I didn't have a Black Badge, I couldn't participate in their official matches. But I did come to all their weekly practices. I also went several times a week on my own.

Compared to other shooters in the club, I was starting to get a reputation. I was often in the top ten percent. Those CQB matches were starting to pay off.

One day I was at the range on my own, and a couple of guys were there firing off a number of weapons. I went over to their bay just to have a look.

There was one interesting rifle there. It looked like the AK47's Randy was training me on. But it was different. The young lad showed it to me. It was a Cz858. Interesting, the same company who made Alex's handgun.

The young fellow allowed me to fire off a few rounds. I was impressed. It was far better than the AK. It performed better, was more stable, and just over all looked to be a better weapon. "Where can I get one?" I asked.

"You can't any more. The RCMP made them prohibited. But the government over ruled the RCMP so we get to keep them. But they aren't being imported anymore."

One of the other fellows said, "You can usually find a used one on one of the gun forums." He wrote the URL down for me.

That night I signed up, under my pseudonym, to the forum. I went to the Equipment Exchange section. Sure enough, some guy was selling a Cz858. Eighteen hundred dollars. Geeze, not cheap. I emailed to enquire if it was still available.

He got back in just a few minutes. It was still for sale. He provided his phone number, so I called him.

He was in Ontario, and as soon as I email transferred the funds, he would mail it to me. He just needed me to email a photo of my PAL.

"My what?"

"Possession and Acquisition License. I can't sell it to you without one. I assume you don't have one by the sounds of it."

"I'm an American visiting for a few months. No, I don't have one for Canada, but I'm licensed in the States."

"No good. Need a PAL. Sorry."

"Wait, how do I get one?" I wanted to see if he had a different interpretation than I got from the RCMP officer.

He laughed at the other end. "First, a wait of three months to even get into the course you must take. Then four to five months for the RCMP to get the license to you. I'm not waiting that long. I can sell this on the next call."

Swell, same as what the RCMP officer said.

I thought what to do. I didn't want this opportunity to slip by. "How about I send you the money to hold on to the gun for a few days?"

"All of it?"

"The whole eighteen hundred."

I could hear him thinking at the other end.

"You can't lose. I pay you. If I don't get the license in a few days, you keep the money."

"There is no way you'll get a license in a few days. But I'll take your money. Until Friday then."

I email transferred the full amount. Then I called Hollenger. Next day Randy took me to the RCMP detachment. The cute corporal was there again at the counter. Soon as he saw me he dropped his head, then went into an office. He came out with two documents.

"Sign here," he sighed. He handed me the other document. "This is your temporary RPAL. You'll get the proper one in a few days by FedEx."

"You are so helpful." I smiled back.

The look on his face indicated he knew I was being sarcastic.

I took a cell phone picture of the license, then sent it off the seller of the 858. I called him.

"Hi Rick. I just sent you my new license." I continued to smile at the officer.

He paused a few seconds on the other end. Then he said, "I don't know how the hell you did it, but we're a go. I'll mail it right now." I hung up.

"You already paid for it?" the corporal said shaking his head.

"Of course."

"I wish I knew how you did this."

I showed him my FBI badge. "I'm on assignment."

He nodded, but I'm sure he didn't believe me.

"I heard you joined the local gun club," he said.

"I did."

"You missed me. I've seen you there." He shrugged his shoulders. "I'm a member too."

The next month of training with Randy was, well, far more intense than the weeks we did CQB. This was a whole new ballgame. My Cz858 arrived, so I wanted to use it instead of the AR platform. Randy was OK with that.

First thing Randy did was drill out the rivet preventing the magazines from holding just five rounds. "Stupid law anyway," he said. I loaded the six mags with thirty rounds each.

The event was called the Service Rifle Matches. This required a lot of running. We first started at the one hundred yard line. When the targets popped up, we took two shots in three second, then the target disappeared. We did this five times while standing.

Then we moved to the two hundred yard line. When the target appeared, we ran to the one hundred yard line, fired two shots standing, before the target disappeared. Then the rest of the eight shots were at pop up targets of three seconds each double tap.

Problem was, for me, the target disappeared before I made it to the fire line. Randy's team I was shooting with were like tornados, bolting down range. I was out of breath by the time I got there. So when the target appeared again, I fired three rounds, for each of the next two exposures, to catch up.

Then we moved to the three-hundred yard line, and ran to the two hundred line to fire at the target. This time kneeling. That was even harder! I couldn't get comfortable, nor stable with the rifle.

I tried a number of kneeling positions. One was so close to the ground, two of Randy's members had to help me to my feet. That was embarrassing as they laughed.

Eventually, we worked our way back to the five-hundred yard line running to the four-hundred line, and so on. At least the shooting from 300 and beyond was prone.

The very last match, Randy said to shed everything and to keep only two mags of five rounds each. The match started at 500 yards. When the target showed, we went prone and fired two rounds, the target dropped after three seconds.

Staying prone, we waited for the target to appear. When it did, we made a dash to the 400 yard line, went prone and fired two rounds. Randy made sure I made it to the mound before they counted the three second exposure.

I did a mag change at that point to give me six rounds ready.

From there, when the target showed, we ran the next 100 yards to 300, dropped to the ground, and fired two rounds. Next was the run to the 200 yard line, go to our knee and fire two rounds. Lastly we dashed to the 100 yard line, from standing, fired off the last of our two rounds.

One twist Randy threw at us was we didn't know if the targets would just pop up, being stable, or were moving either left or right, for only six seconds.

I was soaked in sweat by the end of the day. The worst part was the kidding I got from the crew. Out of seventy rounds I got only two hits on a humanoid sized target.

And I thought being embarrassed at CQB was humiliating enough. This was a magnitude in scale worse.

As we were heading to the vehicles, I started to get woozy. It was hot and muggy, I figured it was just that. But I broke out into a hot the likes of which I'd never felt before. Well beyond the ambient temperature. I was burning up inside.

Randy sensed something wasn't right. I explained what was going on. The crew poured the last of their canteens on my head. I looked like I was in one of those wet tee-shirt contests. If I wasn't so frustrated at boiling inside, I would have been embarrassed.

"You OK, now?" Randy asked very concerned.

I was sitting on the ground and looked up. "No. I'd better go see a doctor in town."

"You'll pay through the roof. Let us take you to the base hospital."

"I'm OK." I tried to get up, but the heat was unbearable.

I didn't have to wait too long to see a base doctor. The building was air-conditioned, so cold I was freezing. The doctor went through a number of questions in order to pin my situation down. "Heat stroke, I'd say. We'll take some blood just to be sure. Then you go home and rest."

Not knowing made my frustration just worse. I went home and collapsed in front of the TV. Hmm, I thought: Canadians pretty much watch the same shows we do. What was interesting was the lack of shootings in the local news.

I was actually confused at their newscast. They spent five minutes on a man who was a transgender and wanted to change sex. They interviewed him, his family, and his friends.

Ok, I didn't get it. There is so much fucked up stuff going on in the world, and they spend time on this shit? I really didn't care what people like that did, I just didn't see it as "news." With Canada so much less violent than the States I guessed they had to fill their time with something.

Every day we practiced the Service Rifle shoot for three weeks straight. I was so exhausted by the end of the day that I skipped my exercising. Hell, I was running a few miles as it was!

I didn't get another one of those internal scorchings, but I did get a call from the doctor to return to see her.

"You're going through menopause," she said.

What? I went immediately into denial. "That can't be."

"Your chemistry doesn't lie. You may want to go on some hormone supplements soon. The next few years is going to be uncomfortable as you go through more of those temperature swings."

Swell. My mother's depression got worse after she went through her menopause. But she was almost ten years older than me when that happened.

"I'm too young. This can't be right."

"When was your last period?"

I had to think. "It must have been just before Christmas last year."

"None since."

"No, I just thought the beating and healing unbalanced my system."

"You told me you were almost beaten to death, and that precipitated a miscarriage."

"Yes."

"It's not uncommon for trauma like that to induce early menopause."

Swell. I went home, picked up some Bacardi rum and coke on my way. Drunk, I cried myself to sleep.

I had to make one of my weekly calls to Hollenger to keep him up to speed on my progress. He asked if I called the lawyer. I hadn't. He almost ordered I do so immediately.

I called the number. "Hello?" the man said at the other end.

"This is Marg Cunningham."

"Oh, yes, I've been waiting for your call. I'm Karl Zimmerman. I was told you need some financial advice."

"Yes. I want to take the fight to the Outfit, but I don't know how to go about doing real estate transactions. I don't want to use an agent."

"I can certainly help you there, but I'm not sure what your plan is."

"I want to buy up property in the Outfit's domain to compete with them."

"That will make them take notice, and could get reprisals."

"That's the idea."

"How much property did you want to buy?"

"I have some money, but not a lot."

"How much is not a lot?" he asked.

"If I sell my grandfather's stocks, about two and a half million."

"That won't be anywhere near enough. It will buy you a few places, but that won't even show up on their radar. If you want to make a statement to make them take notice, you'll need to buy a lot more than that.

"You will not only need to buy property, but you need to take some of their clients and dependants away from them."

"Like what, for example?" I asked.

"Well, get some store who rents one of their buildings to rent one of yours instead. Allow some of the Outfit's loans to people be paid off and you do the loan. Once they see their cash flow drop, they'll take notice.

"But to do that properly, you will need a lot of money. We can fund your effort."

"Money?"

"Yes. But first I will need to take your plan to our Board of Directors for approval, which if they do, I can front you about five million."

"How... Where does that come from?"

"It's a trust fund. I can't tell you where it comes from. But I can tell you it is a special account for... well, let's just say, it's for good use. I'll get back to you in a few days with an answer." He hung up.

Geeze. A fund. For 'good use'. Interesting.

The next few weeks Randy trained me in ballistics and long range shooting. Out to a thousand yards. This included moving targets at four hundred yards, as well as pop ups, staying visible for only three seconds, at five hundred yards.

The best part of this training was there was no running! Everything was slow and precise, all shot from prone.

Well, that's what I first thought.

I used a number of rifles for this, including a modified Remington 700 all done up with a new frame, made by Canadian company Modular Driven Technologies. I also shot an M14 with a scope on it.

"You really should buy one of these new, now you have your license. It's always best to practice with a personal weapon. The Remington you can get no problem. The M14, that's another issue. The Springfield versions are impossible to find. There's a lot of Norc M14s for five hundred bucks. But you won't be able to take it home."

I looked confused.

"It's made in China, and illegal to bring into the US."

"Then I'll get a Springfield."

Randy started to laugh, then cut himself off looking at me. "You're going to make another call, eh?"

I smiled as I hit Hollenger's number.

It took a few weeks, but I got myself a brand new Remington 700 with the TAC21 frame and a six to twenty-four power scope. The Springfield M14 we picked up at the air force base. It was flown in especially for me.

I couldn't wait to try them out.

We spent several weeks doing nothing but long range shooting, from 300 to 1000 yards. I used the M14 out to five-hundred. The Remington from three-hundred onwards. I was going through 300 rounds a day, for fourteen days. Talk about total immersion. I learned a lot about how to breathe, how to hold the rifle with left hand pushing the butt stock into my shoulder, how to slowly, and gradually put pressure on the trigger until the rifle fired.

Randy was clear, precision shooting meant as little of myself influencing the shot as possible.

The 700 had a trigger pull of just eight ounces. Just touch it and off it fired. The first few times I sucked at trigger pull. Those rifles kick, and to be honest, I was a bit scared at first. Scared I'd hurt myself when the gun fired.

After all I went through, almost dying from a brutal beating, I was fearful of a little bit of rifle kick. Stupid and clearly a psychological issue.

However, Randy told me he, and most of the rest of his crew, at one time or another, had gotten a "scope bite." That's when one's eye is too close and the kickback makes the scope hit you in the bridge of your nose. He said it happened to him once during a competition event. He continued to shoot all the while blood was dripping into his eyes. You could still see the faint scar.

Thus, not so psychological after all. That made me even more scared to fire these powerful rifles. So when I squeezed the trigger, I was anticipating the recoil and I was flinching.

That's a big no-no in precision shooting circles. "If that flinching makes you off my one inch at 100 yards, that translates to ten inches at 1,000 yards, hence missing your target."

So we played a little game. I would face away standing, while Randy would put in a round, or not, before I shot. That way, when I was ready to squeeze off a round, I had no idea if it would pound my shoulder, or just go click.

The other trick he used on me was to balance a dime on the end of the barrel. If the dime fell off when I squeezed the trigger, I was flinching.

It worked. By the week's end Randy could clearly see I was no longer anticipating when the round would fire. As he put it, "It should always be a surprise."

I learned a lot about the physics of flight when a bullet is going down range. Plus MOA, that's minutes of angle. One MOA was an inch at one hundred yards. But out to 1000 yards, that angle meant five inches down range.

I learned what hold over meant. That's raising the crosshairs such that one of the bars, or dots, below center was on the target.

I learned to read the wind, and how much to hold over to compensate. It was a lot to take in, but I got the hang of it. I was able to get most of my shots into a twelve-inch circle even at 1,000 yards.

The last week Randy threw in a twist. I was to load up all my gear, all my ammo, 250 rounds, and march through the bush with the crew. We marched for a couple hours, through dense bush, to get to the range. Then we did our shots. The difference with this shooting was we didn't shoot from specific range markings.

I had no idea how far away the targets were, so I had to use the classroom training to figure out the distance, then how much to adjust the vertical turret.

It was both a physical challenge, because I was drained walking all that way with a heavy rifle, and heavy ammo, plus my water and food for the day. But it was also a mental challenge too as I had to figure out the math.

That night I crashed in bed, after a quick rum & coke. But, even with the A/C off I was freezing in bed. I couldn't get enough blankets to keep me warm. It kept me awake the whole night, hence I missed the next day's shootings.

So now I understood why my mother went crazy those years.

By the afternoon of the next day, I was back to normal. Just slept.

Back at it on a bright Monday morning, I was taken to a gym on base. Randy and crew were there in full gear, except no guns.

Randy came over with a belt that had a large knife attached.

"What are we doing today?"

"Up and personal killing," he said.

What? Randy let me watch as his team paired up and practiced knife maneuvers. Attacking both from the back and from the front. The knives were rubber, of course. After about half an hour, he called me over.

"Sergeant Watts here is going to knife you."

What?

I stood on the mat as Watts came up behind me. He grabbed me around the mouth with his left hand, then drove the rubber blade into where the neck and shoulder meet.

Randy came over. "Most people think we stab under the ribs into the heart. But if your assailant is large, you can miss the heart, or hit a rib and not penetrate far enough.

"But here," he put his index finger to the side of his neck, "if you jab the knife down on an angle you sever the carotid as well as the windpipe.

"Of course, it has to be a long sharp blade. We use M16 bayonets." He pulled his out of the holder, called a frog. It looked identical to the rubber ones. "They're just long enough for the distance while thin enough that a good force will get that maximum penetration.

"Once the blade transects the windpipe, your prey cannot yell. They can't take a breath either. So with the blood cut off from the brain on one side, and them unable to scream out, you kill quickly with complete silence.

"Sometimes it's vital that silence and stealth are key. Now you try on the sergeant. Start with a frontal attack first."

One step at a time, he walked me through the motions. He showed me how to hold the knife, blade pointing down in the right hand concealed behind my back. Walk up to the prey. Get nose to nose. Left hand reaches around to hold the back of the head and with my right arm thrust the blade into the neck.

It was creepy. In fact, the thought of it made me nauseated. It made me think of what it must have been like in the era of wars fought using swords and axes.

"I don't know if I can do this," I said, as I backed away from Watts.

"What's the problem?" Randy said.

"Too close. Too personal." I had to come up with some excuse. "I'm going to get covered in their blood slicing the artery like that, aren't I?"

"When you take the knife out, maybe. Not when it goes in. There will be almost no blood if you do it right. If you wait for him to die before you take the knife out, you won't get squirted on."

That was it. I'd seen my fair share of blood and gore. That little girl who emptied the shotgun only six feet away from the drug dealer was quite the mess. But this. This was just so up and personal being so close.

But Randy made me practice more. Both from a rear attack and frontal attacks. It was a long day, and I was so exhausted by the time I went home that I didn't bother to go to the gym.

For a few days we did a number of CQB and pistol training to make sure I was still honed. I used the Cz858 instead of the M4 for the CQB. It was definitely a better weapon, I thought. But I'm no expert.

I also like the fact it used a larger round, 7.62, instead of the smaller 5.56. That meant more stopping power. And that I was sure I would need.

Again, I practiced mag changes until I could do it with my eyes closed. I took two of the banana mags for the 858 and taped them together into a double. That was a potential of having sixty rounds ready to go. I got so good at switching mags in a second that I taped up two more pairs.

By the end of August, Randy snuck me into one of their tactical simulation practices. There were a few hundred soldiers participating, from all over Canada. I even got dressed up in a Canadian Forces uniform. I felt like one of the boys.

"You up for this?" he asked, with genuine concern.

"Thanks, Randy, I haven't had a hot flush for a couple weeks now."

It was way cool to go through some of their scenarios. Most of it was with blank ammo, or laser tag. That was lasers attached to the rifles, and vests that detected the hits. They wouldn't let me do a live fire exercise. I was disappointed about that.

Randy realized I wanted to do the live fire, so he planned a real treat for our last week of training. To put it all together, he said.

"Being in a firefight is like nothing you've ever experienced. The brain does weird things, prioritizing anything that would keep you alive. Adrenaline floods the body, and things both slow down, but also speed up. You simply do not have time to think. Unless, that is, you have the training to overcome what your brain wants to do."

"How do we simulate a firefight?" I said.

"Paintball," he said with a big grin.

"Paintball..." I was skeptical.

"Yep, we put you into a firefight situation using paintball guns." He paused. "Don't you cops train with paintballs?"

I just shook my head cocking it to one side, shrugging my shoulders. I'd never done that. I don't even know if our department trains that way. I knew a bunch of cops went to play it on their own time. But I never thought of it as anything but a game.

"Well, anyway, you'll know when you get hit," he continued. "It stings like hell. Which is what we want. We want your body to want to recoil from being stung. That's the fear part. But we want you to be trained to ignore the fear and do what has to be done."

"You can suppress fear in a fire fight?" I asked.

"No. That's impossible, but also not desirable. What you can do is ignore the fear. It will be there, and you need it there to tell you when you really are in trouble. But what this training will do is show you how to keep thinking, how to keep rational, so your logic of what has to be done is side by side with your fear."

"Sounds impossible," I said, disbelieving.

"Every special forces personnel have been trained for that. There is no underlying reason why you can't be."

"I guess the only way to know is to find out." I shrugged.

Randy gave me some literature on the psychology of firefights to get me prepared for what was coming.

"Just remember one thing," he added. "Your opponents won't have this training. They will ultimately succumb to their instinct of fear and want to flee. They will pause. You exploit that."

We arrived at a facilities set up like rooms in a building. He handed me a weapon that looked like an M4, much shorter, but with a fat barrel and a tank underneath. It was a paintball gun. I also got a paintball handgun.

The only protective gear was the face shield. All we had protecting our bodies was our thin clothes, and the paintball guns.

We split into two teams. One would set up inside, while the other would go in and infiltrate to rescue "captives", which were just cardboard panels of people. We spent every day having a riot, shooting at each other. But the key was getting used to the fast pace and unpredictable issues with confined quarters. Plus how to flank your enemy and kill them from behind.

One of the missions scared the shit out of me. I was leading a three person team into a dark building. We had to light our way with the flashlights on the guns.

We came down a hall that had a number of doors leading into rooms. I had the paint ball gun at the aim.

As I came to one of the doors, which was open, a man jumped right in front of me into my face and planted his rubber bayonet into my neck.

I had never jumped so high in my life. My heart stopped. I even dropped to the floor. When they helped me up, the light from my gun reflected off a yellow fluid. I had pissed myself too.

I paused looking down. I was embarrassed at first, but then it hit me. A tear welled in my eye as I remember that day. The day I was hit so hard I pissed myself. The day my Alex was killed.

My attacker was Sergeant Watts. "Are you OK there, Ma'am?" He gently held my left shoulder.

"Yeah, I'm OK. Just scared me that's all. But I need to change."

We had a good chuckle about it after. They said my screech could have broken glass. But, boy, was that an eye opening experience.

When it came to my turn to be the criminal holding the hostage, I think Randy played me, again (he likely played me with the knife attack). We were supposed to have three of us in the room with the mannequin sitting in a chair. But the two of them said they would be right back and left, closing the door. I was alone.

Sweat started to pour down my face, fogging my face shield. I could hardly see in the dim light of the room, which had no windows.

I could hear them coming. The sound of paintball guns going off got closer. Then they barged into the room, and before I could fire I felt several stings in my right leg and I fell over. More shots hit me in the chest and stomach. I screeched out.

Randy took off his mask and laughed.

He wasn't kidding. Getting hit from close range stung like a dozen bees.

"What the fuck was that?" I said in anger. "I was hidden behind my captive and you still got me?"

"Your leg was exposed. Totally exposed. Soon as you see something you can exploit, you take advantage of it right away. Do not think. Do not pause. Take that shot. Then take the kill shots."

When I got home I had welts all along my legs, arms and stomach. I would have thought that my beating would make anything else mild in comparison. It didn't. Each splat of a ball full of yellow paint was followed by a scream from me.

Randy was also right. You can learn to ignore the threat of pain and do what has to be done. By week's end I was getting far more aggressive. I was taking the battle to the enemy, as opposed to cowering, afraid of getting hit.

By September I went through some ten thousand rounds of live ammo and an uncountable number of paintballs. I was more physically fit than when I was twenty. It was time to go home.

I took one last trip to see the Kiley's in Fort Mac. It was a game chang-er. We were sitting around the dinner table after finishing a nice meal, when Scott passed me a slip of paper.

It had a number and a password. "What's this?" I asked.

"A bank account with two million in it. It's yours."

WTF? "Why?"

"To find the killers of our son," Laurie said. "It's everything we have. We mortgaged our house."

"I can't take this."

"Do you need funds in order to carry out your plan?" Scott asked.

"You don't even know what my plan is."

"We trust you, Honey," Laurie said. "Please. Do what you have to do to find our son's killers." Tears welled in her eyes.

This was so moving. I thought about it. I did have some funds, and the call to that lawyer set up even more resources. "Ok, tell you what. If I need it, I'll use it. But I think I'm OK for the time being. I can't thank you enough."

"No thanks needed. We thank you for avenging our son," Scott said.

As I left, the three of us did a group hug. "You're part of the family now," Scott said.

"You're not alone, Honey." Laurie said.

I drove off in tears, but also determined to get a plan formulated, and executed. "Executed" being the operative word.

Randy and the boys took me to the airfield. My FBI plane was wait-ing for me. Each one took the time to say goodbye. What a great bunch of guys. I was going to miss them, but most definitely not forget what they taught me.

Randy was last. "I sure hope you get what you're looking for. Here." He handed me a DVD. It was Battlefield 4.

"A computer game?"

"PS3 Actually. You should play this as often as you can."

"It's a kid's game."

"No, it's a lesson on the psychology of intimate combat."

I looked confused.

"Look, it's simple. In this game, you will be up against real people, under as real combat as you're going to get. Consider it a type of computer simulation of the real world.

"People are not only unpredictable, but also predictable. You need to learn how to read the difference. With this game you will soon learn when to anticipate each. Remember what I told you during paintball. Flank your enemy. Good luck, and good hunting, Detective Margory Cunningham." He shook my hand.

I embraced him in a hug, and kissed him on the cheek. I was choked up. I said thank you, and got on the plane.

As we taxied off the tarmac, they stood in a line all in salute. I waved back as we rotated out of their view.

I was sad to leave my new friends, but at the same time I felt like I'd been born again. Not religiously, but emotionally and physically. I was a different person, no question.

CHAPTER 14

THE BRONZE STAR

I was flown directly to Florida City. I had a number of things I needed to do first before heading back to Chicago.

Angel met me at the airport, and we drove to the villa.

There waiting for me was my package from the Pentagon of my father's records. It had arrived not long after I left for Canada.

I started to read the documents, skipping the records of his pay, his basic training, and other stuff that could wait. I wanted to read the reports of his combat experience, especially getting that Bronze Star.

There it was, near the end. I couldn't put it down.

The mission began on 19th of November in 1965 when Sergeant Don Cunningham, with a six-man Ranger crew from G Company, 75th Infantry, took a chopper ride to a ridge top on the eastern side of the A

Shau Valley, west of Hue, just east of the Cambodian border.

Don's crew included the last two of his high school friends, Sergeant John Sly and Sergeant George Karnes. The other crewmen were Special Forces medic Steve McAlpine, Corporal James Duren and Sergeant Chuck Donahoo.

Route 547A, a hardened dirt road running through the valley, was an NVA transport route. Recent intel claimed that NVA tanks and other heavy equipment had been recently using the road. The team's mission was to mine the trail.

The LZ was a saddle of ground near a ridge in the valley, with the road to the east. The thick treed steep slopes on either side were beyond the tall elephant grass that filled the basin. Bomb craters from previous B52 strikes excavated the area.

They were also tasked with setting up a radio relay. That was dangerous business. Previous radio relays had been taken out by the NVA because they had sophisticated Russian directional locators allowing the NVA to triangulate the relay's location. Don's orders were to routinely move the station around the ridges.

Don's corporal, James Duren, took the point at the ridge but immediately caught automatic fire from an SKS, hitting him a number of times. Before they even started they had been detected by at least one bunker high up the west slope.

The rest of the crew dove into a crater nearby.

Duren wasn't dead. He was able to return fire. But the NVA tossed some grenades at his position. He took more injuries, becoming pinned down on the ridge.

Don's team couldn't locate the NVA position; it was too well hidden in the jungle beyond the grass.

The team made a couple attempts to reach Duren, even launching M-203 grenades into the general location of the bunker, but the small arms fire was just too intense. It was coming from a number of angles.

Eventually, the team's Special Forces medic, Steve McAlpine, managed to crawl out to Duren and set up an IV.

Don called in a medevac and for reinforcements.

A nearby Huey, piloted by Capt. Louis Spiedel from Bravo Troop 2/17th Cav., intercepted the transmission and came in to evac the wounded soldier. They were on route to another mission and had a number of Rangers on board.

As the chopper touched down under small arms fire, Staff Sgt. William Vodden dove out and sprinted to Don's team. As the Huey lifted off, it took heavy enemy ground fire causing it to flip upside down, with a body falling out below it. It crashed some one hundred meters north of the LZ. A small amount of smoke churned up from the elephant grass.

Five men managed to come out from the wreck. The door gunner emerged last and tried to limp towards the Rangers' LZ. But he dropped from sight amongst more enemy fire.

Vodden raced from his position to retrieve the wounded door gunner. Carrying the wounded man on his back, Vodden was hit and fell. They were trapped. The only thing saving their lives was the tall grass they disappeared into.

"We need to get them," Sp4 Isaako Malo said and started to head out. Don grabbed him, and pulled him into their crater.

"What's the matter with you? You'll just end up like them. Stay put."

Along with Malo, Sergeant James Champion, PFC Charles McKinsey, and South Vietnamese Major Nguyen Van Nho appeared to be the only ones to escape the chopper. Champion was rambling incoherently about PFC Charles E. Crafts falling out and being crushed to death.

A medevac helicopter from Eagle Dustoff came in low from the south. It was piloted by Captain Roger Madison, with WO Fred Behrens. The Huey attempted to land at the yellow smoke grenade near Duren's position, but took a heavy volume of enemy fire.

When they landed, with Don's crew giving covering fire. Sergeant

John Sly rose from cover, ran over and helped McAlpine drag Duren toward the waiting medevac.

Behrens jumped from the ship to help get the unconscious Duren on board.

Regardless of enemy gunfire, the helicopter pulled away, heading back east toward the field hospital at Phu Bai. Sly and McAlpine dashed back to Don's location, followed by the snaps and spikes of dust from 7.62 bullets. Meanwhile, the Crew Chief from the downed Huey, Lee "Shorty" Comstock, managed to crawl to Vodden's position. He told Vodden that the two pilots from his chopper were trapped upside down with their legs pinned in the wreckage.

He couldn't help the wounded Vodden, so he tried to make it to Don's crater. But heavy enemy fire forced him to turn back, making it as far as his downed bird.

An hour later Madison's medivac chopper returned to the scene hovering over Vodden looking for a place to put down. Don threw a number of smoke grenades to mask the chopper from the enemy.

Circling around over the LZ, the ship dropped to the earth just a few meters from the hiding crew. Don sent Malo and Champion over to assist the Cav door gunner and Vodden get on board once they landed.

Before the ship could set down, the smoke had cleared exposing it to several hard hits – two striking WO Behrens in the foot and upper body, another killing Madison, the pilot.

The engine sputtered with smoke pouring from it, then shut down. The chopper auto-rotated, pan caking down just south of Vodden's position near a bomb crater.

Malo, Champion and Comstock bolted from the dead beast to the crater. Comstock, from the Cav Chopper, ran over to see if he could help anyone.

Don called in Cobra gunships from the 2/17th Cav. Within a few minutes the Cobras made several passes over the NVA position. This prevented the enemy from overrunning the LZ. The Cobras made as many runs as they could until the sun set. The Cobras radioed good luck, they would return at daybreak.

Everything went eerily quiet in the darkness. Don had his crew set up claymores around their perimeter. He crawled over to his two friends in their crater.

"Hellofa day," he said to Sly.

"Kind of wish Cherry was here," Sly said.

Don thought for a second. Then realized, "It's been a year since he was killed." He pulled out a photo of the four of them in football uniforms from their high school days. "I miss him."

"Yeah, me too," Karnes said. "But I don't miss his endless stories of his popping cherries. How many girls did he claim?"

"Six," Sly said.

"No, seven," Don chuckled. "He sure liked to brag about his name didn't he?"

"Made me sick, man. I haven't even gotten laid yet!" Karnes complained.

They laughed.

"So, now what, Sarg?" Sly said. "Two choppers down, and who knows how many killed."

"There's got to be more than one bunker up there," Karnes said.

"I tried to count," Don said. "I think there's at least four."

"Come morning, they'll come after us..." Karnes lamented.

A claymore went off with a scream afterwards, which slowly died down.

"Looks like they still are," Don said. "You guys get some sleep."

Don crawled through the tall grass the 75 meters east to the crater where the crew of the Cav Chopper was hiding with Malo, Champion, McKinsey, Van Nho and Crew Chief Comstock.

"How bad is it?" Don said to Comstock.

"Real bad, man. They're hanging upside down in their seats. There is no way I can get them out. Their legs are pinned real bad, man. We're going to need equipment to cut them out. I managed to give them some roots I found to chew on for fluids. But, man, the one guy looks real bad. I don't think he'll last the night."

"Horrible, slow death," Milo bemoaned. "Fucking Charley!"

"Shit. They send in more choppers and they'll just get hosed too," McKinsey complained.

"I just hope the NVA don't find them in the night, man, they'll slit their throats," Comstock added.

"That may be better than a slow agonizing death," Milo said.

"You want to go back there?" Don said.

"Yeah, man, it's dark enough." He slithered off into the darkness.

Just before dawn Don woke them all up. "Sly and I are going to flank these mother-fuckers and take them out. Give us all your nades, and what ammo you can spare."

Once loaded up, Sly and Don went east into the jungle, turned south for a kilometer then crossed the valley into the jungle on the west side. They made their way along the side of mountain. They waited for the light.

Just as the sun rose, Karnes dropped into the crater with the Cav crews. He said that he heard on the radio that an NVA battalion had been spotted heading south their way. They were getting a shit load of uninvited guests by midday.

Sly and Don slowly made their way towards the enemy bunkers. Being dug into the ground, and very well camouflaged, they would almost have to drop into one first.

As they came slowly through the jungle an NVA soldier was coming down the slope right in front of Sly. They got into hand to hand combat, as Don tried to intervene. He drove the butt of the Thompson into the soldier's neck, but not before the NVA stabbed Sly with his bayonet.

Don stuck the soldier in the throat with his knife, but Sly lay there crying holding the wound just below his heart.

"I'm done. He's killed me." He winced in pain. The wound was bleeding through his fingers.

"Let me get you back to the LZ," Don said.

"No. I'm done. Medevac will be here too late. Go finish the mission. Take those fuckers out. Give our boys a chance. Now go."

Don got a tear in his eye. He didn't want to lose another of his boyhood friends. Sly pushed him away, "Go, now!"

Don went off, looking back at his friend. "I'll be back," he whispered.

One of the bunkers opened up on the LZ not a few meters away. Don crawled up close to the entrance. He pulled the pins on two pineapples, allowed the handles to fly, counted to five and then threw them between the flashing barrels.

He rolled away just as they exploded. The concussion reverberated in his chest.

He could hear more fire from another bunker just about fifty meters north. He made his way to it. The NVA crew of three were in the open, firing from a shallow pit behind some logs. Don opened up on them with bursts from his Tommy.

Hearing another bunker, he ran over to it and threw two more nades into that dugout of four NVA, throwing bodies out onto the jungle floor.

Impacts erupted around from a number of Aks north of him. He backtracked to Sly's position, but Sly was dead.

Hearing the NVA hot on his trail, Don bolted south, then east to the tall elephant grass, back to the far east side of the valley.

He dropped into the crater with the last of his crew. He gave Karnes the bad news. Their quartet was down to just two.

Don spent the rest of the day radioing Cobra gunship runs on the enemy to their west. Once they ran out of ammo, Douglas Skyraiders came in to fill in the gap. Don brought ordinance to within their own perimeter as NVA came out from the trees to attack.

Just after noon, Don was informed over the radio that a couple of aero-rifle troops from the 2/17th Cav had inserted just north of them in an attempt to fortify their position as well as bring medical aid to the two trapped Cav pilots.

Within ten minutes of their landing, they managed to contact Don to say they were caught by the NVA battalion and were pinned down with many casualties. They weren't even four hundred meters north.

This was turning into a kill zone quickly. For Don it was looking like they were not going to make it.

"Fuck it," he said. "We're getting out here. Karnes and Donahoo, you guys E'nE out of here, east to the tree line."

"It could be loaded with NVA by now," Karnes protested.

"Better than becoming chopped hamburger here. Save yourselves."

They came back about an hour later with McAlpine in tow followed by projectiles from small arms impacting around them.

"Couldn't, Don," Karnes said.

"But we came across McAlpine here," Donahoo said out of breath.

"I was with Vodden," McAlpine said. "He's too badly wounded to move. So I hid him in a hole in a nearby crater. He's too shot up to carry. Hopefully the NVA won't see him and we can rescue him later. The door gunner is dead, I'm afraid.

"Oh, and earlier I managed to make it to the Cav's perimeter. I saw dozens of dead and wounded troopers inside their small perimeter. The NVA had mauled them during their insertion. I don't know how many are still alive. They're probably hiding somewhere."

"Swell," Don said. "Cluster fuck." He got on the radio demanding exfil.

Just before dusk a medevac arrived, about a hundred meters north of the first downed chopper. It dropped down long enough to extract a batch of the wounded Cav's.

"Do we know of anyone else alive?" Don asked McAlpine.

"A few. Behrens is hiding out by the chopper somewhere. He got hit a couple times by a sniper. But I think he got the fucker with his Tommy. He almost got whacked by friendly ordinance earlier today, though."

As the light faded, friendly aircraft repeatedly strafed and rocketed the area immediately around their position. Night enveloped them again. Radio from base said they would return the next morning to exfil them all. That did not sit well with Don, nor the rest.

They rested quietly in their craters, eating a bit, and using the last of their water. Any sound made them jumpy, as they knew the NVA would try to slide in and knife them.

Don watched silently as he could see faint images of NVA came out to drag off their dead and wounded. He could hear enemy soldiers rustling around in the tall grass.

Throughout the night, the Cav Crew chief stayed with the two pilots still trapped in the wreckage of the downed Huey trying to keep quiet as NVA moved about in the grass. They must have figured no one was alive as they didn't check the wreckage. But the wounded men needed to be evacuated soon as daylight arrived. They were getting worse.

Two NVA's fell into Malo and Champion's crater. The Americans managed to dispatch them with bayonets, but they couldn't take it anymore and decided they would try to E'nE (escape and evade). The crew chief decided not to go as he was armed only with a revolver.

Champion and Malo made it to Vodden, who was still alive. Vodden gave his remaining magazines and frags to Champion and handed his map and compass to Malo. They disappeared into the night, never to be seen again.

An hour later, Don and crew heard a Thompson firing in the valley east of them, followed by AK47 reports. Sergeant James Champion's "last stand."

During the night, on two occasions, Don heard gunfire from Vodden's direction. He had fired at a silhouette of a man standing over the edge of his crater. For good measure, Vodden also tossed a grenade over the crest of the hole.

Crew Chief Comstock came into Don's crater, almost being shot at, to say that one of the pilots, First Lieuy Donald G. Cook, had died during the night.

Don knew he couldn't just sit there and watch more Huey's trying to rescue them get shot down. He had to do something.

"You're going back to the chopper?" he said to Comstock.

"Yeah, man."

"Can you get one or both M60's from the ship?"

"I'll try, man."

"Bring them back here."

Don crawled through the night into the crater where McKinsey and Van Nho were trying to keep low.

"Does the Huey still have the two M60's?" Don said.

"Yes, hanging from the frame," McKinsey said.

"You think you can slither over there and get them both? And all the ammo you can carry?"

"I think so."

"Do it and meet us at our foxhole." Don dashed back to his crater.

Once everyone was assembled, Don laid out the plan.

"When I was running back from the bunkers, Charlie sent at least a dozen or more after me. If we do it again, with the appearance of being more than we are, they will send more south. Then we attack with the M60's up the hill and come in behind them."

"Gutsy move, I must say," Major Van Nho said.

"No choice. We've got to thin their ranks to give the choppers a chance. I need volunteers, two to make the diversion."

They each looked around expecting someone but them to raise their hand. After a few awkward moments, Karnes said, "I'll go."

Don wasn't too pleased. He didn't want to lose the last of his school buddies. "Anyone else, or do I have order someone?"

"Who put you in charge?" Sgt. Donahoo objected.

"Maybe the major here should be then. Well, Major, do you want to take over this outfit?" Don said.

"I'm just an interpreter. I wouldn't know about combat tactics. But I like your plan."

"Then it's settled. Donahoo, care to volunteer to go with Karnes?"

Reluctantly he nodded.

"Ok, take the Tommys and some grenades. Make as much noise as you can. Don't stay in one place for too long. Make yourselves look like a platoon."

"Gotcha," Karnes said.

"Be safe, and when we start shooting get low. I don't want you guys hit by friendly fire." Don looked at his watch. "It's 4:30, you have an hour. At six we attack."

It was a long sixty minutes for Don to wait. It was all hands on deck for this assault. There was one M60, with two belts each, plus their M16s and all the ammo they could carry for each of the four them left: McKinsey, McAlpine, Comstock and Don. Major Van Nho stayed behind to mark the LZ for the incoming medevacs.

Pops started south of their position, it was 6 am right on.

Don pulled out the Walther P38 he'd bought off a local merchant and handed it to Van Nho.

"What's this for?" the major said.

"In case I don't come back. Best you have it than it fall into the hands of Charley."

"I'll give it back to you when I see you next. Go get them."

Don and crew slithered through the grass in the dark. They had only forty-five minutes to sunrise.

They made it to the slope with no resistance. Pops still occurred, but it started to get mixed with the unmistakable sound of numerous Aks to their left and south.

The crew headed through the jungle towards the gunfire as the rising sun parted the darkness, lighting up the canopy floor.

It wasn't more than a hundred meters in front of them. The first of the enemy crouched behind trees came into view. Don and crew waited to get a better examination and a count. They spread out, then made their way into the fray blasting with their M60's at any NVA.

Coming in from behind totally confused the enemy. Most never got the chance to turn and fire back. They were cut down.

Don was personally killing one every few seconds as he ran through the enemy lines. He even tossed a few grenades, the blast of which threw several bodies into the air.

Eventually they ran out of targets.

Don and crew stopped. "George! George Karnes, are you there?" he yelled.

"Over here," Donahoo yelled. "He's been hit! Medic!"

Don raced up the hill, the worse fear took control. He found Donahoo, gun at the ready, kneeling in front of the wounded Karnes. He'd been shot three times in the stomach.

"McAlpine! Get your ass over here now!" Don screamed.

Off in the distance, Van Nho saw a long string of helicopters approaching. The rising sun glistened off their canopy glass. Twelve Huey's loaded with Rangers were arriving. Van Nho threw a yellow marker into the grass.

Six of the birds thundered low overhead and landed just past the downed Cav chopper. Men bailed and formed a perimeter.

The other six choppers turned and landed just south of the original LZ. Crew poured out setting up another perimeter.

Don heard the choppers as he held Karnes in his arms. The boy was still alive, just barely. McAlpine was trying to stop the bleeding. He looked up at Don and gave a small shake of his head. He stabbed Karnes in the leg with a morphine vial.

"I'm sorry, Don, my good buddie," Karnes said quietly. "I'm going to see the rest of the boys."

"Don't talk like that. You're going to be fine," Don lied.

"Boy, we sure had some good games in school, didn't we? We kicked some real ass."

His voice cracking, Don said, "We sure did. We had some great games. We'll have more."

Karnes didn't reply. There was no movement in his chest. His pupils dilated. He was gone.

"I'm sorry, Don," McAlpine said, with his hand on Don's shoulder.

After a few moments, McAlpine told Don to lay his friend down so they could carry him off. Don stood up. Then he stumbled into McAlpine's arms.

"Shit, you're hit," McAlpine exclaimed.

Don dropped to the ground. "It's just a flesh wound. I'll be fine."

"That's no flesh wound. That's right where your appendix is."

McAlpine looked at Don's back, there was an exit hole. He dressed both wounds, then stuck Don with a morphine vial. He and McKinsey carried Don down to the waiting medevacs.

Don was loaded with Madison and Vodden into a Huey. All of them had IVs strung above them. Off they went to the field hospital.

The story was very confusing. There were a lot of names of people all over the place. Too much was going on. It was the Vietnamese Major who wrote the report. He didn't do a very good job at explaining things. There were a lot of spelling and grammar mistakes.

I had a hard time picturing what happened. I read it more than once.

I even wrote all the names on PostIt notes, drew out what seemed to be the layout of the valley and, as I read it a fourth time, I moved the people on the notes around.

It finally made sense what happened.

Then it dawned on me. The coordinates of the valley were in the report. I entered them to Google Earth and had a bird's eye view of the battlefield. Of course, it was fifty years later, and much had likely changed.

I was compelled to go there and see the location for myself. I Googled for more on the battle and found a number of photos of the area.

Digging further into the box of documents, I found the citations. According to the records, Dad received his Bronze Star and Purple Heart while in hospital in Honolulu in March of the following year.

I poured myself a rum and coke and sat back in one of the comfortable layback chairs to ponder what I had read.

This was such a moving tale. My father used deceit and finesse to carry out his plan. Clearly, that event alone would have changed him. Losing two of his friends in his arms in Nam. Then losing his partner, again in his arms, while on the force.

It just brought back the grief for my Alex.

The last week of September was Pam's wedding. They postponed it from June. The wedding was in the courtyard of the villa, near the pool. There must have been three hundred people there. Flowers were everywhere. There was a huge arch over the altar, which was adorned with beautiful yellow and blue flora that had been boated in from Cuba the night before.

The men were all in white tuxes. I had to admit Angel looked quite handsome. His three older brothers were to his right. The Catholic priest was all dressed in a white robe ornamented with yellow trim.

On the left of the rows of witnesses was Angel's mother in the front row, with Maggie in her arms. I was a bit jealous about that, but she had far more experience with babies. I had one, which was so long ago I might as well have had none. That was my excuse anyway.

The organ started, and there she came, arm-in-arm with her father. Yes, she insisted he and his family come. She was all dressed in white, with a low cut front. A long train followed her, being carried by three of Angel's nieces. Behind them a nephew and niece carried cushions with the rings.

I had to admit, I was a little miffed about her father. I hadn't seen Kevin in, well, since before Pam was born. The years as a cop, chief of LAPD fraud squad, in California seems have taken a toll on him. He looked very old, but handsome at the same time.

Alex came to my mind. He should have been here.

Kevin's wife, Stephanie, was still a striking petite blonde. When faced with a choice the men go for the little blondes every time, I thought right then.

I'd never met Stephanie, but Pam showed me a few pictures. Their three girls were bride's maids for Pam.

In a way, I dreaded the awkward moment at the reception with Kevin and his family that was yet to come.

Pam was so beautiful. I actually felt envious. But at the same time so proud of her. I also thought about those many years she was out of my life because of a stupid mistake on my part. I should have told her about her father much sooner. But all was well now. It was history, and here she came with her future in hand.

I felt a mild hot flush form deep inside. Not now, not now. Please, not now. It faded.

The vows were very moving, Angel's in particular. I joined everyone with a tear of joy at the "I do" from each. After the priest pronounced them man and wife, the congregation clapped.

As with everything Cuban, they had a tradition to maintain at the reception. The dinning hall was adorned with flowers of all colors. The customary national dish of vegetable and meat stew, called ajiaco, served with plenty of white rice, was the main course.

Rum and wine flowed like a waterfall. Many times, glasses chimed to prompt the couple to stand and kiss.

I thought I might end up sitting with Kevin's family, but instead I was at the table with Angel's parents. Though Kevin did dart some glances my way.

I was so happy for Pam.

Then came the wedding cake. I didn't think such a cake could be so large and intricate. Cheers and claps filled the air as Pam and Angel made the first cut. The cake was devoured within minutes.

At dance time, I just sat nursing a rum 'n coke. Kevin and Stephanie came over to my table. Here we go.

"Marg, it's so good to see you again. You look great. You haven't met Stephanie yet."

We shook hands. They sat at the table.

"Marg," Stephanie said. "We're adults. We don't need to be enemies. Pam looked so beautiful. She clearly takes after you."

"You're kind, thank you. I guess I should also thank you for bringing her up during my lost years." I felt a bit guilty throwing the snide remark.

"Well, I can tell you, Marg," Stephanie continued. "She was a handful, wasn't she Kev?"

"That she was. Out late with friends. Disobedient, the usual teenage stuff, you know. Lucky for you you missed it."

No, not lucky that I missed those years with Pam. I didn't reply. We chatted a bit more. Then Stephanie had to remind me.

"Pam told us about Alex, and you being in the hospital. I'm so sorry it happened to you. You OK now?"

"I will be when I'm done."

"Done what?" Kevin said.

I just shook my head.

They stayed a few more awkward moments, then, politely excusing themselves, went off to the dance floor. I didn't talk with them the rest of the night. I guess they thought I was a bit snobbish. Too bad.

At midnight, it was time for the bride and groom to say their good-byes. Pam threw the bouquet to lots of hands attempting to capture it. Cheers erupted for the young lady who held it.

Angel took the garter off Pam's leg, held it high to cheers then tossed it to the eligible bachelors.

Pam came up to me just as they were ready to leave. It was a tearful meet. She thanked me, and hugged me tight. I was so proud of her. I was joyful I got my daughter back as a friend.

They left the compound, flanked by a number of guard vehicles, as they headed to the airport for their honeymoon.

The dancing and partying went on all night.

The following day, hung-over, I made my way to the kitchen. I desperately needed some coffee.

Luis was up, had been for a while. Don't Cubans ever sleep? He was making breakfast for himself and offered to make mine.

"I hope the newlyweds made it OK to Cuba," I said.

"Angel texted me that they arrived. I don't expect them to surface any time soon."

Angel's mother, Evelyn, came in with Maggie. We sat together for eggs and bacon. Except my stomach wasn't cooperating. The smell of the eggs and pork made me nauseous. I refused the plate Evelyn passed to me.

"You don't look so good, Marg," she said.

"I need more black coffee. Lots more coffee."

I finally got some quality time with my granddaughter. I even had the privilege of changing her diaper, gross, but still, my granddaughter.

After breakfast I asked Luis, "You have video games in the basement?

I saw the room the last time I was here."

"Sí. For the kids. Some are down there now."

I pulled out the CD Randy gave me. "I was wondering if I can try this."

"Sure, go ahead, those kids know everything about games like that. I have no time for them."

I went into the games room. Half a dozen kids, as old as fifteen, were playing various video games. I couldn't remember all their names, nor who they belonged to, but they were very cordial.

One young lad, Mark, said, "Battlefield Four. Great game. Little old now. PS3."

Within a few minutes he had the game running.

"Look," he said handing me the controller, "you will start at the very bottom. I don't play it anymore. We're playing Star Wars Battle Front on the PS4 over there. So, I'll log you into my old account and you can play with my loadout. Play the Locker map. It's the best."

Operation Locker was set in a prison which was built into the side of a mountain. Most of the map was inside the complex, but you could also go out into the outside winter conditions to get back inside from several doorways.

I found myself playing it for hours. I had to admit it was very addictive. It was certainly an experience playing with live people around the world.

Of course, I sucked at it. Every time I turned around I was getting killed.

Mark came over after several frustrated choice words on my part.

"Look, let me show you. You play, but I'll tell you what to do."

"I keep getting killed. But I can't seem to get any of them."

"You have to flank them and come in from behind. So look at what is happening. The enemy is clustered in that one room. Go outside."

I moved my character to the outside. There I made my way to behind the enemy. Coming inside the complex, I came into the room.

There the enemy players were together keeping our guys from advancing. They were all facing away from me.

"Throw a nade into those guys at the right. Then hose the others with your machine gun."

It worked. I had no idea how many I killed, it happened so fast. I got quite of few of them until one of them came in behind and knifed me.

"There, see? You got seven of them, all at once. Good shooting," Mark said. "Keep going. You'll do fine." He went off to play his game.

That so much reminded me of what my father had done in Nam. He came in behind them and just hosed anyone he saw with gunfire. But this was just a game.

I definitely needed to set this up at home. I needed to get good at the tactics. Find out what works and what doesn't.

The week before my flight home the dentist came and finished my new teeth. It was wonderful to be able to chew normally again.

I was packing up the last of my stuff for my flight home when Pam with Maggie came in.

"You're leaving. I wish you would stay."

"I have to, Honey. I have to finish this."

"But you could get killed, or badly injured again."

I went over to her. Maggie stirred. "It's not safe for me to be here. It's not safe for you two to be here as long as I'm here. Eventually, I'd have to leave the compound, and the Outfit will be waiting. Or, they will get to you to get to me."

"We can deal with that. Luis said he can get you work here."

"Picking vegetables for the rest of my life? I don't think so."

"No, he needs more security. You should at least talk to him before you go."

"OK, I will. But regardless, I have to see this through."

She sighed. Maggie made some sounds. I picked her up and kissed her. "I'd love nothing more than to be here with you. I will. I'll be back. I promise."

I found Luis in the court, he was waiting for me so he could say good-bye. He too tried to talk me out of going. He said they need more security as people from the cities, poor people who were having severe financial problems, were starting to raid his fields.

But he understood I had to do what I had to do. The offer was an open invitation that wouldn't expire.

CHAPTER 15

DECEIT AND FINESSE

Derik met me at O'Hare Airport. He actually gave me a hug and said he was glad I was well. At the baggage claim I picked up my three gun cases.

"Guns? What the fuck is this?" Derik said. "Guns. You... With guns..."

"I'm a changed person."

He just shook his head.

We drove to the Super 8 Motel not far from the airport. When the receptionist asked how long my stay was going to be I said, "Maybe a couple months. I'll pay up front."

I looked at what they had available. "I'll take the king bed non-smoking, please." I paid the girl in cash for two months.

Once I was settled into my room I called Hollenger. I asked him to come and visit. I needed to talk one on one. Something was bugging me, had been since I was laid up in the hospital.

After the call, I hit the internet looking for a house I could buy and quickly move into.

Hollenger came by on his way home. We sat at the small table. "What do you want to know?" he said.

"How did the Outfit find us at the Stardust? Someone talked." I even had to suspect my own boss.

"We've been compromised. No question. You didn't hear about it. But one of the cops who took you there was found shot inside his apartment. It was made to look like a suicide. But co-workers deny he was depressed. We think he infiltrated the department. He was a plant from the beginning. Once you escaped, the Outfit killed him to tie up loose ends."

Swell. The Mob had moles in the department. Why wasn't I surprised?

"The FBI wants to talk with you too. Can I tell them where you are?"

"Have they been infiltrated too? Rudd said the Outfit would be waiting for us to take him in and shoot the car up."

"Not that I'm aware."

"Guess I have to trust them."

"If you want to see this through, you'll need their help. And ours. Have you decided what you're going to do?"

"Maybe." I had decided, while I was at the villa, exactly what I was going to do, and how to do it. But I wasn't going to tell Hollenger, nor the FBI, at this point. Especially now I knew the CPD was compromised.

A few days later an Asian FBI agent came to meet me at the motel. She introduced herself as Special Agent Joan Lim Loo. She was young, much younger than me. She came with a message.

"There was a shootout in Florida. Between the Mob and local Cubans. Your daughter is married to one of them, isn't she?"

My heart sunk. "When? I just left there a few days ago. Is my daughter..." I stopped at the thought she and the baby had been killed.

"Everyone is fine. Your daughter and grandchild are all fine."

"What happened?"

"Seems your daughter and her husband were driving back from the airport when they were broad-sided by a truck. Some men got out and attempted to abduct the car's occupants. But what the Mob didn't know was your daughter had an escort of armed men. They opened up on the abductors killing them all."

Burning brewed in my gut. The only thing I could think of saying was, "Any of the Cubans hurt?"

"No."

I immediately called Pam. She was fine and the baby was fine. It scared her a lot, she said. They were staying in the villa until this all blew over.

After I hung up, Joan said, "Look. I'm sorry about Alex. We all liked him very much. I know I can't replace him..." she obviously didn't know we were in love, "...but I've been asked to be your liaison. So I'd appreciate it if you can keep me posted of whatever it is you plan to do. We can help."

I didn't say anything.

"Of course, we can't sanction anything illegal you do."

I didn't say anything.

"Well," she fidgeted, "we can start by you looking at some photos. Maybe you can figure out who was at..." She paused. She must have understood how bad it was for me. "What can you tell me about the men who beat you?"

I told her about the man with the cigar.

"Holy shit," she said as her eyes popped out of her head. "That's The Rib. Joe Ribaudo. Just a second." She went through the photos. Then handed me one. It was from a distance with other men standing in front of a restaurant.

"That's him, on the left," I said as rage filled my body.

"Jesus Christ. You're sure that's the man who questioned you?"

"That's what I said."

"We think he's their top enforcer. He could be number two or number three in the Outfit."

She pulled out an organization chart of the Outfit, as they knew it. There he was, right up there.

"Enforcer it says under his picture," I said.

"Yes, he's the boss of the enforcer soldiers. We think it's something new with their attempt to reestablish their power.

"I don't know how they expect to do that with all the competition that infects the city: the Russian Mafia, the Nigerian Mob, the Chinese Tong gangs. Not to mention all the other gangs in the city. Violence would be the only tool they could use."

"They must be getting desperate," I added.

"Likely. Like a wounded animal, no telling what it will do."

Oh, yeah. This wounded animal is going to show them what I can do, I thought. I looked carefully at the photo. Joan listed the names of the rest.

"That social network that Alex made from your father's notes has all these guys, except Ribaudo. They were all much younger in your father's day.

"But, there is one big hole in our information. We don't know who runs the Outfit. Someone is giving the orders, we just don't know who. It's definitely not any of them there."

"Where was this taken?"

"The Capone Spaghetti House over in Elmwood Park. It was taken six years ago."

I looked back at the chart. Who's this?" I pointed to another box containing the name T.J. Ribaudo.

"That's Joe's younger brother, one of two. We think he runs the financials of the Outfit. He has a PhD in Economics from Harvard."

I glanced up.

She shrugged, "Only the best money can buy."

"You said one of two. Who's the other?"

"Dead. Killed back in the 1990s. A murder never solved. Speaking of murdered, The Rib's son, Joe junior, was also murdered last year. We had him in a Federal prison on weapons charges. He got into some kind of fight and was stabbed before he could get to trial."

"Oh, that must have made him really pissed."

"Very likely."

"So now we know who Ribaudo is, are you guys going to arrest him?"

"We can. We could, if we knew where he is. But we'll let CPD know and maybe they can catch him."

"I'd rather you didn't."

She looked at me sideways. "I have to. Sorry, Marg."

Leaving, I thanked her as she gave me her card.

I was driven by one goal. Kill every one of those fuckers I could, or at least get as many of them into prison as possible. Utmost was to find Ribaudo and put a bullet in his brain.

But I had to do this systematically, and I needed a base of operation. I needed to find myself a house. I didn't want to use my apartment. I felt it too difficult to set it up the way I wanted.

Getting a house shouldn't be an issue with so many on the market, and that prices had collapsed, though the economy had stabilized from the past six-month fall.

I picked a realtor out of the paper. I gave her what I was looking for, a small two story somewhere in the south side, preferably one which was vacant for quick possession.

It didn't take Angie long to pop up a list while I had her on the phone. She emailed me the website links.

I picked half a dozen and the following day we went to have a look at them. One we looked at was on the market, empty, for eight years, bank foreclosed. It was a medium sized detached one and a half story on South Emerald Avenue. The inside needed some work, but it was livable. A rare feature was a driveway to the front street. I liked that.

The price was perfect, $55,000, of course that didn't matter to me. Still, we wrote up an offer of $35,000 cash, no conditions and immediate possession. Angie passed it to the bank, doubtful they would accept.

Within two days Angie called that they accepted the offer. That's how desperate the banks were to get rid of inventory.

Two weeks later it was mine. I used father's money. It was interesting to see the bank manager's face when I counted out the cash. I wondered if he thought it was drug money. In a way he was right. But he likely was pleased to get one off their books, regardless why.

The home needed some work, such as new windows, new flooring, and a new furnace, but what else I had no clue.

Down the street a house was in the last stages of renovations, so I went to talk with the foreman.

I walked into the front door to a cloud of drywall dust.

"Can I help you?" a voice from the inside said.

"I need my home done. Just wondering if you boys would like some more work."

A young man emerged from the cloud. He was completely covered in white powder. He pulled off his mask and we went outside. It was actually comical to see a black man completely white except the oval of his face.

"Which house?" he said.

I pointed three houses up across the road.

"Oh, I was going to buy that place next. If you don't mind me asking how much did you pay for it?"

I told him

"Hmm, yeah, I thought that a bit much actually. This house here, I paid $11,000 for it. Can you believe that? Ten years ago it sold for $140,000. But I guess the owner lost his job. It's been in the bank's hands for seven years. It was completely destroyed inside. We had to gut it and start over from the shell."

"I guess there's a lot of that."

"Hell, yeah. You see all those empty lots around here? Well, they used to have homes on them. They either burned to the ground, or were torn down they were so dilapidated."

Such was Chicago's economy, still is.

"How much to do a reno like this?" I asked. I wanted to get an idea how much I was looking at for my home.

"I've put about forty g's into it. I was hoping to sell it for $135,000, but in this market I'm not so sure now. I have three unsold homes I've poured money into renovating."

"So I assume then, when you're done here, you won't have any projects?"

"That would be correct. I was getting worried I'd have to lay these guys off. What do you want done and when?"

We went back to my place to have a look. He made a list, then gave me a quote on the spot, $25,000.

I hired him.

I also hired a company to install security, lots of it. Cameras covered every angle. The windows and doors were all set up with detectors.

The home was livable in six weeks. Thereafter, I had to buy a house worth of new furniture. The salesmen at the stores were falling over themselves to help, trying to oversell. Definitely a tell-tail sign things weren't well in the economy. People abandoning their homes are people who are also not buying anything new.

During that time I bought a brand new Ford F-150 pickup. A good rugged four-wheel drive vehicle. I needed it just to move my stuff in.

The security company suggested a gun store in Riverdale for artifacts of personal protection. Chicago had managed to close down every gun store in an attempt to curb gun related crime. Of course, like their attempt a few years back to ban all handguns, their policy backfired, pun intended. Gun crime had just gotten worse.

I bought two double-barreled shotguns, one tactical shotgun (a Derya Arms Mk-10, an AR style shotgun made in Turkey), and five Glock semi-auto 9mm handguns.

The shotguns were loaded, and placed in strategic locations around the house. Same with the handguns: one in the fridge, one taped under the kitchen table, one under the dining room table, one in the bathroom behind the toilet, and one in my bedroom.

I had a good chuckle. I remembered Captain David Doroszuk, my former captain, slept with a loaded 1911 handgun under his pillow. If he could see this, he probably thought I was going a tad overboard. But if my plan played out, I would need this firepower scattered around the house.

My fortress was established. It was time to poke the bear.

But first I needed some reassurance.

The October air was signaling another cold winter ahead. But at least on the day I went to visit my parent's plot it was sunny. There was no snow on the ground, yet.

I sat in front of the headstone that had both their names on it.

"Hi Mom. Pam's wedding was fairytale. She's in good hands. Maggie is such a great baby. She feeds a lot, like a lot. It certainly helped Pam fill out her wedding gown." I chuckled.

"Dad. I know now what you did. I'm so sorry I doubted you."

I paused.

"I need your help. But you're not here. I wish you were here to help me. I need your strength."

I paused.

"Funny. Me asking a dead person for help."

I shook my head.

"Ok, I just needed to reassure myself, I guess. I'm going to finish your work, Dad. Wish me luck."

I kissed the ends of my fingers, and touched the top of the headstone. "I love you both."

The Capone Spaghetti House was in a strip mall in Elmwood Park on North Harlem near West Cortland. I pulled into the Mexican restaurant parking lot a few doors down, and walked to the Capone front door. The plain front gave no hint of what was inside. There wasn't even a sign on the building.

I came in and looked around. The place was a monument to the gangster. Pictures of him were everywhere. There were wooden barrels of whisky stacked, and placed around the room. Newspaper articles from the thirties about the man hung in frames.

There was even a full-life sized mannequin of the man holding a real Tommy gun right at the front door.

Behind a glass panel was some kind of Teletype with a short length of perforated tape hanging out of it. Beside it was a very old slot machine. On the wall behind were more hanging paper clippings.

His famous baseball bat hung on its own in a gold trimmed wooden plaque.

On the opposite wall at the front door was another panel with G-Men comic books, a Dick Tracy comic book, a set of handcuffs, and a shotgun. Clearly, the symbolism of confrontation between Capone on the left, and the FBI on the right.

A sitting area was further in on the left, with a number of tables. A few patrons were spearing platefuls of spaghetti and meatballs. On the right was a long bar, most of which had people sucking back beers while watching the Friday night football game.

At the very back on the right was a large round table. In front of it, in the aisle, was a PRIVATE sign. A large man in a suit guarded the entrance. A dozen or so old men could barely be seen through the thick cigar smoke.

I pretended to go to the washroom, which was past the guard. I came up to him and said, "I need to pee."

He flagged me through. As I past the table I tried to see if The Rib was there. He wasn't. They were all just old wrinkled men chewing on Cubans, and throwing back shots of booze. Some of them glanced at me as I passed by.

In the washroom I looked into the mirror to get some composure. I was shaking. My hands were uncontrollably trembling. I took a deep breath, then flushed a toilet to finish my ruse.

Exiting the room I stopped at the table. "Good evening, gentlemen."

They paused and looked at me.

"No need to pretend you don't know who I am. Oh, I'm sorry, you're all so old. I forgot you're suffering from Alzheimer's. I'm ex-cop Margory Cunningham, daughter of Chicago Police Department Detective Don Cunningham."

A few fidgeted in their seats. One old guy with gnarled hands, and yellowed eyes, gave me a deep scowl.

"I'm looking for the Rib, Joe Ribaudo. If you know where I can find him I'd be real appreciative."

I looked around at the dumb and dumber silent group. The guard came up right beside me.

"Oh, come on, boys. You know who he is. I just want to talk with him."

The old man gave a nod to the guard, who then grabbed my right arm hard. As he proceeded to forcefully escort me out I said, "Tell him I will find him." Other patrons stopped eating to watch me be pulled to the front door, and pushed through it.

Done. Message sent. Now to grab their balls and squeeze them tight.

Next was the moneyman. I called my contact.

"I'm ready. I'll need some of that money you offered. But first, I want you to know I'm going to use my father's money first."

"Don't do that. Keep it as backup. Look, I can front you up to fifteen million. What do you plan to do?"

That was three times the previous quote. Clearly they were taking me seriously.

"Buy real estate and replace some people's loans at a cheaper rate. So how does this work?"

"You don't actually get the money. What you do is submit to our committee what it is you want to buy, or who you want to lend to. We check these. We vet them. Then we deposit that amount in a special account. It will appear to be in your name. But it will only appear that way to anyone who checks."

"Let's be clear. You won't have free reign of the money. It's ours. And whatever property or loans you buy legally belong to us."

"Who's us?"

"Not a question you ask."

I called Joan and told her to meet me at a food and liquor store on Blue Island Avenue. She asked what was going on.

"I'll explain when you get there."

I waited outside the store for her to arrive. She was late. I saw her walking along the sidewalk to the store's door. "Joan," I said. "Don't go in yet." She came to the pickup and got in.

I explained what I was about to do.

"That's entrapment. It's illegal," she said.

"For cops it is. Not for me. All I need you to do is be my intimidation. You go in first and look as if you're a customer."

"OK, I'll play along." She went inside.

I followed a few minutes later. A woman was behind the counter. "Is Mr. Campenni in?" I knew he was as I'd seen him open the store in the morning.

"Yes, he's in the back."

"Please, can I speak with him?"

She called him to come out. We shook hands. He remembered me from my investigation of De Luca last February.

"Look, Mr. Campenni, I know your store is a front for money laundering, and it's costing you big time. How much rent do you pay for this place?"

He was silent, looked shocked at the allegations. He fidgeted a bit then said, "Why should I tell you anything?"

I pointed to Joan, who was looking at the produce. "See that woman over there? That's Joan. She's with the FBI. She can shut you down right now if she wanted to. So, take your pick, talk to me or be out of business."

He didn't look too happy. "Ok, what do you want?"

"Again, how much are you paying in rent?"

"Twelve hundred and fifty per month."

"And add to that the profit charge your landlord is demanding you pay. How much is that, five percent?"

He paused. Shook his head looking downwards at the counter. "Six."

"Plus you're forced to have some customers pay far more for things than the sticker, and that money is then paid to your landlord for building updates. How much is that?"

He looked at Joan. "If I told you that happens, she would arrest me."

"She isn't going to arrest you. I have a proposition for you, which will not only save you money, it will also get the Outfit off your back. You'll be able to run a lawful business."

He looked at me, paused then said, "Bullshit. How?"

"You know the building just up the street that was for sale?" He nodded. "I bought it, and I'm willing to let you rent it from me for half what you pay now. I won't charge you a profit tax, and you won't be dinged for those monthly upgrade invoices, the one's that clean the dirty money."

He laughed. "If I did that, they'd be on me in a second. I don't want to wind up in the hospital."

"You won't have to worry about that. That's also why Joan is here. They intimidate you in any way, she will arrest them."

"Are you crazy, woman?" he laughed. "You do that and they will be all over you."

I smiled back.

"It's either play with me or Joan'll have a team in here within the hour to shut you down."

He thought a few seconds. "When did you want to do this?"

"The store is ready. You can move any time. It's a bigger store too. That could be your excuse to your current landlord for the move. You want to grow and provide more to the community."

"It's a big job moving all this."

"I'll hire the Westside Movers to do it."

"When?" Campenni asked.

I placed a contract on the counter. "Next month is fine. Sign this."

He read it over. "I cannot sign this now. I have to think this over. You come back in a day or two."

I thought for a second. He was going to call his Outfit contacts. That was fine too.

"Ok, I'll give you a couple days." I walked out, with Joan following me.

Outside, Joan got into my truck. "I don't understand how this is going to work. You do realize he is going to call the Outfit."

"I'm counting on that."

She looked confused.

"Trust me," I said with a smile.

"OK, but assuming he does move into your building, how is that going to work?"

"Every building I've bought and renovated has surveillance installed. You'll be able to watch it go down live on the internet. Soon as one of the Rib's goons try any kind of intimidation, you'll have it on disk."

"You do realize I can't be part of this. This is clear entrapment."

"I don't want you to be part of it. So it won't be entrapment. I want you to be ready to swoop down and make arrests when this goes down."

"I may have to arrest you too."

"In a way I hope you do. Then you can let it out that I made a deal for my freedom."

"You're playing a very dangerous game here," she said.

"Just be ready to arrest."

"I still don't understand," she continued. "You're going to hire the moving company owned by the Outfit to move that business? That's ballsy."

"I want to send a message. That will certainly do it."

Campenni declined my offer. He said he didn't relish the thought of having his legs broken. Didn't matter, he had made the contact. The message was sent.

The following weeks I made deals with a number of people, mostly businesses, who owed money to the Outfit. All names from Rudd's list. It took a lot of persuading. But the prospect of paying four percent interest, compared to the eight percent or more the Outfit was charging, was too compelling for some of them. The rest, like Campenni, were too scared of the Outfit.

That didn't matter. The Outfit was realizing I was becoming a potential thorn.

One in particular who eagerly accepted my offer was Clark Hall, the man who lost his nephew last year.

"Did you get your loan for your car shop, Mr. Hall?" I said when I called him.

"I did, but the rates are killing me. I couldn't get one from the bank, so I went to a private company."

He gave me the name. It was on Rudd's list. It was the private bank the Outfit owned.

"How much interest is the loan?"

"Nine percent. How can they charge so much for a loan? I don't understand how that is legal."

"Is the loan open? Can you pay it off any time?"

"I think so."

"How about I give you a loan for two percent."

There was silence at the other end.

Then he said, "What's the catch?"

"No catch. I can lend you two hundred grand tomorrow at two percent. Say a ten-year loan. Could you handle that?"

"Handle that? Of course I can. I can use the rest to buy some half decent equipment. The economy may be bad, but people are keeping their old cars running instead of buying new ones. More business for me."

"I'll be by in the afternoon tomorrow then with the cash."

Another dart thrown at the Outfit.

I also bought nine more buildings, and moved three businesses from Rudd's list who were fronts for money laundering. Ten businesses I contacted refused me for fear of retaliation. But that was fine too, because the message would be passed up the food chain.

The timing was just right. I had all this finalized just before Thanksgiving.

This year, I was invited to Alex's parents for the spread. His brother and sister's families were there. We had a great feast, but we also gave a prayer for the vacant seat at the table.

Around the fireplace, Scott and Laurie asked how things were going. I explained what I did with the businesses. Scott was very concerned.

"The Outfit will retaliate against you. They'll kill you. Legally, anyone arrested, if they find out where your money came from..."

"It was all borrowed." That wasn't a lie. This money really was on loan to me.

"Still, I can see a defense lawyer making good hay out of this in court."

"Not my problem. I'm not a lawyer. It's the principle of the issue at stake here. It's retaliation for the death of Alex and our baby at stake here."

They understood.

"I don't need the money you offered, but it was a very nice gesture."

Laurie went upstairs. She returned with a small blue box. I opened it. It was an engagement ring.

"We found it with Alex's stuff from his apartment. I was with him when he bought it. That was just before last Valentine's Day. I thought he'd already given it to you. But I guess he never got the chance."

"No, he had to leave..."

I stopped mid-sentence. My God. Alex was going to propose to me. My heart sank. My mind filled with his face. I could picture him getting on his knee to present me with this ring.

"That makes you our daughter," Laurie said. And we gave each other a big hug. I had a new set of surrogate parents. That felt comforting. I put the ring on the correct finger.

At some point the Rib would have to make a move.

A move did happen, just not quite what I expected.

I had arrived at a building I bought on South Oakley Avenue. All the windows were spray painted with graffiti; a six sided star with III in the middle. The Black Gangster Disciples. They were marking their territory.

I went to the door to make sure it was secure when I was swarmed by half a dozen black men. I stood with my back against the door, and a wall of men with baseball bats.

I pulled Alex's Cz handgun from under my shirt and pointed it at them. "You come after me and I'll take some of you down first."

Two backed up, but the rest just stood there.

"What do you want?"

"Yo on our turf. Yo costin' us chedder. We're here to B.O.S. Mob yo azz," one said.

I recognized his bandana. "Black Gangster Disciples aren't you?"

They didn't say anything for a moment. Then the same man said, "Yo need to move on and leave our kingdom."

"You guys are being conned, not by me, but by the Outfit. You've had members gone missing, am I correct? You think it's the Vice Lords or the Latin Kings? Right? It's not. It's the Outfit. They're pretending to be your friends, all the while they've been tunneling into your territory."

"Yo lie."

"No, I'm not. I don't want you guys. I want the Outfit. I need to talk to your Minister." With my Cz pointed at them with my right hand, I passed a card to the man with my left. He took it.

"He can contact me any time," I said.

Slowly they left. I gave a great sigh of relief. I was trembling. This was taxing emotional work. I got a cold sweat from head to toe that lasted well into the night.

The next day my cell rang. All the man said was "Empty lot, 77th and Kedzie, One PM."

"Wait, no. Somewhere very public."

There was a pause. "OK. There's a McDs on Western. Two PM." He hung up.

I had just finished my Big Mac and fries when four black men came in. I noticed them because they stood out from the rest of the patrons enjoying their lunch.

They were well dressed in expensive business suits and ties. And very well groomed. This must be who I'm meeting with, I thought.

The very tall and sleek individual, with lots of jewelry, mostly rings on his fingers, sat across from me. The other three flanked my seat.

"And who are you?" I asked.

"Let's just say I'm Bishop." Ah, the local area Black Gangster Disciple minister. "I know who you are, Detective Cunningham."

"If you know who I am, then you should also know I'm no longer a cop. I'm a private individual doing business."

He laughed. "Right. You're buying up property and making loans. For what end? Piss off the competition? That kind of business can get you—"

A bunch of children passed by with their mother. A lttle girl with her hair bundled up in lots of pink ribbons smiled at the Bishop. He twitted his fingers at her and smiled back.

He looked back at me.

"Look, there's no way we're talking here with all these people around. I assume your vehicle is outside. That gray pickup?"

"Yes."

"I assume it isn't wired."

"It's not."

He got up. The other men followed him out the door. They stopped and stood by my truck. I dumped my garbage, and picked up my Coke.

The two of us got into my vehicle, while the men surrounded the truck. Being on the tall side he didn't fit well in the seat, with his knees pressed up against the glove box.

First thing the Bishop did was to pull a small twenty-five caliber revolver on me.

"You think this is some kind of fucking game?" he said with a stern look.

"Life's a game," I replied, sucking on my straw as if nothing was amiss. But I was scared shitless inside.

"I don't play nice games," he growled.

"I know that."

"Then what the fuck are you up to? You throw money around buying up businesses, have renters leave the Outfit. Renters who I use to clean my... My proceeds. How am I to do my work when you interfere with my business?"

"Are you going to shoot me here in broad daylight, in front of all these witnesses?"

"This city is rampant with senseless murders. But you already know that don't you, Detective."

"You would know since you're the cause of some of it."

His eyes squinted. "You're very up front and blunt aren't you?" He put the gun away. I knew he was just intimidating me, but I still gave myself a great sigh of relief inside. I couldn't show him any weakness.

"But I'm also a reasonable man," he continued. "You can't run an organization if you're not a reasonable man."

Run an organization? He was just a minister for his area. But then I got to thinking. This guy was their "Chairman of the Board." He ran the Disciples!

"You told one of my employees that the Outfit is ripping me off. I don't take such accusations lightly. Do you know how many of my employees have been..." He paused. "I've lost?"

"I don't."

"Twenty-three." He looked sad. Their loss seemed heavy on him. "Most of them were my junior employees. All have gone missing, likely killed." He paused and looked out the front window. "Taken out in the prime of their lives," he said in a tone of remorse. "Mother-fuckers." He looked back at me. "All along the evidence has pointed to the Latin Kings. I've had to..." He stopped.

He started to fidget in the seat, feeling around at the door. "I'm cramped, how do you..." He reached around the front, found the release, and let the seat lunge back.

He sighed. "That's better." Continuing his thought he said, "But you seem to think it's the Outfit screwing with us."

"The FBI found a farm in Iowa, where bodies were fed to pigs. So far, last I heard, at least a hundred people's DNA had been found there. The farm was a front for the Outfit."

He looked hard at me, then turned to stare ahead. "I've been to that farm. They convinced me to put money into it. Mother... fuckers!" He pounded his fist on the dash.

"They're trying to expand their territory at your expense," I said. "Actually, not just you exclusively. They're going after all the major gangs, all the while making you think it's each other."

He slowly turned to look at me. "Why are you telling me this?"

"I don't want you to retaliate against the Outfit. I want you to stand down and let me finish my work."

"And what is your work, exactly?"

"They killed my fiancé. We were to be married." I showed him my ring. "I was carrying our child. They tortured me. They also went after my daughter and granddaughter. I want to nail their fucking balls to the wall."

He paused for a second, then looked outside the front window and pointed. "You see that man to the left of your truck?"

"Of course."

"He's married to my daughter. She's pregnant. My first grandchild." He thought for a few moments. "Having your own children puts new perspectives on things." He looked back at me. "Something you clearly understand. You understand what happens when someone fucks with your family."

Then he chuckled. "But you're chipping away at them. For what purpose? You want them to retaliate?" He paused. "Fuck me, you do want them to retaliate against you."

"To flush them out, in particular, Ribaudo."

"Oh, I know that mother-fucker. He's one mean dude. But that doesn't tell me what you plan to do, exactly. Kill them all?"

"I'm playing my lower cards to finesse out their big suits."

He looked confused.

"I'm setting them up for the FBI. But let me be clear, I am emphatically not working for the FBI. I'm just going to take out the trash for the FBI to pick up, so to speak."

He paused for a few seconds. "Can you swear to me that neither the cops nor the FBI will come after me?"

"I can't speak for them. But my focus is not you and your operations. It's the Outfit. I get them taken out and you would be able to fill their void."

He laughed. "I have to admit it. You're one hellova liar."

I was taken aback. He didn't believe me.

"I'm not lying," I tried to reassure him.

"Oh, yes you are. You're lying about setting up the Outfit for the FBI. You're planning some kind of reprisal of your own aren't you? Anyone who threatens my family, let alone kill someone in my family, doesn't live to see the next sunrise."

I didn't say anything. I sucked up the last of my Coke with one eye cocked in his direction.

"Let me speculate for you, then," he continued. "You want them to go after you so you can T.O.S."

That's gang lingo for "take out on sight." I just gave a small smile.

He looked ahead again and nodded his head. "Ok, I'll lay off the Vickies, and I'll hold off on some of my money problems for the time being." He got out and closed the door. Then he stopped and turned back to the vehicle. Knocking with his rings on the glass, beckoning me to lower the window. I dropped it down. Leaning in he pointed his right index finger at me, "You're playing a deadly game, woman."

He left. I watched him in my rearview mirror calling over a vehicle. They all got in the black Mercedes and drove off. I held onto the steering wheel with both hands and dropped my head between them, and my heart started to beat again.

Hollenger called me. "We got the Rib. I need you to come down and identify him in a line up."

"Where did you find him?"

"A beat cop pulled him over for a traffic violation. He recognized him from the APB."

Swell. He's going to go through the legal system. I wasn't going to get him.

A man in a suit, obviously Ribaudo's lawyer, accompanied Hollenger and myself into the booth with the two-way mirror.

Five men were marched into the room behind the glass. There he was, the fourth from the left. There was no way I was going to miss that face.

"Take your time," Hollenger said to me.

If I pointed him out, that would be it. They would arrest him, and off to prison, the "college" as the Outfit called it. That would mean he would be out of my reach. Prison was too good for him. He had to die, and I had to be the executioner.

"He's not there," I said.

Hollenger swung his head around fast. He was pissed. "You're sure?"

"He's not there," I repeated.

"Look carefully and take your time..."

"She made her choice," the lawyer interjected. "Let my client go."

Outside Hollenger laid into me. He went on about we could have put him away. It would have been justice for me and Alex.

"No." I said. "I dish out his justice."

"And how do you— Wait. I don't want to know. Get the fuck out of here."

On December 20th, the city held a vigil at ground zero for the first-year anniversary of the bombing. I was surprised most of the buildings had been repaired. You wouldn't have even known that the faces of some of them were completely rebuilt.

The "L" line was not yet completed. They were close to finishing the new station. Wabash and Madison were still closed to traffic. But the businesses were back to normal, as best that could be.

I attended the event. The Mayor and the Governor made very patriotic speeches. A plaque with the names of the dead was unveiled on one of the pillars of the new station.

On Christmas Eve morning I flew to Florida to spend the week's holidays with Pam.

Cubans certainly know how to celebrate Christ's birth. It's a massive event. Everyone who worked at the villa was there. Neighbors were also invited.

Traditionally, the main event was Christmas Eve dinner. I arrived as they were preparing the feast, which was an all-day event. Pam pulled me to the main court behind the pool where they were roasting three pigs, with their heads still on. It gave me the shivers to recall all those people who had been fed to the pigs at the Outfit's farm.

Luis and Zamira Sotolongo came up to me and gave me a hug. "Thank God you're here and safe," Zamira said. "Come, we could use another pair of hands in the kitchen."

There must have been a dozen women preparing food for the night's party. I was introduced to them all, but there was no way I would remember their names. With big crowds like that, I would have expected everyone would have nametags.

"So what can I do?" I asked.

Zimira explained the dinner arrangement. "We're just getting the deserts started. You can help prepare the plantains, yuca, and sour oranges. Just make sure the plantains are completely green and devoid of any spots. That will take you a while."

The other women were making large bowls of cascos, orange, guava, with grapefruit shells in sweet, heavy syrup; and baskets of buñuelos, plus fried sweet dough.

It all looked so delicious. Hours of preparation, but consumed in a few minutes.

Once done I was looking out the back window towards the smoke rising above the searing pigs. None of the men were tending the BBQ, they were just sitting around drinking beers and telling jokes with a lot of laughter.

The air was full of the tender aroma of the roasting pork.

Zimira came up to me and said, "Pam told me about the farm. You don't have to worry. Those pigs were grown locally. Luis picked them out this morning." She handed me a beer. "Brewed right here," she said.

More of the Noche Buena – the party goers – kept pouring in for the banquet. It lasted until midnight when they then held their "misa del gallo" or "Mass of the Rooster." A Catholic priest in his full white robe gave the mass and sermons. It was the same priest who married Pam.

After that, the partying continued. I packed it in around 2am.

On Christmas day they feasted again. How these people weren't 400 pounds was a mystery. The big event of the day was the exchanging of gifts. Hundreds of them filled underneath the tree. It took an hour just to hand them out.

I relished the next week, recovering from the constant partying of the last few days, only to be thrust into the next party event: New Years.

The dinner's main food was black-eyed beans. Apparently it was to bring luck. For me, it just gave me gas.

The dancing, singing and beer drinking went on until the clock struck its chimes for the New Year. Just minutes before, Luis had left the front door open, as well as the back door.

He told me this was a tradition to let the old year out the back, while the New Year came in the front.

I thought I'd have a week to recuperate, but, in fact, I had to come home from all the festivities, which lasted practically that whole week!

The next four months progressed nicely, in spite of another long deep cold winter with lots of snow. Maybe that's why things went well. Too damn cold for the Outfit to deal with me.

By May, my infringement into the Outfit's territory was starting to pay off. With the aid of my hidden cameras, the FBI and CPD had made seven arrests, and six of those went to conviction. They were all junior enforcers, however. But it was still chipping away.

I was playing my small cards, and the Outfit was playing theirs, and I was taking them with my open hand cards – the police.

The best part was some anonymous people were calling in giving up more Outfit members, those higher up in the food chain. Those mostly involved in money laundering. These "concerned citizens" were telling the cops where and when certain major meetings were taking place. The Bishop was doing his part.

It was only a matter of time before those in the upper hierarchy in the Outfit would have to play their face cards. Me, the Black Lady, would be ready.

CHAPTER 16

RETALIATION

One morning in mid-June a black SUV was parked on the opposite side of the road from my house.

At first I thought nothing of it. But an hour later and the vehicle was still there. The windows were tinted, so I couldn't see inside.

I walked across the street towards the vehicle, looking right at it. It started its engine, and sped off.

I snickered. The Outfit had taken my bait.

The next day it was back. Again I went out, with my baseball bat this time, but the car took off before I left the front step.

On the third day it was there again. This time I went out the back door, got into my pickup, which was parked behind the house. I backed out of the drive with the SUV directly behind me. I didn't turn onto the road. I went straight backwards until my bumper just touched their side.

I then put the truck into four-wheel low, and gunned the engine, pushing the SUV sideways over the sidewalk, into a tree on the neighbor's property.

I forwarded into my driveway and got out. I stood there and watched, baseball bat in hand, as they tried in vain to get away. No way. They were stuck, as one of the tires was pulled off the rim.

No one got out of the vehicle as I stood watching, patting the bat in my hand.

A few neighbors came out to see the commotion, but quickly went back inside. Funny thing is, no cops came.

About an hour later a tow truck showed up and they were rescued.

Not long after, twenty or twenty-five minutes, there was a knock at my door. Out the living room window I could see a cop car parked outside, with two uniforms at the door.

"Hello, fellas," I said. "What can I do for you?"

"We got a report that there was a traffic collision across from you," the taller cop said with a pen and pad in his hands.

I had to wonder, what took them so long? Could they have been sent by The Outfit to harass me?

"No, I'm sorry. I don't know anything about it."

"You don't," the cop said, clearly not believing me.

"Yep, I don't know anything about any accident."

The cop started to look inside my house, and made a move to get past me. I put my arm up to the door blocking his attempt.

"What are you doing?"

"I just want to look around."

"Not without a warrant, you don't. You do know who I am, don't you?"

He just gave me a glare.

"Let's go, Bob," the shorter cop said tapping the tall one on the shoulder.

"Have it your way," the tall cop said. They left.

If they were real cops, of that I had no doubt they were, they definitely were spying for The Outfit.

I never saw the SUV in front again. They parked several houses down for about a week. I wondered when they would make the move and storm my house. I was ready if they tried.

I had to get some food, but I also wanted to see if and how they followed me. As Randy said, get to know the behavior of your enemy by testing them.

I was driving in my pickup to the Watkins food store not far from my place over on South Western Avenue. As I turned onto West 79th Street, a silver Audi pulled in behind me. I could see three men inside. I started some maneuvers, passing people to put some space between me and the Audi.

Yep, it made similar moves to close the gap.

The food store was packed with people in a line up, which extended well out into the parking lot. Rationing of produce and meats had become a recent norm. Processed foods were still available, but like all the rest, prices had doubled over the previous year.

As I drove around looking for a parking spot, a fight broke out between a few people impatient at having to put up with the multi-hour wait for meats.

I decided not to join the line, so I got just a few items that I didn't have to wait for.

When I came out of the store, my silver shadow was parked along Western. I loaded my groceries, and headed out in the opposite direction the Audi was facing

I looked in my rearview mirror, and saw it make a "U" turn in the middle of the road, with other drivers screeching and honking. It soon got in behind me again.

Instead of going directly home, I turned north on South Ashland Avenue, then into the Food-4-Less parking lot. They followed.

Signs on the windows said, "Out of meats." Still the place was full of people attempting to stock up. I didn't park as the lot was full. I went back onto the road and headed south on Ashland, back where I came from. They followed.

I got on my phone to my old partner. "Derik, go to the Home Depot over on Clinton Street. Meet me at the front door."

"What's up? I'm on a case."

"I'll explain later. Get going now, please."

They continued to follow me.

The Home Depot was far enough away that Derik would make it before I did.

My phone rang as I got close.

"Marg, I'm here," Derik said.

"Wait at the front door. Almost there."

I found a parking spot on the roof of the Home Depot near the stairs to the store. They parked not far away.

I got out and walked into the stairwell. Out of the corner of my eye, as I glanced back, I saw two men get out and follow me in.

Soon as I got down to the doorway, I scurried as fast as I could out the door where Derik was waiting. Off we drove back up to the upper parking lot and waited as far away as possible, with their car still in view.

I explained to Derik what was going on.

After about twenty minutes the two men emerged from the stairwell, and briskly walked to their car. One was on his phone.

They waited another half hour watching my truck, expecting me to come out from the store.

Eventually, they gave up and drove off.

We followed them into the Brighton Park area. They stopped on South Archer Street, got out and walked into a small restaurant.

Derik dropped me off in front.

"Thanks, I owe you," I said.

"Want me to wait for you?"

"No, I'll take a cab back to the Home Depot. Thanks again."

I went in.

It was a small Italian restaurant, one of the fronts on my list. The kitchen was against the right wall, with two rows of seats on the left against the windows overlooking the side street. There were only a few people eating. But near the back, in one of the booths, there they were: my three admirers.

I picked up a fork and knife from an empty booth. I was nervous as hell on the inside, determined on the outside. I dropped myself into the seat forcing the one man into the window. I was opposite the other two.

"Hello, boys," I said.

Their jaws just dropped. One paused mid drinking his water.

The man directly opposite me made a move to the inside of his shirt.

I stabbed the man beside me in the thigh with the fork. It was well seated. He winced, clearly holding back his pain. I held the knife against his belly, in clear view of the other two.

"Tell your boss," I said in a firm authoritative voice, "there is nothing you can do to stop me. You boys try one thing against my family..." I gave the fork a bit of a twist. The man yelped. "...and I'll do much more than this. You've been warned."

I got up, pulled the red tipped fork out and dropped it on the table. I let the knife go on the floor. "Here..." I said, picking up the man's ice water, and pouring it into his lap, "...this should dull the pain." I walked out, not giving them time to say anything.

I was shaking like a leaf in a windstorm in the cab ride back to my pickup.

After several days, I needed more food. This time I wasn't going to take any chances. I was sure my poking their eyes was going to escalate things.

Even though I kept Alex's Cz85 on me at all times, I also kept my Cz858 carbine in back behind the seat of my pickup, with three loaded magazines beside it. I covered it with a blanket. Got in and headed into town.

Sure enough, before long. As I turned onto West 79th Street, I saw a black car behind me. Best I could see, there were two men inside.

As I came up to the lights at South Halsted Street the car sped up on my left. Through my side mirror I could see that the rear passenger window of the car was open.

Soon as the vehicle came beside me I looked right inside. A shotgun barrel was pointed at me. I hammered on the brakes as he fired. The pellets peppered the roof post, some bouncing off the windscreen shattering it.

They sped on through the red light, barely missing cars. I floored the gas, navigating around the stopped vehicles.

Traffic was bottled up at the next lights forcing them to slow down. I slammed into their rear. They turned into oncoming traffic, and blew through the red light. I followed full throttle, other cars screeching to miss us.

Twice more I bumped into their rear, almost forcing them off the road. Again, traffic required them to slow as they steered through a green light.

I followed full force, slamming into them a fourth time. Steam started to pour out from under my truck's hood.

They were just about to try to turn right at Racine Avenue when I did a fishtail hit into them spinning the sedan off the road onto the sidewalk. It careened to a stop against a power post.

The maneuver forced my truck into the middle of the intersection skidding sideways where the engine sputtered and shut off. A cloud of steam rolled into the air.

Through the right window I saw the shotgun man emerge from the car. He started firing.

People scattered for their lives away from the intersection, abandoning their vehicles.

I bailed out the door as pellets splintered plastic and shards of glass all around me with each blast. I opened the back half-door, retrieved my carbine, racked the action, and hunched down as low as possible. I was scared shitless. Where the hell were the cops?

I was on my own. I'd have to defend myself. My training with Randy kicked in.

I peered under the truck to see the man's legs almost at the grill. He was still blasting away. I had lost count how many he volleyed.

I pointed the rifle to just over the hood above the driver's door. Soon as his head appeared in the scope I fired one round.

His body thumped onto the asphalt in front of me with the shotgun bouncing away.

There was silence for a few moments. Then more gunfire erupted from a loud weapon. I dropped to the ground as a bullet whizzed by my head after coming right through the sides of the truck.

I adopted the modified prone aiming through the underside of the pickup. Through the scope I could see the passenger side door of the black car was opened, and someone was behind it firing a handgun. It looked like a Desert Eagle. Another man was on the opposite side of their car, shooting at me over the roof, also with a Desert Eagle.

They must have seen me under the truck as impacts near by threw chunks of the road onto me.

I held my breath. I put the cross hairs right in the middle of the closest man's head and fired. All I saw was a red mist where he used to be. I quickly acquired the second man's head, who was still firing, and popped off a third round. He disappeared.

I paused, taking a deep breath. I had to advance to the car as there was one more assailant, the driver. I had to move fast. If I stayed in place any longer fear would take over.

With rifle bearing on the vehicle, I walked around the back of my truck towards the black car. I could hear sirens in the distance. The driver got out in a hurry. He started to run across in front of me.

I wanted to shoot him, but rounds would have gone into the storefront behind him. Couldn't chance that.

"Stop! Or I'll put you down!" I yelled.

He stopped, and dropped his head down. Turning towards me I said, "Get on the ground!"

He did.

I went right up to him, put my foot on his neck, and held the barrel right against the back of his head. "Give me a fucking reason."

Two cop cars screeched into the intersection.

I stood back, put the rifle on safe, and held it high with my left hand. My right arm was also in the air.

Several cops drew their sidearms. Pointing them right at me they yelled, "Put the weapon down now!"

I slowly put the rifle on the ground, making sure the barrel pointed away from the cops. I got prone on the pavement, putting my hands behind my head.

Two officers held their guns at me, while a third, kneeling on my back, which hurt like hell, pulled my arms around my back and cuffed me with one of their zip ties. It was too tight.

"There's still a round in the chamber," I said.

"Shut the fuck up!" said the one cop, with his Glock only a few feet from my head.

More cop cars arrived, squealing their sirens. It was a traffic jam.

I was picked up by two officers, and stuffed into the back of a cruiser. The man I let live was placed in another car.

Now the inner emotions came forth. I was shaking in a cold sweat. I'd done it. I was alive. I thwarted my assailants. I had to make sure I thanked

Randy.

I didn't feel guilty, not at all. I didn't feel anything but satisfaction. I was worried what this would mean for my freedom though. I could very well go to prison for the rest of my life for this. But then again, it was self-defense.

I was taken to District Seven station and put in an interrogation room. I didn't bother to say anything until a detective came in.

Finally, after what must have been an hour, a woman, tall with black hair, somewhere around late thirties, walked through the door. She was well dressed in an expensive looking suit.

She sat opposite me, took her glasses off and said, "You're Marg Cunningham aren't you?"

"That's me."

"You're supposed to be off the job. Is that not correct?"

I was, kind of, at least to the public I was. "Yes," I lied.

She put her glasses back on and looked at some papers. "Three dead. All head shots." She looked over her glasses. "That's some fine shooting. Want to explain this?"

"They were following me. I had already warned them I'd use lethal force to stop them if I had to."

"Hmm. So, how do you know they were the same men who followed you before?"

"The one with the shotgun will have four small holes in his right thigh. You'll find a fork fits perfectly."

She leafed through the files in her hand. Stopping at one, she smiled. Looking over the rims she said, "OK. Stand up, please." She got out her handcuffs.

Swell, I was going to be arrested.

"No, I'm not arresting you. You're being transferred."

Me... A cop... In handcuffs... I was quite embarrassed.

We left the room. At the front desk I saw why I was brought out. Hollenger and FBI Special Agent Joan Lim Loo were waiting for me.

Joan didn't say anything. She just headed out the door. But she looked pissed.

Hollenger said, angrily, "You're a disaster waiting to happen. Shit, you make shit happen."

"What—" I tried to say, but he interrupted me.

"Don't say anything. You're in my custody. Let's go."

We headed out.

Outside Joan was leaning against her car. "You sure know how to make a mess of things," was all she said.

The comment passed me by as I was focused on something else. A black SUV was parked across the road, it was the same one I backed into as the dent in the side was still noticeable. It's engine started, then pulled into traffic forcing a couple of vehicles to squeal to a stop.

Joan looked around. "That's them?"

"That's them," I said.

Shaking her head, she said, "This isn't going to end well. I'll be calling you in the next few days. We need to talk." She got in her car and left.

Hollenger took me by the arm to his vehicle. He opened the passenger door, got out his key and undid my cuffs. He leaned inside the door and grabbed Alex's handgun. "Here," he said as he handed it to me.

"What gives? I thought I was under arrest."

"You are, well technically you are. You're going to be under house arrest as this gets investigated. Get in."

As we pulled into my drive he popped the trunk open. "Your rifle is back there."

I smiled at him.

My poor truck was a write off. But I needed transportation. The dealership was great. Though, I didn't tell them exactly what happened, only that I got into an "accident." It hadn't been released from the pound yet. Soon as it was the dealership would see the damage.

They lease me another truck until my insurance came through.

While in the dealership office about to sign the papers, my phone gave the Dragnet theme.

"Hi, Joan."

"Detective." Her tone was flat and to the point. "Meet me at the White Castle, Roosevelt and Western. Three P.M. Don't be late."

She didn't give me time to say anything.

I got my rental and headed to the restaurant.

I parked beside her in the back lot. We got out and stopped at the back of her vehicle.

"What's up?" I asked.

"Do you have any idea how much of a mess you've created with your stunt?"

Yeah, I know you said that when I got out of jail. "Stunt? They went after me first. I was—"

"I don't want to hear about it. Let's eat. I'm starving. My treat."

As we went inside, she said, "Great seafood here."

I noted the dented black SUV pulling into the church parking lot across the road.

Joan ordered first. "I'll have the Sriracha Shrimp Nibblers, onion rings and a Sprite. What are you having, Marg?"

"What's a slider?" I said to the young brunette behind the counter.

"It's just our burgers."

"I'll have the Savory Grilled Chicken then. With fries and Coke."

Joan sat at a table with the view to the SUV. "Can I trade you places?" I said.

"Why?"

"Look over there." I pointed to the lot.

"Damn. That's the Outfit staking us out."

"Yep. They've been tailing me since you guys got me out of jail." We sat so I had a good view of my fans.

"So, what did you want to discuss?" I expected to get a major tongue-lashing.

"Look, I understand they attacked you first. But you did slam into one of their vehicles in front of your house."

"That one, actually, see the dent? What can I say, I missed the brake pedal when I pulled out."

She shook her head. "Look, you really should leave this to the professionals."

"Professionals?" I chuckled. "You guys have been trying to end the rule of the Outfit for what, a hundred years?"

"And you think you can end it?" Joan said.

"No. I have no delusions of that. I just want to get even. I want to avenge the death of my Alex and our child."

""How far are you willing to go for that? Murder Ribaudo?"

I didn't say anything, just slurped my Coke.

"I won't be able to keep you out of jail if you do anything like that. You'll go to prison for the rest of your life. You want to miss watching your granddaughter grow up?"

"No."

"Well, that very well could happen."

"Joan, do you have a family?"

She put her food down and wiped her face. "I know what you're trying to do. You want to know what I would do if someone killed Jerry or my two daughters. Well, I would want to kill them. But at the same time we have the rule of law. We need to let the law deal with criminals. Otherwise we just have anarchy. But you already know that."

She resumed eating her shrimp with a somewhat pompous look.

"I'm not going to get into a debate about the merits of our criminal justice system," I countered. "But I would argue we already are in a war of anarchy. How many homicides do we solve now? Twenty, maybe thirty percent? The criminals rule this city.

"Hell, the violence is so bad that wealthy people are leaving the city in droves. They're worried the entire city will erupt into anarchy. With the civic finances in the toilet, and getting worse every day, they're probably right. We've already lost the war."

"I saw that article too. You planning to contribute to that chaos?"

"No," I said.

"But you are planning something."

"Only to defend myself."

"But you just said you want to get even. I don't understand. Are you or are you not going to provoke a fight?"

I now kind of regretted saying I wanted to get revenge. Tipped my hand too much to my plan. "If I told you anything, would you try to stop me?"

"I can only act on your actions. But you're on notice about doing anything the law would deem criminal. I can't protect you. Officially, I have to say that, right?"

"I understand perfectly," I said.

"There's another thing. Have you considered you might get killed yourself? Sooner or later, the Outfit is going to put out a contract on you, if they haven't already. Every thug in the city will be after your head."

"They have, according to Hollenger."

"And that makes no difference in you choices?"

"Of course it does. But as with all war, we must do what we must do even if it causes our own deaths. Some things are worth dying for."

I didn't need this kind of negative thinking. I needed every ounce of confidence I had.

"If you don't mind me asking, Marg, are you religious? Is this some kind of crusade?"

Here we go, the Thou Shall Not Kill lecture from a Christian. "I don't know any more."

"Well, I am, marginally," she said. "Religious that is. I don't go to church, but I have to think there is a higher power. A purpose for all of this, some kind of plan."

"And an after-life?" I asked.

"I suppose so. Yes."

"Then it doesn't matter if I get killed, or kill the Outfit. As the saying goes, kill them all and let God sort them out." Hmm, I kind of blurted that out.

She looked at me hard. "Rather cynical. I have to be honest, you sound like a psychopath."

"You want me committed?"

"No. We only commit people who have done unspeakable acts. Are we going to see unspeakable acts?"

"Only if they come after me first."

"That's your plan is it? You want them to come after you? Then it's all self defense then, isn't it?"

Shit, I've already said way too much. I've fallen for the very trick I was trained to do. Get your opponent to open up and reveal their plans. I needed to end this conversation now. I clammed up and quickly consumed the rest of my lunch.

"Well, for your sake I hope you know what you're doing," she said.

Once we finished eating, and were getting up to leave, Joan said, "I have to admit, you did an amazing job of dispatching those men. They were top ranking enforcers. It's gotta cut into the Outfit's abilities."

That was nice to get some more ounces.

We parted on amicable terms, but with another stern warning against making something happen.

Yeah, right...

A few days later, I was getting into the truck in the driveway when I noticed a slip of paper under the wipers. It read:

WE HAVE JOAN WE WANT YOU

There was a number.

Shit. Fuck. Bloody hell. This wasn't supposed to happen. They were supposed to come after me in my house.

They would torture her like they did me. There was no way I was going to let that happen.

I walked to the end of the driveway. Parked six doors up was the dented SUV. I'd have to shake their tail somehow.

I went back into the house and paced up and down the hallway.

I had to think. They took her to get at me. How was I going to get her back? If they thought I was angry before, now I was really pissed.

I called Hollenger. He was flabbergasted. "Don't do anything stupid again. No killings! We'll do everything in our power to find her."

"Bullshit," I snarled. "By the time you find her she'll be dead. I can find her." Unless, that is, they feed her to pigs. I shuttered at the thought of poor Becky Clarke.

"How?"

I remembered the chip all FBI agents get. "Check with the FBI. She has a location chip."

Hollenger called back a few minutes later. "They aren't getting any signal. They think it could be jammed or they removed the chip from her. So now what?"

I thought for a few seconds. "Oh, I know. What was that beady-eyed lawyer's name, at the line up?"

"Ribaudo's lawyer?"

"Yeah, him."

"Why do you want to know his name?"

"He'll know where Ribaudo is."

"Do not see him! Look, Marg. The FBI is looking for her. Stay out of this."

"Never mind. I'll Google him." I hung up.

Sure enough, Ribaudo's name showed in a number of newspaper articles.

His lawyer's name was right there, Stewart Bergson. I Googled him and there he was, with his own Facebook page.

I checked my watch, it was 5:00PM, past closing time according to his hours. Hopefully he was working late.

However that tail waiting outside for me was a problem. I'd have to prevent them from following.

Dressed in black pants and a long sleeved black pullover I loaded up my truck with my gear and weapons. I couldn't be seen from the street.

I pulled up the road to the SUV and stopped beside them. I got out, walked over to their vehicle and fired my Derya semi-auto shotgun into the back driver's tire. As it deflated I fired into the front tire, then for good measure, I double tapped into the front grill.

As I got in I yelled to them, "Where I'm going you can't follow." And I drove off.

I waited outside Bergson's West 51st Street office. He was there as I could see him through the window.

The issue was the call. The Outfit was waiting for me to phone them. I'm sure the crew I immobilized made their update to Ribaudo. So they knew I was on the move.

I'd have to make some gesture. I thought about the Jack Reacher movie I watched when I was at the villa recuperating.

Same scenario: damsel in captivity and the hero of the story has to rescue her. Many bad guys get killed in the process. Typical Hollywood.

It was the calls he made to the bad guy that made me laugh watching it. I wished I could remember his words as he turned the table around on the enemy to buy time. I'd need to do the same thing.

I dialed the number on the paper, but Bergson drove out from the back lot in his BMW. So I cancelled the call and followed him to a ritzy area in the north of town. I drove into his driveway after he entered his home.

He opened the door at the knock. "Stewart?" I asked.

"Yes."

I barged past him into the large foyer, pulled out Alex's handgun and pointed it at is head. He backed up against the wall gasping. His wife came out of the living room and screamed.

I pointed the pistol at her. "Get into the living room, both of you," I demanded.

The Jewish icon-filled room was huge, with three couches circling a fireplace.

"Sit," I ordered. They sat together holding hands. I sat opposite, barrel pointing at them.

"What, what do you wa…" but Stewart stopped. His eyes bugged out.

"I, I know who you are…" He cut himself off again. He shook his head.

"Who is she, Stew?" his wife asked. "What does she want with us?"

I expected Stewart to tell her, but he lied.

"I… I'm mistaken. I… I don't know you. What do you want?"

"Oh, you remember me. You're Ribaudo's lawyer."

He tried to signal me to shut up, but his wife saw. Her face went deep red. "You told me you were through with that piece of shit years ago? You're still representing him? He's Mafioso!"

"I had no choice, Laura. He, he would have us both whacked if I left him. Who do you think pays for all this," he said with his hands in the air.

"You lying sack of shit!" she screamed as she beat him with both hands. He tried to hold off the punches, but she got in some doozies.

She stopped, sobbing. Whimpering she said, "You promised me. You promised me. You promised me..."

I finally decided it was my turn on Stewart. "Ribaudo kidnapped an FBI agent to get to me."

Laura's weeping stopped as fast as it started. Her hands covered her wide-open mouth.

All Stewart could say was, "Oh, shit."

"Do you know where he would take her?" I asked.

He thought for a few seconds. "He wants you? Then... This is not good. Then he's taken her to lure you in?"

That's what I said, is this guy slow? He sure looked like he was nervous, or maybe scared shitless. "Yes. Now, where would he take her?"

"He would never make any trade where he has her. He... He'd do it somewhere... Why do you want to know where she... Fuck, me. You want to rescue her? You're insane!"

I pointed the gun between Stewart's eyes. "I won't ask again, where would he take her?"

Stewart paused thinking.

Laura pounded one of his legs with her fist. "If you know, tell her!"

"Ow! Stop that. Shit, woman, I'm thinking. Oh, oh, wait. I had to represent Marconi, I mean, Macchi... One of Ribaudo's men in court today. As he left, he said something, what was it exactly? Shit, it was... He said they were all ordered to his mansion. Rib's mansion. That's over near Michigan City. That's not nor... That's unusual. Bet that's where they took her. But you'll never get in there. It's, well... It's a fucking fortress."

"Stew," Laura interrupted. "You must help her."

"If I do that, Rib will have us both at the bottom of Navy Pier."

"Not if I eliminate him first, he won't," I said.

Stewart laughed aloud. "You? Kill the Rib?" He laughed more. "People, lots of people, have tried to kill The Rib, and every one of them is now terminated, burned, a ghost. And he's still here."

"You think you can take out Ribaudo?" Laura asked.

"Of that, I have no doubt," I replied, lowering the Cz.

"How? How the fuck are you going to ki— I mean, get at him? Just walk in the front door?" Stewart said.

"Maybe not the front door. But there's got to be a way in."

"Never. He'll— Rib'll have at least a dozen armed men at that house. Armed to the teeth, I might add. You'd be full of holes before you got into the— Shit, before the gate."

"He's not expecting the way I'll arrive," I said firmly. "Show me his place on Google Earth."

"No, it's suicide," Stewart sniggered.

"Why do you care if I don't succeed?" I asked. "If I succeed, you'll be free of him and honor restored to your lovely wife."

She smiled at that. Then she turned to Stewart and gave him a pound on the leg with her fist saying, "Show her now, or you'll be dealing with my wrath!"

He looked at her angry face, then at me. "Ok. Ok. Ok, but it's a..." He got up shaking his head. Pointing, he said, "In my office."

We looked at the home and property using Google Earth. Then at the residence with Street View.

Laura brought me a hot cup of coffee.

Fortress was an understatement. It was in the middle of nowhere, in Indiana near the lakeshore.

"It's a big house, much bigger than mine. Three stories," Stewart explained. "It's surrounded by a block wall, with only one gate to get in." He shook his head. "It's, it's— No way. It's impossible."

I clicked to get out of Street View. "Print this," I said. I took the map.

"Looks like another entrance to the house here at the back."

"Good eye. Yeah, two actually. There's the main entrance out to the pool here, but there's also a door here to the kitchen. It's for his workers, his staff, the cook. But it's code locked." He paused. "I, I... I know the code."

I looked up at him waiting for the number.

"I saw him punch it in one day." He shrugged. "I have a photographic memory for numbers. It's one-three-six-four."

I wrote it on the back of the printout.

"One-three..."

I got it, thanks. That should be it then. Thanks for your help. I'll leave now."

"Wait, you have another problem. I mean, there— assuming you succeed in ki— I mean, dispensing with The Rib, you'll have to contend with his brother, TJ. He will never stop coming after you. But... Maybe you can get him first."

"I'm listening."

"This is Friday night. Every Friday he visits a broth— I mean, an escort service. You know to— To satisfy himself. It's down on West Ontario Street. He always uses the back entrance so no one will see him."

"I had to wonder how he knew this, did he accompany TJ and dishonor Laura? I hate that. "Tell me you didn't..."

"No, oh, no. Skanks— I mean, prostitutes aren't my thing, AIDs and all that, you know? Anyway, TJ is fond of beating them up when he can't, well, you know, he can't, um, perform as he thinks he should. I've had to get him out of a pickle more than once." He looked at the handgun. "You good with that thing?"

"Good enough."

"I hate guns. They scare the shit out of me. But my suggestion is you need to, to, well, deal with the brother first, if you catch my drift. At some point you'll have to. His name is TJ. Just TJ." He wrote the address down and handed it to me.

"Why are you so helpful all of a sudden?" I asked.

"Um, because, well... Because one day I'll no longer be useful to Rib." He looked at Laura standing at the door. "When that day comes, because I know so much..." He looked back at me, "he'll have me eliminated. It's just a matter of time. So if there's just one little chance of him being, well, put out of business, so to speak, I'll jump at it. And if you survive this ordeal, and you do, well, you know, I'd be happy to, no duty bound to defend you, gratis."

"That's nice to know. But let's not count our chickens just yet, shall we? I still have to get in there."

"I'll say it again, how are you going to do that?"

"Not sure yet."

"One thing I can tell you. One day I was there they thought the Latin Kings, they're a large rival gang in Chicago—"

"I know who they are."

"Right, of course you do. Anyway, they thought the Kings were going to storm the place. So he beefed up security, as I suspect he has done this time.

"He positions his guards in pairs, one pair at the front door, some traversing the compound. Others are stationed in the house. But always in pairs, never more, rarely less."

I nodded.

"Well, if you want to meet TJ, you'd better get going. He arrives at the brothel about eleven pm. Good luck, and good... Well, I hope you..." Stewart shook my hand. So did Laura as I was heading out the door.

I couldn't help but wonder if it was all a ruse. Would Stewart call the brother and warn him? Laura's outrage seemed pretty genuine. I had no choice.

I waited in the back alley behind the hot-sheets hotel. It was very dark. No way TJ could see me. A man, as large as Ribaudo showed up, got to the door when I came up behind him and said, "TJ Ribaudo?"

He turned, "Who wants to know?"

My 40 cal Sig was already aimed at his head, not ten feet away. I fired. He dropped with his brains spattered all over the door.

Shit. I'd actually done it. Randy's training was taking over. I couldn't see much of the body, the alley was too black. Good, because I probably couldn't stomach the scene.

I nonchalantly walked out the alley towards West Ontario Street. There, I mingled with a crowd of people.

Gun shots. A normal Friday night occurrence that most people just ignore now. Six hundred and thirty-three killings so far this year, more than fifteen hundred shootings over all. Several a day is normal for this city.

Funny thing to think, as at that moment we could all hear more gunfire in the distance, from across the river. About half-a-dozen reports.

The crowd looked up briefly, but then shook it off and went on their way.

I deviated off into the parking lot where my pickup was waiting. I walked across the park from my truck to the river edge. I glanced around to make sure no one was looking, and said goodbye to my Sig as it disappeared into the black of the water.

The execution of TJ, pure cold-blooded homicide, was starting to sink in. Logic dictated it was best to eliminate him first than have to try to stop him later. I had full control this way. That was my excuse.

Except cops would be all over the crime scene, and I had to make sure ballistics didn't come back to anything I owned. I couldn't take the risk of being stopped before I could finish my mission. The Sig was new, so there would be no record of the barrel markings.

I even made sure I wore gloves when I put the rounds into the magazine. There was no way I'd be able to fish out the casing in the dark of an alley.

I sat in the idling vehicle for a moment. My hands were trembling on the steering wheel. Then my mouth filled with the contents of my supper.

I dove out of the truck onto my knees and puked a mass onto the pavement. Some of it even burned the inside of my nose.

It was that industrial waste sized chunks of puke, a thought of that line from a movie came into my mind as I spat out the last of it. Then I reached into the cab to get a bottle of water. It took a few washes to get the disgusting taste out.

I got back into the truck and finished off the water. I sat there staring at the lights of my city.

My first cold-blooded execution. I didn't count the ones I dispatched who shot at me, well, because they were shooting at me. But this, this was a preemptive strike, a deliberate, calculated ending of someone's life. It had to be done, if not then, later when TJ went after me.

I had to keep telling myself this.

The convincing worked, as I should have felt bad. But I didn't. I actually started to feel good about it. It gave me confidence. And TJ wasn't going to be the last I was going to send to the afterlife. Getting Joan back alive was all that mattered.

I still hadn't made the call the Outfit was expecting. Soon as someone answered at the other end, I just said, "I'm on my way."

I headed to Michigan City.

The drive was just over two hours. During the trek, I thought more about what I had just done. Some reflection started to sink in. Long drives give too much time to think.

He may have been a low life scum, but I had taken his life. Was I now any different than them? I wondered what my father felt as he ran through the NVA lines shooting anything and everything he could.

But then I remembered, Dad likely executed those two Outfit soldiers for killing his partner. I bet he did it exactly as I had just done. Point blank, double tap to the head. And I expected he felt the same as I did: satisfaction, with a touch of guilt.

"Fuck! Shit! How fucking stupid!!!" I realized I should have taken the Sig apart and kept the barrel. I could have thrown it along the roadside. I wondered if it would be found one day and the rifling matched to the slug that passed through TJ's brain. "Fuck, nothing I can do about it now."

I was thinking so much about the execution and what I may have to do soon, that I wasn't even watching the road. Completely on autopilot the two hours flashed by.

I entered the road that Ribaudo's home was on; Beverly Drive, off US 20, just south of Michigan City. The area was well secluded, not far from the lake. His mansion was the only home in the expansive woodland.

I called Hollenger. Before I could get a word out, he was screaming at me through the phone. He knew I was up to something. TJ's corpse had likely been found. I managed to get in that Joan was at Ribaudo's home and where it was.

"Where I'm going next. Send in the cavalry." I hung up before he could say anything.

I popped the hood open, and took the bulbs out of the front lights. The moon was near full, and there were few clouds. So I'd have no problem navigating the road. I just didn't want my vehicle to be seen. The shadows of the trees would see to that.

The time was just after 2AM.

I stopped at the side of the intersection to Beverly, about 500 meters from his home. The road went straight, then, before the gate, it made a left turn carrying on northward.

I got out and set up my modified Remington sniper rifle on its bipod on the aged asphalt. I lay in front of the pickup and sighted to the gate.

Through the scope at full power, I could see the front steps leading to the main entrance. Two guards, fully armed, marched back and forth along the top of the landing. I adjusted the zoom so that one of the men occupied two bars of the reticle, just as Randy taught me.

I checked the reading on the M1200 Hi-Lux scope, it was indeed just around 500 meters. I was ranged.

In the canyon of trees along the road there was little effect from any wind. I was set, and ready.

I went back into the truck and checked the rest of my gear. I had ten magazines for my Cz858, all taped into pairs. That was 300 rounds. I checked that the scope was set on two power, perfect for close quarters combat.

Alex's Cz pistol was loaded with the hammer forward, a round in the chamber. I had six mags of sixteen rounds each stashed in a number of pockets, and pouches.

I put on the simple webbing gear I bought from a tactical supply store. It gave me the most mobile abilities. I applied dark battle paint, used by the airsoft guys in their re-enactment displays, over my face.

Lastly, I tied what little of my hair I had into a ponytail. I forgot to visit a barber and have it all cut military short. Hopefully, that's all I forgot.

I was ready. D-day was upon me. I was nervous. But at the same time confident my training would kick in. Run off instinct, as Randy hammered relentlessly into me every day. Don't think, just do. I remembered his words, "Soon as the crosshairs are on target, fire. Do not spend time trying to aim."

I lay back down behind the 700. I cycled the action, putting a round in the chamber. With my finger off the trigger, I sighted on one of the men on the steps. I had to wait for him to stop moving. He did to light a cigarette.

"Those things will kill you," I muttered.

My heart was racing. It was affecting my aim. Randy told me under such times in order to slow my heart down was to take in as much air as I could and hold it. The pressure of my lungs would prevent the heart from pounding and it would slow it down. It worked.

I aimed. He stood there taking puffs. I held my breath as I put the nine ounces of pressure on the trigger. The rifle went off in a deafening report, echoing throughout the trees.

Down he went. I cycled the action again. The other man on the step came over to him and bent down. I fired at him. He dropped on top of the corpse.

I got back into the truck and drove towards the gate. Lights were coming on all over the compound. I got to within a few feet of the iron gate and slowed.

I engaged the cruise control, which remembered my highway speed, and got out. The pickup raced through the gate, throwing them wide open. The truck careened at full speed onto the driveway.

Near the house, only a few hundred feet away, it turned to the left a bit, dove into the pond and stopped. Its rear end protruded into the air. Steam rose from the hot engine.

Oops, so much for my dealership's rental.

The proverbial cliché of 'All hell broke loose' became reality.

Two men came running across my view towards the truck and opened fire with full automatic weapons.

I had snuck through the shadows into the compound, my diversion worked as planned. Before I arrived I'd used the overhead Google Earth image to locate every tree I could use as cover.

The first one was just inside the gate on the right. I was there, kneeling. My 858 aimed at the ready. I wasn't much out of breath with the one hundred meter dash to the tree. The training was paying off.

The perps were stopped, still firing. I let go a double tap into each of the two shooters. They both dropped.

A rapid succession of snaps and impacts into the tree from my right forced me to take cover behind the massive trunk.

Swell, someone saw me. Or saw the flash from my rifle. I peered around the tree, and sure enough I could see two flashes in the distance. I fired back, leaning out from behind the tree. The two men stopped shooting, and I could see their dark outlines running towards the house.

I aimed a bit in front, two mil-dots, as I'd practiced so many times, and popped off some rounds. One went down, and I was sure I clipped the other. He went in behind a corner of the building. I remembered from the layout it was nothing more than that, a small nook, so I knew he was trapped.

Time for walk and shoot. I got out from behind the tree and started to lay a barrage of fire as I briskly walked towards my prey. Without thinking, I switched the mags over to the other coupled full one. I continued to lay shots at the corner as I quickly made my way to it.

I came around, carbine leading me, where I found the man on his butt, his gun on the ground beside him. I got a piece of him all right.

"Please don't kill me, please," he pleaded.

"Where's the FBI agent?" I demanded, the barrel only a few feet from his forehead.

He didn't say anything.

"Fuck you then," and I fired.

I changed to another pair of coupled magazines to give me a fresh slate of 61 rounds, dropping the almost spent mags on the ground. Slowly I made my way along the wall, rifle pointing in front of me.

The kitchen door wasn't too far, just around the next corner. There were enough tall cedars to give me plenty of cover. Shooting was still happening behind me. What they were targeting was a mystery. So much for professionalism.

I got to the door. "Now we see if Stewart was right." I entered the code. The door clicked.

I slowly opened it. There were no lights on in the kitchen. I let the door close quietly behind me. Now I was without direction. Stewart gave me a vague description of the interior. I knew where the door to the hallway should be.

I turned on the flashlight attached to my rifle's fore stock. There was the door. I turned off the light, and I slowly opened the door just a crack. That part of the hallway was the back of the main entrance.

Two men were opposite me, one at each corner of the foyer. Each was aiming Ak47s towards the front door. I targeted the furthest one first, firing a single round, putting him down.

The sound in such a confined area was deafening, but I had put in my ear protection soon as I got into the kitchen. The other man closest to me turned, but not fast enough, my shot put him down. But he wasn't dead.

I went over to him, pulled out my Cz handgun, with my thumb pulling the hammer back. That was just for intimidation, of course.

"Where's the FBI agent?" He didn't answer. He was groaning in pain. I put the muzzle of the pistol against the top of his forehead. "I won't ask again."

"Third floor bedroom. At the back. In the middle."

"Thank you." I fired.

Besides the main entrance staircase, there were two sets of side stairs at each end of the house leading up to the top floor. Each went up to a landing, then made a 180-degree turn between each floor.

With my carbine proceeding me at the aim, I slowly made my way up the left steps.

As I came to the second floor, I peered around the corner, muzzle first. No one. Upwards I continued to the third floor.

This time I got right down on the floor before I let my muzzle enter the hallway. Sure enough, as I expected, someone was at the door to the room guarding it, AK in hand. But he was looking at the other stairway.

If I fired it would tell my prey I was near. I had to be stealthy about this, but also neutralize that guard. There was only one way, and my stomach wanted to jump into my mouth at the thought.

The door opposite me was partly open.

Four bedrooms occupied the back half of the house. The guard at the door showed me which room Joan was in. I suspected Ribaudo would be in there, likely with a few guards.

I dashed across the hall into the open doorway. I slipped into the dark room just at the door. As I suspected, the guard saw me and followed me into the room.

I allowed my carbine to drop onto its single point sling in front of me as I grabbed my bayonet.

Soon as he made it to the doorway, I pulled right in front of him, grabbing the back of his head with my left hand, and impaled his throat with the knife in my right hand.

We were nose to nose. His eyes bulged staring blankly into my very soul. He tried to scream out, but the knife not only severed the carotid, but also cut through the windpipe preventing any air movement into his lungs.

It took longer than I thought, but eventually the life in his eyes evaporated and he fell into me, putting both of us onto the floor.

My leg was pinned under his bulk, I wanted to scream from the pain, but I held back. It took several tugs on my leg, and pushing of the carcass, to free myself.

I left the knife planted in his neck. It acted as a plug. If I pulled it out, blood could have squirted all over me.

But then I realized, being dead there would be no blood spraying out. Fuck it, just leave the bayonet.

I stood back staring at the skewered corpse. I wanted to throw up. I told Randy I wasn't comfortable with such a personal way to inflict death. I closed my eyes, took a deep breath as I raised my head into the air.

Looking back down, I let the air out, and raised my rifle to the aim.

All four rooms shared a back balcony. The entire back of each room was all glass. I went out through the sliding doors. Slowly I let the muzzle creep into view of the adjacent room.

There she was tied in a chair. She looked in good shape. It didn't appear that she'd been battered like I was.

Ribaudo was beside her with a handgun. Two armed men were near the door, one on each side of Ribaudo. Their MP5's aimed at the door to the hallway. It was the same two who roughed me up in that factory. The Mallet was on the right.

As Randy said, people do predictable behavior. They were expecting me to barge through the bedroom door. And, as I had done in that game so many times before, I had out flanked them.

I took a deep breath and held it as I fired a double-tap through the glass at the Mallet. Then quickly targeted the second guard with another double-tap before he could turn. Ribaudo was all alone with me.

I walked through the destroyed window into the room, all the while maintaining aim on Ribaudo. He had crouched down behind Joan, the handgun against her head.

"I underestimated you, Cunningham."

Being a larger man, he had a hard time keeping himself hidden behind the petite Joan. His right knee was fully exposed. Not being more than five yards in front of me, I fired a round right into the knee and it exploded. He screeched, dropping the handgun. I came around to get full view of my target.

"Don't kill him!" Joan yelled.

Alex in my arms flashed in my head. "He doesn't get to live."

"You're both dead," Ribaudo winced. "You kill me and my brother will hunt you both down."

"Again, you underestimated me. I planned this carefully. Your brother is lying dead in a dark alley. His brains splattered all over a wall."

"No, you lie!"

"Did you think I wouldn't get revenge after you tortured me and killed my Alex? Killed our baby? Time for payback, you fucking prick."

But first there had to be justice. I let the rifle hang in front of me from the single-point sling. I pulled out the handgun and pointed it at his head.

"This is what I used to bring down your man who beat me, and killed my unborn child. This is what I used on that man who killed the father of my child. This is Alex's handgun and I'm going to use it to kill you."

I fired a round into his head.

That was it? It was all over? For over a year I wanted this moment to come. All my effort, all my energy, my entire soul was poured into this very day, this very instant. Anticipation of this consumed me, ruled over me.

And it was over.

Just like that.

I didn't feel relieved, not even satisfied. I still wanted to do more to him than just this. I felt disappointed it ended in a flash.

I stood there looking at the corpse. Blood flowed out onto the carpet into a pool. I was pissed at Ribaudo even more that my desire to inflict my own long painful butchery of his soul didn't happen.

Cuban style, I spat on the fat carcass.

As I was cutting away the zip ties holding Joan to the chair she said, "I told him you'd come for me."

Once free she gave me a big hug. "No time. We need to get out of here now." I handed her Ridaudo's pistol.

"Stay behind me." I changed to another coupled mag for the 858, keeping the partly spent mags in case. As Randy kept reminding me during our simulations, always have a full mag swapped in when you get the chance.

"Stick to me like a Siamese twin," I said.

She walked with a pronounced limp.

"You're hurt," I said.

"They found the microchip and cut it out. I'm OK, let's get out of here."

We went back out onto the balcony and into the room I came through. At the aim I could see through the opened door to the stairs. Someone was there ready for us to emerge from the Ribaudo's bedroom. Bad mistake. I fired a round as soon as his skull hit the crosshairs. His carcass slid down, disappearing behind the stairs.

There was likely a second shooter at the other stairs, I figured. "Go fast across the hall," I said.

"You want me to go first?"

"Yes, he won't have time to shoot. Then I'll engage him when he tries."

She gingerly stepped over the impaled man at the door, then made a dash to the stairwell. The shooter in the opposite stairwell fired off a burst, but she was already behind the wall. As I made my tear across the hall, I fired into his direction.

Joan started to go down the steps, avoiding the body. I grabbed her. "No, we don't go down. Follow me. Always attempt to flank your enemy and come in behind."

Joan looked confused.

We went back into the third floor hallway towards the stairs where the other shooter was.

Slowly I crept down each step, muzzle preceding me. Before the landing at the bottom floor, I peered over the banister. Yep, sure enough, he was waiting for us to come out of the other stairwell.

I fired point blank into the back of his head. Crimson sprayed out along the white marble floor.

As we rounded the bleeding body, Joan said, "Oh... My... God...

That's... Just... Gross..."

We got to the corner where I had previously felled one of the guards near the kitchen. Someone opened up on us from the foyer. Rounds splintered wood and drywall around us. We hugged the wall.

"Your boss is dead," I yelled. "And I've killed all of your buddies. You want to be next?"

There was silence except for faint sirens in the distance. The cavalry was arriving too late.

"The cops'll be here soon," I said. "I'm giving you the opportunity to drop your gun and surrender with your life."

"How do I know you won't just kill me?"

"I give you my word. I came to get Joan. I've done that. All I want to do now is get her out of this house. You're standing in my way."

An AK slid in front of me. Someone emerged with his hands in the air. He was just a young man, likely late teens. He was scared to death.

With my carbine pointing at him I said, "Get on the floor. Hands behind your head."

It was over. I succeeded.

The Indiana State SWAT team stormed into the foyer, M4's aimed at us.

"Drop your weapons!" "Get on your knees!" "Hands behind your head."

Joan and I complied.

We were taken to their District Division in Lowell, Indiana.

I was in the interrogation room for, well, I couldn't tell how long. But I was hungry, as well as starting to get a headache, which I do when I go without my coffee too long.

I also felt completely spent.

I looked at my hands. They were trembling. My whole body was trembling. I read about this in the documents Randy gave me on firefights. This was the adrenaline withdrawal process kicking in.

A hot flush permeated my body. That's all I needed now. My mouth was dryer than the Sahara. I needed a drink. But I knew they wouldn't give me any water, to increase my discomfort.

For hours I was visited by a number of police, asking the same questions.

"Do you think you're some kind of Special Forces executioner?" Was typical in trying to get a response from me. Tactics I'd used on my own interrogations many times.

All I gave them was Hollenger's cell number. I said nothing more. Their questions were answered with stares from me. Eventually, they played the waiting game. A game I knew all too well. Who would break first? It wouldn't be me.

Whitman came to mind. Fucker played that same trick on me. I crossed my arms, and dropped my head to make it look like I was catching some zees.

At least my trembling had stopped. The rush was over.

I just wanted to get some sleep, truth be told. I was totally exhausted. Compounding that, I needed to eat. And I needed to pee.

I made that request to the next cop who came in as she wanted to know if I needed anything.

"I do, unless you want to get a mop and pail and clean up my piss from the floor. And it's fucking hot in here, can you up the A/C?"

Two officers came in, unchained me from the desk, and escorted me to the bathroom. I also cleaned the camo paint off my face and hands. They returned me to the shackles of the desk. They didn't turn on the A/C.

"Now, I need to eat."

"You get nothing until you talk."

"I don't talk until Hollenger gets here."

The cop left the room.

I folded my hands, and closed my eyes.

My mind drifted to what I had done. How many did I kill? Let's see. Two at the main door, two more after that, that's four. Then one who was running, that's five. Six with the one cowering in the corner. Two more in the hallway, that's eight.

Nine guarding the door. Two more in the room made eleven. Ribaudo made an even dozen. The one on the stairs made thirteen. Then fourteen with the other one at the bottom of the stairs.

Ribaudo's bother was fifteen.

Not bad for a night's work, I thought. Then it dawned on me. "Oh, shit," I said under my breath. I shouldn't have thrown the Sig I used on him into the river. It could be found one day and matched to the bullet that excavated his skull.

"Damn it." I said. Oh, geeze, how simple a problem I could have solved. All I had to do was take the barrel out, throw the rest into the river, then throw the barrel away somewhere else. Now I was worried it may come back to bite me.

Nothing I could do about it now. Anyway, so add the other three at the intersection that made eighteen I'd eliminated of the Outfit. That had to put a huge dent in their numbers.

My father's events in Nam came to mind. Him running through the jungle, with a belt fed machine gun, he must have killed many more than I just did.

Then I realized I had killed eighteen people. I got the feeling I was going to be branded a mass murderer. I started to get nervous about my predicament.

A female detective came in the room. Another trick to try to get me to open up: she was the "good cop," I'd wager.

"You're one walking kill zone aren't you?"

"Did you talk to Joan, the FBI agent yet?"

"I ask the questions here. First, who the hell are you?"

"Detective Marg Cunningham of the Chicago Police Department."

"No, you're a former detective. You quit last year."

"It only appears that way. So you do know who I am and why I'm here."

"Doesn't matter who you were, or who you think you are. You're nothing in this state. You're going down for mass murder."

Not the "good cop" after all. She read me my rights.

"I demand to speak to a lawyer."

She slid me her phone.

"I need the number in my wallet."

She rummaged through it and pulled a card. "This one?"

I looked at Bergson's card. "Yep, that's him."

She left the room for me to make my call. Stewart was pleased, and astonished, I had succeeded. He said he was on his way. And not to worry.

The female cop came back in with a McDonald's breakfast, with a large coffee. Thank God! I wolfed it down, then laid my head on the table on my crossed arms. I drifted off.

I dreamt of Alex, how we enjoyed ourselves at the restaurant in Chicago. I was startled awake mid delight when the detective came in, with Bergson and Hollenger.

The detective undid my cuffs and said, "Reluctantly, you're free to go. Get out of here before the Governor of Indiana changes her mind. And stay out of our state in the future."

CHAPTER 17

I'M ALL ALONE

The three of us drove home together. Stewart Bergson was driving. I was in the back. I realized, "Hey, they got my vehicle and my weapons."

Hollenger looked back over his seat at me. "You're lucky that's all you got taken away from you. Deputy Strong called the Governor of Illinois who called the Governor of Indiana to secure your release. Apparently, you destroyed years of work. They were homing in on Ribaudo."

I snickered. "Well, I just saved their state millions on court costs then."

"Yes, that you did."

Stewart piped up, "Hey, that's lost revenue for us too, you know."

Hollenger looked back again. "You also killed TJ, didn't you."

"Don't answer that," Stewart snapped looking at me in the mirror. He then looked at Hollenger, "She pleads the fifth."

"Just another senseless killing that will never get solved because of lack of evidence," is all I said on that subject. But I was kinda worried something may implicate me.

Once past the State line, Hollenger made a call. "You have him?" There was a pause. "Good, we'll be there soon. Keep him on ice."

He turned to me. "That was Joan. That kid, the one you didn't kill?"

"Yeah."

"You'll never guess who he's the grandson of." He smiled. "John Torrio, who, in turn, is the grandson of 'Papa Johnny' Torrio."

"Interesting, and?"

"And, the kid's talking."

"Wait, how did you get him? I'd think he'd be in Indiana's hands," I said.

"The FBI took him this morning. They have him in their building. He's talking."

"How long has it been since you slept," Stewart asked, looking at me through the rear view mirror.

"Couple days, I got a power nap in the interrogation room."

But the reminder made me yawn.

"Look at you," Stewart continued. "You're dead on your feet. You need to sleep. We'll take you home first."

"No, I want to talk to this kid first." They protested. "Just go," I demanded. "I'll catch a couple winks while we drive."

They woke me when we pulled into the Chicago FBI building on Roosevelt Road.

As we emerged from the fourth floor elevator doors, Joan was there to greet us. "I didn't get a chance to say thank you for saving my life," she said to me. She couldn't hold back, and she hugged me.

"It was because of me they took you. It wasn't supposed to go down like that," I said. "I'm sorry."

"Couldn't be helped. Funny, though. The whole time I was there I had a feeling you would come for me. Let's see what this little prick has to say."

I went into the interrogation room with just Joan. Frank Torrio was there, chewing on the ends of his fingers. He looked up nervously. "I'm sorry I shot at you. I didn't know you were a cop. I didn't want to do that. I didn't even want to be there. I want to make a deal. I don't want to go to prison like my father."

During Alex and my research, we knew that the Outfit's former boss, Frank Torrio senior, was in prison for life. Put away some ten years ago. He was convicted of embezzlement, money laundering, and bribing a public official (one of our former mayors).

The best part was that a Catholic priest and the prison chaplain were sending messages to the Outfit so he could maintain control. Both of them where charged, and convicted, some five years ago. That severed all communication to the outside world.

Of course, since then we couldn't figure out who was running the Outfit, but Frank junior here was the closest in the family to wearing the crown.

"What can you give us worth making a deal?" Joan said.

Nervously he looked the two of us over. "Can you please sit," he asked in a low voice. Joan and I looked at each other. "Please," he said again.

"This is going to take some time."

We did. Frank seemed to settle down. "I'm nineteen. I have my whole life ahead of me. I want to make something of myself, not go to prison for life.

"Look, I've met a girl. I want to marry her. I also want to go to university. I've been accepted."

"Taking what? Criminal law so you can bail your family out?" I said, sarcastically.

He looked surprised. "No. No. I want to take geology."

"Geology..." I said, with a tone of disbelief.

"Yes. Geology. I love the earth sciences. Plate tectonics, igneous rocks. I've been accepted at Laurentian. That's in Sudbury in Canada. You know, that's right on a meteorite impact crater. Some 1850 million years ago. Boom! What a blast that must have been..."

He paused. There was no doubt he was very passionate about this.

"I'm sorry," he said, sheepishly.

"No. It's OK. We believe you," I said.

"What can you tell us of the family? I'd bet you know a lot," Joan said.

"Enough to put them all away."

"Tell us, Frank, who runs the Outfit? It's definitely not you," I asked.

"My grandfather."

"John Torrio?" Joan said.

He was one of the old geezers at the restaurant, I remembered. Mother-fucker. Under my nose all this time.

Frank nodded.

"You're sure?" I asked.

He nodded again, looking right in my eyes.

"Look," he said. "When my father went to prison, and was cut off, Grandpa wanted to bring the Outfit back to its glory days, when he ran it thirty years ago. He ordered the hit on De Luca. He ordered your abduction and the hit on you." He looked at me.

"And Ribaudo?"

He nodded. "Yes, his father and my grandfather worked together to run the Outfit long ago. Ribaudo's old man was the enforcer. He murdered lots of people. The apple didn't fall too far from that tree, I can tell you.

"Ribaudo and Grandpa wanted to rebuild the empire."

"You have some proof we can use?" Joan asked.

"He ordered my father to kill my mother."

Joan and I looked at each other. I looked back at the kid. "Says in our files that your mother committed suicide some ten years ago."

"No, my father shot her to make it look like a suicide. It was just before he was to go to trial. The last one where he was convicted. My mother couldn't handle it. She was a heavy drinker as it was."

"And your grandfather ordered your mother to be executed? How do you know that?" Joan said.

"I was there."

"You saw it?" I said, excitedly.

"Yes. They didn't know I was there."

"You were, what, eight?" I said.

"Almost nine. My father and grandpa were arguing about the case. Grandpa was worried my mother, if they put her on the stand, would spill it all and they all would go to prison."

A wife cannot be compelled to testify against her husband, but that immunity didn't include father-in-laws.

He started to choke up. Tears welled in his eyes. "My pop put the gun below her chin. She was passed out on the bed with booze. And he pulled the trigger."

He paused. "I cant get it out of my mind... Her brains all over the wall." He sobbed.

We waited for him to regain his composure. I really felt for this kid. I knew exactly how losing someone hits you.

"Where were you to see this?" Joan asked.

"When Mom and Pop argued, and he started to slap her around, I would hide in my mother's bedroom closet. I saw it all. I heard it all."

He brushed a tear off his cheek.

He paused. He started to shake his head. "I can't take this anymore. Ribaudo's house, you barging in like Rambo and killing them all... That was the break I needed. I'm not afraid any more. Not of them. Are you going to arrest Grandpa?"

"Oh, of that you can guarantee," Joan said.

"You're a brave kid, Frank. For cooperating like this," I said.

He smiled. "I guess I'll... I have to testify in court, won't I."

"Yes, you will. In the meantime you will be in protective custody."

"And Steph too?"

"That's your girl?"

"Yes, she's started her studies in paleontology right here in Chicago."

He paused. "I have access to all the Outfit's records. All our holdings. All our loans outstanding. I have it on CD. I'd been copying it off computers for the last four years. They thought I was getting ready to take over the Outfit."

He paused some more. "It's all mine... I guess I'll inherit all this now, don't I?"

"Marg, outside, please," Joan said.

After closing the door we watched him in the mirror, chewing on the ends of his fingers.

"Think it's legit, or is he playing us?"

"Looks genuine to me," I replied.

"Well, too bad for him, because he won't be getting a dime. Once we execute a RICO indictment against these guys, we'll gut the Outfit of everything they own. Just like we did in 1992. Anyway, I'll get started on the warrants."

Just as she was about to leave the room, she said, "And you, Detective, need to go home and get some sleep."

By the time we finished processing Frank and his girlfriend, setting them up in seclusion for the grand jury, I didn't get home until well after 10PM. I decided to go to my old apartment. I hadn't been there in months. Besides it was closer.

I had to have one rum and coke to settle myself down before collapsing in bed. I looked at my chart on the wall. "I can take you down now." I raised my glass in a toast to my father.

I had to laugh while watching the late-night news. They showed the bust at Ribaudo's mansion.

"It was a text book case of cooperation between the FBI, Chicago Police and State police here in Indiana at the home of Mob boss Joe 'The Rib' Ribaudo in the early hours of the morning."

They showed the three of us in handcuffs being taken away.

"The task force felt little resistance as they stormed the home. There was a small firefight as Ribaudo barricaded himself in his bedroom."

They showed a black body-bag on a gurney being loaded into an ambulance.

"But he lost that fight as expert SWAT killed him."

I turned the TV off.

Joan, two beat cops, and myself entered the Capone Spaghetti House restaurant. Like the first time I entered, the old geezers were clustered around a table at the back. It was the same ten withering old farts.

The bulky guard put his hands out in front to stop us. I pulled my badge and my sidearm out (I never did get Alex's Cz back, nor my rifle), pointed it at his head. "Get the fuck out the way."

He moved over.

"Arrest him for assault of a police officer," I said to one of the cops.

I came up to the circular table. The air was thick with cigar smoke. "Johnny Torrio, I have a warrant for your arrest for the murder of Mary Torrio, Roberto De Luca, Detective Becky Clarke, and Special Agent Alex Kiley. Please stand."

He looked up at me with old yellowing eyes. His wrinkled thin face showed no emotion. His gnarled and distorted hand lifted a glass of booze to his mouth. He finished it off, and stood up.

One of the officers went around behind and cuffed him. He winced in pain.

As they took him from behind the table into the aisle, I said, "Your grandson is a good boy. He's given you up for the murder of his mother." I looked at the cops, "Take this piece of shit away."

I was alone with the remainder of the reminiscing club. "You dinosaurs are done. Your time is over. Go wither away and die off."

I left the restaurant.

It was a wonderful September day. The sun was bright, and it wasn't too hot. I came up to Alex's gravesite and placed a bunch of flowers against the headstone. His mother and father must have been there earlier that Sunday morning, as another bunch of fresh flowers were already neatly in place.

I sat down on the grass. "I just want to bring you up to speed. It's all over. On Friday they gave Torrio life on four counts. At eighty-three he isn't going to make the four hundred years he was sentenced to. I got him for you my love."

I paused. "The kid was great. He's gone to Canada. He told me at the court he was going to sell what was left of what Outfit owned. After what the Feds took, that is. He forgave all the loans people owed. He's going to use the money to fund research and scholarships for kids who can't afford to go to university. I think one day he will make a fine scientist.

"The Outfit is done. We arrested about a dozen more as the dominos fell. The rest have fled.

I snickered. "One hundred years the Outfit ruled this city. It was all brought down by a nineteen year old pissed off kid."

I paused some more. I looked around at the surreal landscape of differing headstones. Other people were paying their respects to their buried loved ones. A funeral was happening across the way.

I smiled. "You'll be proud of me. I've been nominated for the Superintendents Award of Valor and the Police Blue Star Award. We'll see if the Awards Committee accepts them though."

I stood up. "I'm going to your parents for dinner tonight. We won't be able to play hearts, or bridge, because you won't be there. We all miss you very much."

I kissed the ends of my fingers of my right hand, and touched the top of his headstone.

"I love you so much. I always will."

"Read between the lines of what's fucked up
and everything's alright.
Check my vital signs to know I'm still alive
and I walk alone."

Boulevard of Broken Dreams

Author's Note

The Vietnam combat scene was an actual event as described by someone who was there. The names of the soldiers are real, with the addition of some fictional characters for this story line. That section of the novel is dedicated to those brave men, especially those who never came home.

AUTHOR'S PREVIOUS NOVELS
AVAILABLE ON AMAZON.

BLINDING WHITE FLASH

"There are too many excellent elements of "Blinding White Flash" to list in one review. The author, J. Richard Wakefield, has created a masterpiece about the lengths ordinary citizens will go to in order to defend their country from foreign invasion. While many books in the military/war/action-adventure genre are thrilling to read, "Blinding White Flash" thrusts the reader into the heart of war with all of its pain, bloodshed as well as heroism and valor. Wakefield gets down to the nitty gritty of the conflict between the force made up largely of Canadian volunteers who give blood, sweat and tears to stop the Chinese government from seizing Canada and its resources. It's obvious that Mr. Wakefield has a strong knowledge not only of weaponry but military history and strategy as well. The battle scenes are gripping and spellbinding at the same time: the intensity, the hardships the men endure are all captured.

The tone of "Blinding White Flash" truly fits the description of war: bloody, traumatizing, at times heart-wrenching. No punches are pulled here. The characters in the book display the type of selfless valor and bravery that has exemplified the Canadian soldier from the trenches of Vimy Ridge to Afghanistan.

In my opinion, "Blinding White Flash" should be either a blockbuster movie or a television series. In some ways, this larger-than-life story resembles Leo Tolstoy's iconic tale of love and fighting War and Peace. Like the Russian soldiers who fought valiantly to drive Napoleon's forces from their land (and did 150 years later when Hitler invaded the Soviet Union) the Canadian fighters are often outgunned and outnumbered by superior Chinese forces. Also, they use the brutal cold of the Canadian winter as a very effective weapon against the invaders.

From start-to-finish, "Blinding White Flash" holds the reader in its grip and doesn't let go."

BLINDING WHITE FLASH: INVASION

"It's hard to believe that Invasion is even better than the almost flawless war story *Blinding White Flash*. *Blinding White Flash: Invasion* has a bit different tone to it than the original book.

Invasion starts in British Columbia. Groups of Canadian soldiers and civilians are preparing to defend Canada from tens of thousands of Chinese troops that are landing on the west coast. The action moves inland to the BC interior and onwards into Alberta.

While Blinding White Flash is a masterpiece of thrilling action sequences and a strong storyline that features amazing characters, Invasion is much more intense. The sequel delves more into the politics behind the conflict that is ravaging much of the world. In same ways, the book is a commentary of the unstable times we live in globally.

The author has intensely-researched every fine detail of the book to make every bit of the story factual and even believable. Even the villains, namely the Chinese general, are not merely one-dimensional characters but have strong and weak points, as well as reasons for doing what they do.

Blinding White Flash: Invasion is a mind-blowing read that is phenomenal from start to finish."

THE BARN

Nick Easton, owner of a business, finds himself captive in the basement of an old barn. He doesn't understand why. But after months of hell, gets confronted with a choice.

Marg Cunningham is the detective tasked to find Easton. The trail leads in many directions, but she is convinced who might have been the kidnapper. She just can't prove it.

Ed Whitman takes 'revenge is a dish best served cold' to the extreme. He waits ten years after Easton fired him to take Easton hostage, not for money, but to make a choice.

This story is a four part mystery from different perspectives of a kidnapping, but not for money. Easton's world view is challenged for the first time in his life, and must make the most important choice, the most expensive risk, of his life.

THE LOYALTY PARADOX (BEING WRITTEN)

In this sequel to *The Cunningham Arrests* the United States is being torn apart. Islamic attacks intensify, government deficit spending runs out of money, and the country is crippled by an energy crunch. Deep cold winters destroys crops, causing food prices to skyrocket, empty shelfs are common. Deadly riots abound.

Being pulled by several factors, the Department, the US Constitution, and family, Chicago Police Detective Marg Cunningham has to decide where her loyalties lie in a world of increasing instability and chaos.

www.ingramcontent.com/pod-product-compliance
Lightning Source LLC
Chambersburg PA
CBHW051518260626

47170CB00003B/669